DEAD FALL

A.K. Turner's latest crime fiction series features forensic sleuth Cassie Raven, who was first introduced in two short stories broadcast on BBC Radio 4. She also works as a TV producer and writer making documentaries on a range of subjects from history to true crime. A.K. has lived in East London since its prehipster days and recently qualified as a City of London walks guide so that she can share her passion for the city's 2,000-year history; her specialist subject – crime and punishment!

 @AKTurnerauthor

 @akturnerauthor

 AKTurnerCrimeWriter

Also by A.K. Turner

Cassie Raven series
Body Language
Life Sentence
Case Sensitive

DEAD FALL

A.K. TURNER

ZAFFRE

First published in the UK in 2024 by
ZAFFRE
An imprint of Zaffre Publishing Group
A Bonnier Books UK company
4th Floor, Victoria House, Bloomsbury Square, London, WC1B 4DA
Owned by Bonnier Books
Sveavägen 56, Stockholm, Sweden

Copyright © A.K. Turner, 2024

All rights reserved.
No part of this publication may be reproduced,
stored or transmitted in any form or by any means, electronic,
mechanical, photocopying or otherwise, without the
prior written permission of the publisher.

The right of A.K. Turner to be identified as Author of this
work has been asserted by her in accordance with the
Copyright, Designs and Patents Act, 1988.

Extract from 'Macavity: the Mystery Cat' taken from Old Possum's Book of Practical Cats
by T.S. Eliot (c) Estate of T.S. Eliot and reprinted by permission of Faber and Faber Ltd.

This is a work of fiction. Names, places, events and
incidents are either the products of the author's
imagination or used fictitiously. Any resemblance to
actual persons, living or dead, or actual
events is purely coincidental.

A CIP catalogue record for this book is
available from the British Library.

Paperback ISBN: 978-1-80418-159-1

Also available as an ebook and an audiobook

1 3 5 7 9 10 8 6 4 2

Typeset by IDSUK (Data Connection) Ltd
Printed and bound in Great Britain by Clays Ltd, Elcograf S.p.A.

Zaffre is an imprint of Zaffre Publishing Group
A Bonnier Books UK company
www.bonnierbooks.co.uk

For Luca

Chapter One

The sky was just starting to lighten the inky surface of the canal, the peep and quack of the dawn chorus subsiding. Cassie Raven had been walking fast, head bent, eyes on the towpath, replaying the row she'd just had with her boyfriend. Which was how she almost crashed into it.

What the . . .?

A steel barrier blocked the towpath. And a few strides beyond it, a dark red puddle on the ground, the precise shape of a cartoon speech bubble, and instantly recognisable.

Blood, a good litre of it. Going by the colour and viscosity, it had been shed four or five hours earlier, the exposure to air already making the haemoglobin morph into iron oxide – the same compound as rust. Reminding her how the human body was fundamentally just a fancy chemistry set.

A female cop was striding towards her now, shaking her head. 'You can't go through here, you'll have to find another route.'

'What happened?' asked Cassie, lifting her chin towards the stain. *A knife wound?* Stabbings weren't exactly uncommon in Camden, usually drug-dealing related.

'I'm not at liberty to say,' said the cop, eyeing Cassie's tattoos.

Fair enough. The family might not know yet that someone they loved was seriously injured – or more likely dead.

The pool of blood looked too neat and unsmudged to be a knife wound. Squinting up at the building that overlooked the canal – a huge Victorian warehouse, converted into upmarket apartments – she caught a flash of something. A man in what looked like police uniform peering over the balustrade of a narrow balcony.

Nine, maybe ten, storeys up.

An accidental fall? Or a jumper. Either way, from that height, she'd almost certainly be meeting them later at the mortuary. For sudden deaths in the community the cops had arrangements with local undertakers to deliver bodies out of hours.

Cassie treated all her guests with care and respect but having experienced her own moments of bottomless despair she had always felt a special bond with suicides. Before retracing her steps she told the cop, 'If I were you I'd cover up the blood until the cleaners arrive? Just in case the family come by.'

Left the cop looking puzzled at the authoritative way the girl with the punk haircut had spoken.

Losing her rag with Archie had unsettled her. They'd only been living together on her narrowboat for nine or ten weeks but already she was getting that claustrophobic feeling, all too familiar from her one and only previous – failed – experiment in living with a lover.

On the upside, they both worked with the dead – Archie as a pathologist, Cassie as an anatomical pathology technician, aka APT – which meant they could talk about work without the constant self-censorship needed with civilians. She had taken against him at first, pigeonholing him as the entitled posh boy medic, but they'd gradually fallen for each other across the bodies of the dead, and after dating for a few months, she'd finally taken the leap in agreeing to live with him.

He was easy-going, fun company – and the regular sex was a definite plus. On the downside, the narrowboat wasn't exactly spacious and the headroom in the main cabin was only six foot two at the highest point – the same height as Archie – so he was constantly banging his head on the ceiling. It made her wince in sympathy but also irritated the hell out of her, which she knew was desperately unfair. That morning when he'd got up too fast from their bed and cracked his head she had snapped at him, 'For Chrissake, Archie! Every single morning?!' Worse, he hadn't snapped back – just sent her his (increasingly familiar) wounded look.

It occurred to her that maybe she was feeling the same way as he was – that she no longer had enough headroom.

At the mortuary, Cassie took a shower in the ladies' changing room – her regular routine since Archie had moved onto the boat. When the two of them had to get ready for work at the same time it was like a complex dance routine – or a clown act. After donning a clean set of blue scrubs, she put in her lip and eyebrow piercings and scraped her hair up into its topknot, her reflection telling her it was time to re-dye her hair its usual batwing black and get her undercut reclipped. Making a face in the mirror, she pulled out her phone and tapped out a message to Archie.

Sorry I was an arse this AM. I'll buy us a curry later. C xxx

She'd got into work early, to enjoy a few moments of solitude before everyone else arrived. Going into the tranquil chill of the body store where the only sound was the low hum of the giant fridge, she started checking her inventory – or guest list, as she preferred to think of it. Moving along the wall of polished steel, she opened each of the drawers to check the occupant's name, d.o.b. and identification number on the tag of their body bag against the paperwork, chatting softly to the white-shrouded bodies within as though they could still hear her.

'Morning, Mr H, Doctor Curzon will be examining you today, to try to find out why you died, get your family some answers' ... 'Hello, Mrs V, you're leaving us this morning. I hear the service is going to be at your church where you and Mr V got married. That's lovely' ... a few murmured words for each of her ladies and gents, down the line of drawers.

Cassie had always talked to the dead in her care just as if they were still alive. She had always seen the mortuary as a shadow-land where the recently dead hung suspended between life and burial or cremation – an interlude in which they might still have some awareness of their surroundings. Irrational nonsense, of course, and at odds with her otherwise scientific outlook. But it was a belief that gave her work meaning, and made her feel responsible for these souls while she was looking after them.

Drawer number eight housed her latest arrival, delivered by the undertakers during the night. Finding the entry in the check-in log she recognised the address of the canal-side apartment block where she'd seen the cops that morning. It read, '*Adult female, d.o.b. TBF, thought to be S. J. Angopoulis*'. So the person who'd fallen – or jumped – was a woman.

She pulled out the drawer on its runners and started to unzip the body bag – always liking to greet her new charges in person. But at the sight of the face a violent shiver went through her – and not from the perma-chill of the body store. Her autonomous nervous system was sounding a klaxon. The young woman had a depressed skull fracture that had mashed the left-hand side of her head, her face was a livid purple from temple to jaw, but she was still totally recognisable.

Her name wasn't 'Angopoulis'. It was *Angelopoulos*.

Sophia Angelopoulos. Better known as Bronte.

Chapter Two

Pulling herself together, Cassie tried to speak normally as she would to any of her guests. 'Hello, Sophia,' she said softly. 'Long time no see. You're in the general mortuary in Camden and I'll be looking after you. We'll be trying to find out what happened.'

The last time they'd laid eyes on each other they'd been fourteen-year-old schoolgirls, classmates at Camden High. *Classmates but not friends*. Feeling a surge of guilt, Cassie leaned closer and spoke with feeling. 'I am so sorry to see you here, Sophia. I promise we'll do our very best for you, and your family' – wondering whether she might pick up some clue to her last thoughts, as she sometimes did from the bodies in her care.

The first time had been just a few months into the job. She'd been checking in a Mrs M, an elderly lady who'd died of a skull fracture after falling on her front step one icy morning. Cassie had been overcome by a weird sensation – a feeling of slippage into a space between dream and reality, before hearing the single word, *Bugger!* Nothing dramatic or mysterious, just an expression of the old lady's shock, which of course she knew could simply have been a product of her imagination. *And yet . . .*

Now, setting an awkward hand on Sophia's chilly shoulder, Cassie scrunched her eyes closed, and waited, but the only sound was the soft burble of the fridge.

What did you expect? scolded Cassie's internal voice. *Why would she speak to you, of all people?*

Cassie had actually seen the adult Sophia, albeit from a distance, once since school: at Dingwalls, one of Camden's music venues a couple of years back. Sophia had been up on stage singing – transformed from the dumpy little girl into a beautiful and slender woman with a cloud of near-black curly hair, sleeve tattoos inked up both her arms.

Although she'd only been the support act to another band – this was before the media started calling her 'a rising star' – it was clear she had serious talent. Despite her tiny frame, no more than five foot three, her jazz-inflected contralto had an intensity that gave Cassie the shivers, and a bouzouki player among the backing musicians added a spine-tingling roots depth to some of the numbers. She hadn't known who it was when a friend had dragged her to the gig, because this new incarnation of the girl she'd known as Sophia Angelopoulos went by the name of Bronte – the Greek goddess of thunder.

The door to the corridor opened to admit her fellow technician Jason.

'What's on the menu today then?' he asked, sounding bored. 'Jumper?'

'No idea until we see the coroner's report.' Cassie hesitated. 'I knew her – kind of – at school.' Hoping to head off any off-colour comments Jason might be tempted to make: she'd had to tell him off before for calling the bodies 'stiffs', or making comments about the size of a woman's breasts. Like Sophia, Cassie was only twenty-seven – almost half Jason's age – but she was the senior technician and in her mortuary the dead were treated with dignity and respect.

No need to mention that Sophia – Bronte – was a celebrity, appearing regularly in the tabloids, if not always for the right reason. Cassie held her breath, half expecting him to recognise her, but luckily he just shrugged and turned to go, saying, 'Just popping out for a ciggie.'

Cassie fired up the computer. Nothing from the coroner's office yet to say whether Sophia was down for a routine post-mortem – the kind you got when death was unnatural or unexpected but not suspicious – or the full-on forensic version where the police had reason to suspect foul play. It was only just 9 a.m. – aka half an hour since they'd opened but she was impatient to find out more.

'Dorothy? Hi, it's Cassie.'

The warm reassuring tones of Dorothy, the admin assistant, came down the line. 'I expect you're calling about that poor girl by the canal.' A pause as she consulted her computer . . . 'Sophia Angelopoulos?'

So at least her surname had been corrected. 'Does the police report mention her performing name, Bronte?'

A pause as Dorothy checked through the notes. 'Not that I can see.'

So it sounded like the cops had yet to realise they were dealing with a celeb death. *Surprise surprise.*

'What's the deal?' asked Cassie. 'Does the coroner want a routine or a forensic?'

'Just a routine. The police officer who attended – Sergeant Hickey – reported no suspicious circumstances. Apparently she left a suicide note – well, a text.'

Half an hour later Cassie had peeled the clothes from Sophia's stiffening limbs, and laid her out on her workstation. Taking a blank female body chart – the basic outline of a woman, front and back view – she started marking the location of any visible injuries, scars, and so on, with crosses. 'We do this to alert the pathologist to anything that might need investigating further,' she told Sophia quietly.

A cross for the head injury, *obviously*. Rocking Sophia's head gently side to side, she found it as floppy as a puppet's. *C1-C2 cervical fracture*. Another cross for the neck. Working her way down the body, she marked up several contusions and grazes – no doubt the result of the impact – before turning Sophia's arms palm upwards. Seeing the cut marks sliced into the delicate skin inside the upper arm she flinched. *The place to self-harm without being discovered*. They were silver-white, long faded, might even date from her school days – *their school days*. She marked them up, knowing that they'd go down as evidence for a history of mental health issues.

Sophia's left forearm was floppy too, with complex and multiple fractures of the radius and ulna – probably as a result of flinging her arm out reflexively before she hit the ground. The palm of the right hand and the underside of the fingers were also badly grazed – a scatter of abrasions like a galaxy of dried blood – which was unexpected since all the other injuries were on her left-hand side which had clearly taken the brunt of the impact.

With the chart completed, Cassie draped a coverlet over Sophia's naked body below the neck. It wasn't something she'd usually do – bodies were unremarkable, the mortuary's stock-in-trade – but she didn't like the idea of Jason seeing her naked, young and still beautiful, from the neck down at least.

Bit late to start getting protective now, noted her snarky inner voice.

When Dr Curzon breezed in to perform his external examination of Sophia's body she gave him a welcoming smile and even attempted some small talk – albeit through gritted teeth.

'How did your conference go?' she asked him. 'Bermuda wasn't it?'

Curzon frowned: their interactions were usually solely functional, borderline chilly. He had never hidden his dislike of her: an antagonism that seemed to be partly a knee-jerk reaction to her piercings and tatts, etc., but also because she had *Opinions*. To Curzon, *Opinions* were the exclusive domain of the pathologist, not of some gobby technician with ideas above her station – especially one who sometimes had the temerity to question something he had overlooked on a body.

'It was very agreeable,' he said, visibly puffing up. 'I was at The Loren, at Pink Beach? A delightful spot, and my paper was *very* well received.' This last with a smile that aimed for modest and fell at the hurdle of smug.

'It sounds great,' she enthused, before handing him the coroner's report on Sophia's death. There was method in her charm offensive. Curzon could be a slapdash operator at the best of times, keen to get through the list and back to his private practice, but she also knew, via Archie, that Curzon's wife had killed herself, which meant he tended to bring personal baggage to the suicides they saw.

Cassie wasn't about to let Sophia get a raw deal. Still, it must be two years since Curzon had come home to the terrible sight of his wife hanging from a ceiling joist of their garage. *Perhaps he'd come to terms with it by now?*

Curzon glanced down at Bronte. 'Another narcissist who didn't care about wasting valuable police time and resources,' he said, in a voice etched with acid.

Or not.

'What's wrong with a quiet overdose in bed? At least that doesn't upset the neighbours.' He handed the report back to her with a dismissive sniff. 'She was on drugs I assume?'

'The police report says there was what appeared to be synthetic cannabinoid at the scene.'

Reaching out a gloved hand, he flipped Sophia's poor damaged head from side to side, making Cassie wince. 'No doubt as to the CoD anyway. Fracture dislocation of C-spine and significant head injury due to collision with *terra firma*. The lividity suggests she lay undiscovered for at least four hours.'

He was referring to the mauve colour that stained the left side of Sophia's face like a birthmark, which could also be seen on her left shoulder, upper arm, and hip: not bruising, but the result of her blood pooling and coagulating where her body had lain closest to the ground.

'I did notice an abrasion,' said Cassie carefully, turning Sophia's right hand upwards to show him the palm. 'Hard to see how that fits with the rest of the injuries? From the fractures to the left arm it's clear that side took the impact,' extending her own arm to demonstrate.

Curzon's mouth went down at the corners. Barely glancing at the grazed hand, he shrugged. 'She probably scraped it on something on the way down. I think we can file it under "not significant"' – sending Cassie a warning look.

Stay in your lane.

And with that he headed over to Jason's table to meet his next customer.

Cassie bent her head level with Sophia's dark curls. 'Don't take any notice of him,' she murmured confidentially, as if they were back in the loos at school bitching about a teacher. 'He's a professional dickhead.'

Bronte. My name is Bronte.

Cassie blinked. The words seemed to rise from the body in what she remembered as Sophia's fourteen-year-old voice: a slightly harsh tone, aggrieved sounding. As a rational person, Cassie knew that it was probably all in her head, but nonetheless she always respected anything she got from the dead.

'Bronte it is,' she said.

Chapter Three

As the blade of Cassie's scalpel breached the tender skin below Bronte's collarbone, she waited for the usual mental gear shift: the necessary switch from seeing the body she was slicing open as a person to an inanimate object to be analysed.

Nothing. The body was still nerdy Sophia Angelopoulos from Mrs Hooper's Year Ten class.

She felt a flutter of panic. This had never happened before, not even the time she'd eviscerated someone she'd been far closer to.

Come on, she muttered to herself fiercely, forcing herself to make the second cut of the Y-incision that started at the collarbone, meeting at a point on the chest where a pendant might hang. But her hand was shaking.

She noticed that Bronte's eyes had drifted half-open. It was simply the result of the facial muscles relaxing as rigor faded – but feeling that half-lidded gaze resting on her made sweat prickle out on her forehead. Throwing a glance at Jason on the other side of the autopsy suite – who was busy opening his gent's chest with the rib shears – she reached for the blue roll they used to clean up, tore off half a metre and draped it over Bronte's face, her hands still trembling.

'Sorry,' she murmured. 'I just can't . . .'

It worked. Her racing heart slowed, and she was able to make the midline incision.

Ten minutes later, after extracting the viscera in a single 'block' into the waiting white pail, she removed the blue paper mask shrouding the face. Now that the body was an empty shell from neck to groin her usual self-preserving dissociation had finally kicked in. Bronte's body had become anonymous, a puzzle to be solved rather than a person, and would remain that way until the organs were replaced and the body reconstituted.

Seeing Dr Curzon had arrived at his dissecting bench, she used both hands to carry the pail over – viscera were surprisingly heavy even in someone as small-framed as Bronte – and tipped out its contents. 'Do you want the head opened, Doctor C?'

'No need,' said Curzon without looking at her.

Usually she would agree: the severity of the head trauma needed no internal confirmation of catastrophic brain injury. But this time she hovered at his shoulder as he started separating the organs for dissection with swift strokes of his PM40. She lowered her voice. 'Look, I should probably let you know, she's a singer, name of Bronte?' He looked blank. 'Anyway she's a bit of a rising star? . . . So I wouldn't be surprised if the media crawl all over her death. Just saying.'

He shot her a look, picking up her meaning immediately. 'Let's have her brain then,' he said wearily.

She headed back to the body, hoping that Curzon would be covering his substantial arse by giving Bronte a more thorough PM than the usual. A routine post-mortem examination could take as little as thirty or forty minutes. And no wonder: the pathologists only got paid around a hundred quid per body, as opposed to the four-figure fee they charged for the full forensic version.

Jason must have been earwigging because she hadn't even fired up the bone saw before he sidled over to her station. Staring at Bronte's face, he said, 'Is it her? That singer, you know? The one who was in all the papers, off her tits?'

'Yep.' Cassie pictured the infamous image of Bronte in the tabloids. It was night-time and she wore a figure-hugging evening dress but was barefoot and clearly drunk, stoned – or both – lipstick smeared, mascara gone walkabout down her face. Caught at the door to her block she had turned to remonstrate with the paparazzi, face angry, mouth open – a moment illuminated by a brutal flash. Under the unflattering picture one of the headlines had screamed: BRONTE MELTDOWN! And underneath, the faux-concerned subhead read: FEARS THE TROUBLED STAR WILL BE THE NEXT AMY.

Aka Amy Winehouse.
Bastards.

The effort of memory twisted Jason's face before he burst out, 'Bronte! Yeah, that's her. She did "Clean Break".'

Cassie shrugged, frowning.

Jason looked incredulous 'You must've heard it? Biggest dance track of last summer.' Excitement had flushed his already ruddy cheeks. 'We've never had a celeb in before.'

Moving so that she blocked his view of Bronte's body, Cassie fixed him with a look. 'She isn't a celebrity in here, OK? We treat her exactly the same as we would any of our guests, understood?'

Jason shrugged, but as he walked away she could hear him singing the earworm she dimly remembered playing everywhere last summer, '"Break, break, I need a break, break, break. Gimme a break"...'

After she'd removed the skullcap to access Bronte's brain, her eye fell on the stream of water that constantly sluiced the autopsy table, carrying the blood away towards the drain-hole between her feet. She gripped the table edge, pitched back to that terrible moment in the showers in Year 10.

The thread of what looked like blood in the water heading for the drain. Muffled laughter. Then the high-pitched sound of a girl keening.

Chapter Four

On the way home that evening, Cassie picked up a takeout: Thai – Archie's favourite. Aware of how grumpy she'd been recently she'd made a resolution to be 'good girlfriend' tonight. Slowing as she reached the spot where Sophia aka Bronte had fallen she was surprised to see that the police cordon had already gone. In its place was a single massive bouquet of white roses, expensive-looking – no note but perhaps left by her family. Dropping to her haunches at the spot she'd seen the cartoon speech bubble of blood, she scoped the towpath but found no trace of it. She nodded to herself. The crime scene cleaners had done a good job. She hated the idea of Sophia's blood being there for any rubbernecker to see: these days the images would be all over social media in a heartbeat.

Looking up at the balcony where she'd seen the cop earlier, she frowned. It looked like Bronte had fallen more or less in a straight line. Surely you would push off when you jumped? So as not to hit anything on the way down?

She climbed on board *Dreamcatcher*, opened the cabin door and found Archie sitting on the banquette with his knees up, laptop propped there, with Macavity lying beside him. The cat – *her* cat – gazed up at him with an adoration he hardly ever granted her. Still, she had to admit it was a cosy scene, especially with the warm fug in the cabin and the resinous tang of woodsmoke in the air.

'Well done for getting it going,' she told him, looking at the woodstove which was roaring in a way she took forever to achieve. 'What did you do?'

'Gosh, no clue. I just used the kindling and got a good draught going.' He sent her his cutest grin. 'Dib dib dib!'

'What?'

'I'll have you know I was a sixer in the Cub Scouts, the first to get a fire building badge.'

'Of course you were. Was this before your gymkhana career took off?'

Archie might as well have been raised on a different planet to her. Public school in Wiltshire, horse riding, the pursuit and slaying of innumerable fish and furry animals . . . then Harrow, choir, rugby . . . *yada yada*. Meanwhile, by the age of fifteen, Cassie had been bunking school to smoke weed by the canal or drink cider in graveyards with her goth and emo pals, giving each other stick-and-poke tatts. Archie had gone on to do a 'gap yah' in Cambodia and Vietnam before medicine at Oxford; while Cassie had dropped out of school after GCSEs and left home at seventeen to go and live in a druggie squat.

While she served up the food, he reached for the table that pulled down across the banquette. 'Could you check the news for me?' she asked. 'See if there's any mention of Bronte?'

'Charlotte or Emily?' He pulled a frown, before breaking into a grin. 'Kidding. Even I've heard of her, she's that bad-girl singer, with the bad-boy boyfriend, right?'

'She was. She's my latest guest. Jumped off her balcony, according to the cops.'

'Blimey!' Scrolling on his phone, he said, 'Yep, here we go. "BREAKING: Camden Police say woman who fell from canalside apartment was troubled singer Bronte".'

Cassie blinked hard, realising that 'troubled singer' was now her old schoolmate's epitaph, fixed and unalterable: her chances of getting through her turbulent twenties and finding some kind of peace gone forever.

As they ate, she told him about the injuries. 'Cervical fracture, major brain trauma, complex fracture of radius and ulna on one arm.'

He nodded, twirling some noodles onto his fork. 'All pretty standard for a fall from height.'

'I dunno,' said Cassie unhappily. 'She had an abrasion on the wrong hand. And if she jumped, it's hard to see how she landed where she did.' She imitated a jump with her fingers. 'I'd say she ended up less than a metre from the edge of her balcony.'

'Meaning?'

She shrugged unhappily. 'Surely if you jump off a building you travel *some* distance? Seeing where she ended up it was more like she'd been dropped, like . . . a dead weight.'

But then surely the cops would be all over details like that? *Or not.* She pushed her plate away, her green curry half eaten.

'No signs of foul play though?' Archie asked. He put his head on one side. 'It's bothering you, I can see.'

She bit her lip trying to decide how much to tell him. 'I knew her at school.'

'You were friends?'

Shaking her head, she stood to clear her plate and get another beer out of the fridge. How to explain the Year 10 politics at her all-girls' state school – the rival cliques, the brutal food chain with mean girls and bullies as apex predators, and at the bottom, girls like her and Sophia who just didn't fit in.

Sophia leaving suddenly like she did wasn't my fault, she told herself.

Once Cassie might have put in a call to DS Phyllida Flyte to discuss the case, but the last time she'd spoken to the uptight cop was six months ago. Since then she had left the Met after her unofficial investigation into a fellow officer had almost ended in her death. Flyte was now working as an investigator for the Independent Office for Police Conduct, the body that looked into complaints against the cops. Which, given the tsunami of stories emerging about the behaviour of Met officers, would be keeping her nice and busy.

Getting a vivid image of some dodgy cop on the business end of Flyte's icy stare, Cassie smiled for the first time that day.

FLYTE

Earlier that day, former Detective Sergeant Phyllida Flyte had faced her first big test in her new role. She'd felt nervous, but not in a bad way: more than fifteen years in the Job had taught her that a dash of anxiety could give you an edge over your opponent.

And having seen the case file, opponent was precisely the word she'd use to describe PC Ashley Skinner.

Flyte was sitting opposite Skinner and her Police Federation rep for her first interview as an investigator for the Independent Office for Police Conduct. To Flyte's left sat her mentor William Wentworth, veteran investigator and former prosecution barrister.

The interview room was a far cry from the bare and brutal version found at the average nick – it was painted a soothing pastel peach colour and had framed prints on the wall – *for crying out loud*.

After reading the misconduct caution, Flyte looked up from her file and tried to smile. 'As you are aware, this interview is in relation to Katya Adamsky's contact with police and specifically your actions prior to her murder by her husband Pawel. If we decide there is a case to answer you may be referred to a misconduct meeting or hearing which could result in disciplinary proceedings.'

A glance at William to ensure she'd got the legalese right. 'But all that aside, we just need to establish what happened here.'

Ashley nodded fervently. 'You and me both,' she said, pulling her best helpful smile. Flyte noticed she'd had her teeth whitened, probably for the interview.

Ashley's conduct was being investigated for her actions – or more accurately, inaction – in a domestic abuse case that had ended with thirty-one-year-old Katya Adamsky being stabbed, strangled and – just for completeness' sake – battered to death by her husband.

'You were aware that Katya had previously called police about her husband's behaviour before you first attended their address?'

'Yes, but she never said he hit her. That didn't come out till his trial.'

'Hmm.' Flyte referred to her notes 'Nonetheless there was a history of disturbances at the marital home, including neighbours reporting a man repeatedly shouting, "I'm going to kill you." And when you went the first time, it was because Katya had called police to say she was "frightened of her husband". Correct?'

'Yes, but when we attended she said she wanted to withdraw the complaint.'

Flyte sent her an acid smile. 'Hardly uncommon among victims of abuse, especially if the perpetrator is still in the house. So when you turned up with PC Dodds, you interviewed them.' She glanced at her notes with a frown. 'Separately?'

'That's right.' Ashley nodded.

'According to your notes she didn't complain of any violence? But you saw fresh fingermarks on her neck, throttle marks. How did she say she'd got them?'

'She said it was a sex game they played.'

'Right.' Flyte paused and turned a page of her file. 'The husband said the same thing to PC Dodds. In exactly the same words.'

Another nod.

'But according to both your notebooks, these exchanges with Katya and her husband took place at exactly the same time, 11.15 p.m. – in their kitchen-diner.' Putting her head on one side Flyte asked, 'How big is that room, Ashley?'

She pulled an uncomfortable shrug. 'I couldn't tell you.'

'Well, I can tell you that having visited the scene and measured it myself, it is three and a half metres long by two and a half metres wide. So it's clear that you interviewed Katya within earshot of the man who'd inflicted her neck injury.'

'He wasn't listening,' said Ashley, but she threw a look at her union rep.

'Let's take a look at the other actions you took, shall we?' Flyte went on. 'You reported the incident as "medium risk", rather than "high risk", which meant that if Katya called the police again it wouldn't automatically receive a priority response.'

Ashley said nothing.

'How many domestic violence cases have you attended, Ashley?'

'Oh, hundreds,' said Ashley with feeling. 'There's a lot of men out there who can't control their temper.'

The 'red mist' explanation of domestic abuse – which Flyte knew had been proven to be inadequate and dangerous in countless studies. One woman was murdered every four days by their partner or ex-partner, and most of them had previously suffered – and often reported – clear-cut signs of abusive behaviour.

Flyte checked the notes again. 'Katya told you that her husband stopped her going out with her friends, and had taken her car keys away.'

'Yeah, but I made sure he gave the keys back to her. And gave him words of advice.'

'"Words of advice".' Flyte let the phrase hang in the air for a long moment. 'Did it not occur to you that this was a red flag? A classic sign of coercive and controlling behaviour? A pattern of control and abuse that often predicts an escalation to serious assault and even murder?'

'I just thought he was . . . bossy.' She shrugged. 'I mean it's a different culture, eastern Europe, isn't it?'

Flyte just stared at her. 'Have you read the College of Police DASH guidance on domestic abuse?'

'Not yet.'

'Not yet? It's been out for four years!' Flyte heard her mentor William clear his throat. *Steady on*, she told herself.

'Are you aware of the Silent Solution, Ashley?'

'Yeah.' Ashley sat up straight – she knew the answer to this one. 'It allows members of the public to make a silent call to police and press 55 to indicate they're in danger.'

'Yet you didn't tell Katya about it? Even as a precaution?'

Ashley shook her head, clearly realising too late that her previous answer had been a mistake.

The Silent Solution had been created specifically for domestic abuse victims. Katya's mobile phone had been found beside her on the kitchen floor. At some point during her husband's two-hour assault she'd had the chance to call 999 and left the line open, apparently believing the urban myth that a silent call would automatically trigger a police visit.

Hearing no response from the caller, the police operator had hung up, assuming a misdial. Shortly afterwards Pawel had returned to where Katya lay and finished the job.

It had been another hour before Katya's sister, unable to raise her, had let herself in the flat and found her battered and bloodied body. She had rushed upstairs to find Katya's ten-month-old daughter in her cot who, thankfully, had escaped her father's wrath.

'You know what gets me is that they both knew there was a baby in that house but they couldn't have cared less.' Flyte was blowing off steam to her mentor William in a nearby coffee shop. 'They even stopped off to pick up KFC on the way to the callout!'

'It's an upsetting case,' said William, nodding in agreement. After taking a sip of tea he looked at her kindly. 'It can't be easy for you, jumping the fence, as it were,' he said. 'Having to treat people who were once fellow officers as suspects.'

She nodded, squeezing the lemon slice into her Earl Grey, but she was actually thinking how easy she was finding it to hold her former Met colleagues to account. Too often during her time as a detective she had buttoned her lip, and failed to challenge the attitudes she'd encountered: towards women, gays . . . anyone who wasn't white, male and straight – The Other. It had been six months since her brief career as a murder detective had ended in circumstances that had demolished her remaining trust in the police force. When the opportunity to become an IOPC investigator had come up she hadn't hesitated for long before applying for a 'career break' from the Met – serving police officers not being eligible to work for the IOPC. It had been a tough moment, handing back her warrant card after so long, but she'd had no doubts, feeling certain that the 'break' would become a divorce.

'So,' she said, 'will Ashley Skinner be dismissed for the failures that let Katya die?'

'We simply determine if there's a case to answer,' said William patiently. 'As you know, after that it's out of our hands and up to the panel who will hear her case and decide whether she should face dismissal or any disciplinary sanction.'

'She'll probably just get a slapped wrist and further training, right?' – hearing the bitterness in her own voice.

He sent her a thoughtful look. 'Listen, Phyllida, it's entirely understandable that you have strong personal reasons for wanting the Met to clean up its act. We're all working towards that. But personal feelings aside, we also have to consider the best way to produce a better police service.' He leaned in and lowered his voice. 'If all the Ashley Skinners were dismissed the Met would lose thousands of uniforms overnight. We've established that there was a culture from senior officers at her nick around not taking domestic abuse seriously, and she does have seven years of unblemished service.'

'Yes, but . . .'

'Sanctions against officers found guilty of misconduct are important, of course they are, but we must never forget the learning aspect of our work. Identifying and disseminating recommendations for improvements that can make a real difference on the ground.'

Flyte nodded half-heartedly. It was dawning on her that there had been one big advantage in dealing with straightforward villains. As a police officer it wasn't your job to give them learning and hugs, just to catch them and put them behind bars.

Chapter Five

The next morning on her way to work Cassie saw a gaggle of people milling about on the towpath close to where Bronte had fallen.

Getting closer, she saw that some were aiming their phones at Bronte's balcony or taking selfies, no doubt posting to social media. At the junction of towpath and estate there now lay a drift of flowers in plastic wrap, cards – some home-made – and here and there a tea-light holder. As she passed the pop-up wake, a young woman was just bending down to add another bunch of tulips to the canal-side shrine, her face blurred with tears. Cassie avoided her eye: these public outpourings of sympathy for a stranger made her feel uncomfortable.

She'd been sixteen when the news dropped that Amy Winehouse – Camden's most celebrated resident and recovering druggie – had died after a vodka binge. Her feelings of seemingly inconsolable anguish had endured for weeks on end – something that oddly she couldn't recall experiencing after being told, at the age of four, that both her parents were dead.

Cassie and her friends had done the whole 'Amy death trip' – holding an overnight vigil outside her home, making a pilgrimage to all the pubs she'd drunk in, and later, travelling to her grave up in Edgware cemetery to light a black candle and (without any sense of irony) drink a bottle of supermarket own-label vodka. But in the last few years she'd witnessed Amy's transformation from a real person with a huge talent into a brand, and Camden turned into a magnet for death tourists. It made Cassie uneasy: sure, there was genuine admiration but it was clear that many were getting a fix of ersatz angst at the avoidable death of a troubled young woman.

Surely Bronte wasn't big enough yet for her death to have the same impact?

Fifteen minutes later she got her answer. Rounding the corner into the mortuary car park she blinked at the scene that confronted her. There were two TV crews filming the mortuary, a Japanese female reporter in a suit doing a piece to camera, and a bunch of random civilians aiming their phones at the building.

WTF?

Clearly they had heard that Bronte's body was here. Crossing the car park, Cassie felt her blood pressure spike as she bumped into a young woman with a buzz cut dyed pink, who was walking backwards while filming on her phone. Swinging round, she pulled a big fake smile and said, 'Sorry, my bad!' but then fell into step alongside Cassie. 'I'm Charly' – pausing to allow Cassie to introduce herself, an invitation she ignored. 'You look like you work here? It's terrible news isn't it. Did you see Bronte come in?'

Cassie said nothing but it didn't stop the questions. 'Has anyone viewed the body? When will we find out how she died?' By now they had reached the mortuary entrance. 'Could you give me a quote?' asked Charly.

'Sure.' Cassie smiled. 'Go fuck yourself.'

Only then did she realise that the woman had been filming her all along, with her phone held casually at waist height. *Marvellous.*

She swiped herself in as fast as she could, horribly aware of the arc of phones and cameras aimed at her. *Jesus.* Was this a taste of what life had been like for Bronte?

She went straight into the mortuary manager's office. 'Christ, Doug, have you seen . . .?'

'I know, I know.' Doug was a worrier at the best of times, but now his face was creased and pale and he was rubbing his sternum like he did whenever he got an attack of acid.

'What is wrong with people?' fumed Cassie, digging in her bag for some antacid tabs. 'Aren't they trespassing?'

'It's a grey area apparently,' he sighed. 'But the police are on their way: they can order them to disperse to avoid a public nuisance.'

'Thank Christ! Imagine coming to view a body of someone you loved and facing that.' She shook her head. 'Are Bronte's . . . I mean, Sophia's family coming in?'

Doug nodded. 'Yes, her mother and father are due in about an hour – I thought that would give you enough time to make her . . . respectable.'

'I'm not a miracle worker,' she muttered, picturing her damaged face and stoved-in head.

'I know you'll do your best. At least there's no PM list today. Oh, and just so you know, the parents separated years ago, can't stand each other apparently, but they've called a truce to view the body together because it's what Sophie would have wanted.'

'Oh great,' said Cassie, handing him the tablets. Estranged couples could be a nightmare: rather than uniting them, the death of a child often brought old grievances bubbling to the surface.

Doing without a shower, she got straight into scrubs before going to prep Bronte for viewing.

After transferring the body-bagged figure to a trolley she wheeled it into the autopsy suite. Since there were no postmortems scheduled, Jason was rostered off, which meant no dance music on the radio, no whistling and no tacky comments. That helped her mood. You could keep your spa days, whale music and yoga – the solitary moments she spent here with only her guests for company was the closest she ever got to chilled.

Extracting Bronte from the body bag was easier now that rigor was fading. Again she covered her nakedness, this time with the red plush viewing coverlet, before casting an eye over her damaged face and head. After the PM she had carefully padded out her smashed skull with cotton wool and lint, more or less restoring the natural curve of her head, but the lividity that stained her face purple from the side of the temple down past her jaw presented more of a challenge.

'OK, Bronte, let's get you looking nice for your mum and dad.'

Cassie noticed that her right eye had reopened, and seemed to be sending her a hostile look.

Don't be ridiculous, she told herself.

She reached for some cotton wool. Lifting the eyelid gently, she used tweezers to place a wisp on the eyeball before lifting the eyelid down over it. 'The slight friction will keep your eyes closed,' she murmured, repeating the routine with the left eye and smoothing down the lids.

Luckily, the skin over the cheekbone was still intact so it didn't need micro-stitching. Cassie got to work with some concealer and foundation she'd bought on her way in – and ten minutes later was applying a final dusting of powder. The lividity was still there but no more than a shadow now.

She had washed and towel-dried Bronte's long, curly, near-black hair the previous day but it was still damp. Firing up the hairdryer she kept in her locker she lifted each hank of hair to dry over her fingers. 'You always had fabulous hair, so thick,' she said. It proved a godsend now, concealing the neat stitches Cassie had used to repair the ear-to-ear incision over the top of her head.

Having arranged Bronte's hair around her face, she stood back to assess her efforts. Not bad at all given what she'd had to work with, although the one-sided swelling to Bronte's face gave it the suggestion of a sneer.

As if she were saying: *Is that the best you've got?*

Chapter Six

In the reception area Bronte's mother and father looked like a tableau of an estranged couple. Chrysanthi Angelopoulos sat in one corner, as far as it was possible to be from her ex-husband, George, who'd taken the other corner, elbows on his thighs and head in his hands.

As Cassie greeted them, they both struggled to focus on what she was saying, their expressions grief-dazed, still in the zombie-like state inhabited by the just-bereaved: the death of their only daughter not yet a reality.

Minutes later, in the viewing room Chrysanthi stood on the other side of Cassie from George, using her as a buffer zone. None of this came as a surprise: Cassie had seen time and again how sudden, unexpected death could magnify emotions and resurrect long-simmering resentment. She'd even seen grieving relatives throw punches at each other.

Keeping her voice low and matter-of-fact, she prepared them for how Bronte, currently behind curtained glass doors, would look, making eye contact and using the opportunity to check each of them out. She'd thought at first that they were both in their mid-fifties, but now, seeing Chrysanthi's barely lined face and clean jawline in close-up, she decided she was probably only in her forties – perhaps fifteen years younger than her ex?

It was her clothes and the vibe she gave off that put years on her: a dowdy calf-length black dress that hid her shape and sturdy, 'sensible' shoes. She put Cassie in mind of a Greek lady of a previous generation – the kind you might glimpse through the kitchen door of a taverna, or making her way to church in a tiny mountain village.

After ensuring that they were both ready, she pulled the cord to open the curtains covering the glass doors to the anteroom where their daughter lay.

She had arranged Bronte to be viewed in profile, showing her undamaged right side; the coverlet covering her slender body to just below the chin to hide the midline stitching. Chrysanthi's hand shot out, flattening her palm against the glass, a primal gesture.

'Would you like to go in?' asked Cassie gently. Getting a fierce nod in reply.

George – blank-faced, shell-shocked – followed them inside. Chrysanthi immediately took Bronte's right hand, milk-white against the deep red of the coverlet, and bent down so that their heads were almost touching. Chafing the dead hand between hers like she could warm it, she started speaking softly in mellifluous Greek, as if comforting a crying child.

The beautiful words fell on Cassie's ear like music, and she found she could make out a handful of them which had survived the metamorphosis from ancient to modern Greek.

Agape meant beloved; she couldn't recall what *hamartia* meant.

Cassie had got her science A levels at evening classes, but after starting work as a mortuary technician had discovered that ninety-five per cent of anatomical and medical terms were rooted in the classical languages. And so she'd signed up for a final A level in Classics, and was still learning Latin and Greek, for their beauty as much as their practical value. Like *coracoid* – the Greek name for the hook-like process on the shoulder bone – named for the crooked beak of the crow. *Or raven.*

Turning to George, Cassie sought his eyes: most men found it harder to express emotion but that didn't mean they weren't suffering: if anything it probably made it worse. He swiped at his eyes, took a shuddering breath. 'She was my life,' he said, lifting his hand and letting it fall, a hopeless gesture.

The saddest thing to Cassie was that he and Chrysanthi wouldn't be able to comfort one another or share memories of their daughter.

'When can we bury her?' asked George, taking refuge in the practical. He was tall like his wife and had clearly been handsome when he was young – was still good-looking, with a full head of dark hair silvered attractively at the temples. Unlike his wife, he was dressed unshowily but stylishly, in a well-cut dark blue jacket with a shirt and tie underneath. Cassie knew he was a successful businessman who'd also acted as his daughter's manager, so he must have been used to hanging out with music industry types.

'The pathologist will advise the coroner of the provisional cause of death,' she told him. 'And if there's nothing untoward she will release the body.'

George frowned. 'Untoward? But Sophia . . . took her own life?' His voice becoming hoarse on the last words.

'As you know the police found what appeared to be drugs at your daughter's flat and the lab is conducting blood tests.' Cassie hesitated. 'I'm afraid the results might take . . . a while.'

Or more likely months, on a routine PM. 'The coroner needs to know if the balance of Sophia's mind was disturbed before an inquest can be held.'

Chrysanthi's head jerked up, fixing her ex-husband with a look of hatred so intense it took Cassie aback. 'This is *your fault*!' she hissed. 'It was *you* who kept on at her to sing, filling her head with record contracts and getting famous, just so *you* could get some of the glory' – her Greek accent surfacing in her fury.

George just stood there mute, probably knowing that responding would only make it worse.

Chrysanthi wasn't done. 'My little girl was too ... *fragile* for that world.' She pointed a finger at her ex, a look of hatred on her face so implacable it was frightening. 'God might forgive you your sins, Georgios Angelopoulos, but I promise you, *I never will.*'

Chapter Seven

In the changing room, Cassie went through the ritual of replacing her lip and eyebrow piercings which she habitually took out for viewings, in case a grieving family member might find her look a bit hard core.

Eviscerating bodies was a breeze compared to dealing with the poor bastards left behind – and this one had been tough: Chrysanthi's raw grief and her fury at her ex, and the fact that Cassie had known Bronte, had left her feeling shaken.

Because of what you did, said her inner voice.

Cassie shook her head to dispel it and meeting her own gaze in the mirror said, 'I'm looking after her mum and dad as best I can.'

She'd given them both her mobile number, saying they could view their daughter anytime, in contravention of the recent email from the trust saying relatives should be 'encouraged' to wait until bodies were released to the undertakers, where they could be viewed 'in a more appropriate environment'. The kind of official bullshit that made Cassie want to puke: the real reason was to reduce the mortuary workload.

At lunchtime, Cassie took the underground tunnel linking the mortuary to the hospital to get into Camden: it was usually only used by the porters bringing bodies over, but she couldn't face the gauntlet of press and social media ghouls who were still hanging around on the pavement outside where the cops had corralled them behind a barrier.

'Hey, long time, stranger!' said Tina, in a voice gravelled by four decades of nicotine. She'd grabbed a corner table at the little Greek-Cypriot taverna between the High Street and Bayham Street – a rare survivor among the chain outlets that had sprouted across Camden.

'Too long: my fault,' said Cassie with a guilty grimace. She'd always liked Tina, but making friends – and keeping them – had never been her strong point. 'Love the hair,' she said, admiring the lavender ombre rinse through Tina's bobbed blonde cut.

'I'm not dead yet!' Tina was in her sixties but she dressed well and took care of herself – serious fag habit aside.

After they'd ordered meze for two, Tina delved into her bag and handed an envelope across the table. 'Here are the pics you were after. I printed them at the best resolution.'

'You're a total star,' said Cassie, leafing through the police photos from the scene of Bronte's suicide. Tina was a crime scene manager and they had worked together on dozens of forensic PMs over the years. 'Obvs I didn't get them from you.'

Tina shrugged. 'You're all right,' she said. 'I know you get involved with the cases and I think that's a good thing. We both know what some of the pathologists can be like on routines. Sloppy fuckers' – unleashing a laugh so unapologetically filthy that diners at a table nearby stopped eating to watch. 'Anyway, I'm retiring in a few months. What are they gonna do? Fire me?'

Cassie grinned: Tina didn't take shit from any pathologist – or detective.

'So this is the balcony.' Cassie scanned the photo – it was modern-looking, clearly an addition to the original Victorian structure, with a balustrade made of toughened glass with steel edges. 'Regulation height?' she asked.

'Yep. Just over the 1,100 mil.'

'And this gap here, between the bottom of the glass and the concrete footings?'

'All legal. No more than a few inches.'

'I can't see anything here she could have stood on, you know, to jump off? Like a chair.'

Tina shook her head.

'I dunno, Tina. If I was gonna chuck myself off a high building I'd want to make sure I jumped nice and clear so I didn't bounce off balconies on the way down? But she fell really close to the building, didn't she?'

Tina tipped her head, considering it. 'Yes, but if she was in a state, or off her head, she might have just tipped herself over the balustrade. You know there was a suicide note? A text to her mum from her phone.'

'Yeah, it was mentioned in the police report.'

The waitress delivered their meze and Cassie put the images back in the envelope. Was she simply letting her personal history with Bronte cloud her judgement?

Tina was watching her with intelligent eyes. Lowering her voice, she asked, 'You don't think there's anything moody about it?'

Cassie smiled: she hadn't heard anyone use *moody* – Cockney for questionable, dodgy – in years. 'Not really. I suppose I can't get my head round why she would top herself when she'd literally just made it big.'

Tina made a face. 'Pressure? Having all that fame suddenly at twenty-seven can't be easy. You know she had a druggie past? She was in rehab a few months back, after splitting up with the junkie boyfriend. The one who had his own band?'

'I don't know that much about her,' admitted Cassie. She was allergic to social media – had tried Insta half-heartedly for a few weeks but hated the way it constantly nagged at you, like a dog begging at table. 'Do you?'

'Abi, my youngest, was crazy about her,' said Tina, rolling her eyes. 'We've had a lot of tears. You know her breakout hit went viral on TikTok?'

'Vaguely.'

'"Clean Break". That was how she got the record deal. And the single went triple-platinum.'

'So was she minted?'

Tina lifted a shoulder. 'Minted enough to buy that flat.'

They shared a look. Since Cassie had left home a decade ago Camden's property prices and rents had skyrocketed, forcing ordinary people to move out to the suburbs, leaving the centre to the seriously well-off. If it hadn't been for an old mate from her squatting days going to 'find himself' in Goa and letting his boat to her for a token rent she'd be living miles away in some random suburb.

'I can't believe you missed the video of it on TikTok,' said Tina. Pushing her plate away, she picked up her phone, tapped at it.

'Christ on a bike!' Her head shot up to look at Cassie. 'You need to see this.'

Chapter Eight

Half an hour later and Cassie was back at the mortuary, having installed TikTok and viewed the vid about a dozen times.

It opened with a slow zoom out from the mortuary at night, low angle and filtered to look like Dracula's castle, set to a doomy drone. Then it cut hard to a caption, the words against black:

What REALLY happened to Bronte?

Then Bronte's hit single 'Clean Break' – a dance music track with a kinetic beat – blared out over a fast-cut montage of the scrum outside the mortuary, before the voice of the pink-haired girl Charly came on, questioning Cassie. Then the music was dramatically silenced to highlight Cassie's answer: '*Go fuck yourself*' – the audio prissily bleeped to erase the f-word, her lips pixelated. Then jump-cut images of the police herding everyone away from the mortuary followed by the infamous shot of Bronte captured by paparazzi outside her flat. The doomy music returned, this time over a pull-out from Bronte's balcony that swung down to the towpath and the pile of flowers and tributes. Cut to another caption on black:

Suicide? – which evaporated to be replaced by words that loomed out of black:

Or is that what somebody WANTS you to believe?

Cassie had just showed the vid – which already had 310,000 views – to Doug. 'I mean can she even do that?' she asked, pacing his office furiously. 'Put out images of me without my permission?'

Doug shook his head helplessly. 'I have no idea. It's the Wild West, isn't it? Social media. Do you want me to talk to the Trust, get the lawyers' advice?'

Cassie blew out an exasperated breath before shaking her head. 'That would be like pouring petrol on a bin fire.'

'Who is this @Charly_Detective?' asked Doug, peering at the screen with a mystified expression.

'She's one of these keyboard detectives,' Cassie raged. Even a social media refusenik like her couldn't avoid their 'theories' which were increasingly getting picked up by the mainstream press. 'Any time there's any kind of supposedly unexplained death they pile in with their idiot theories just to get more views. This kind of shit is the last thing Bronte's mum and dad need right now.'

Cassie wanted to have a proper look at the pics Tina had given her from the scene of Bronte's suicide without having to explain her interest to Archie, so she texted him to say she was working late to catch up on admin and not to wait up. Archie's reply was a sad face emoji, which made her feel bad, before her guilt swiftly morphed into irritation. What was wrong with needing a bit of time to herself? It wasn't like she was cheating on him or anything.

She wound up in The Black Heart, once her go-to drinking haunt, in a converted Victorian warehouse in the market. It was her first visit in a while, since she and Archie had become a proper item, but she felt instantly at home. Despite the skull imagery and goth memorabilia it had a cosy charm, festooned with fairy lights, although she didn't recognise the barman under the big orange neon cross that still hung over the bar.

Taking her beer to a corner table, she pulled out her phone, having photographed the crime scene images and protected them with face ID.

But an hour later, any idea she'd had of spotting some clue the cops has missed had well and truly faded. The photos all fit with the police report which had found no sign of forced entry or violence.

But . . . was it her imagination or did the photo of the kitchen table in Bronte's flat feel like a still life? Like something posed? Her smartphone, green Rizlas and pack of Marlboro Reds were arranged alongside a psychedelic packet – the kind that synthetic cannabinoid was sold in. Cassie smoked a bit of weed, took the occasional pill, but she wouldn't touch the stuff, knowing it had been linked to psychosis and increased risk of suicide in the vulnerable.

Bracing herself, she opened TikTok, and flinched to see Bronte trending. Putting in her earbuds to cut the sound of The Cure coming through the pub speakers she listened again to Bronte's breakout hit 'Clean Break', which had already clocked up more than half a million new plays since her death. The hook 'Give me a break, break, break/I need a break, break, break . . .' was horribly catchy – a club anthem that conjured up a sea of waving hands.

From the lyrics the 'clean break' had a double meaning – reffing her split from a man who'd left her 'broken and broke', but also from 'pills and spills', and 'JD and coke' – the latter delivered with an audible wink that made it clear she wasn't talking about Coca-Cola. It sounded like a hundred other dance numbers but was elevated by her punchy contralto delivery: the voice of a woman who wasn't taking any more crap.

As Cassie closed the app she found herself wondering whether she was any different to all the ghouls out there. Perhaps some dark hidden story was somehow easier to accept than the grim but simple truth: that a twenty-seven-year-old with the world at her feet could smoke some dodgy gear and tip herself into the void.

Chapter Nine

Cassie's route home took her past the turning to the mortuary, where she was relieved to see that the rubberneckers of earlier had gone, at least for the night. She slowed her pace, struck by a sudden thought. *Had she turned off the body store lights when she'd left to go to the pub?* It wasn't like her to forget something like that but still . . . Swearing, she dug out her security pass.

Once inside, she opened the door to the body store – and found it pitch-dark, and silent but for the murmur of the giant fridge.

You're losing it.

She flicked the lights on. 'Goodnight again, everyone,' she said, picturing her guests slumbering behind the wall of polished steel. Her eye fell on the drawer marked 'Sophia Angelopoulos' and she added, 'Goodnight, Bronte.'

Her head whipped to the right. *What was that?* A faint scraping sound from the autopsy suite next door. Then silence. With every sense on high alert she edged towards the door and into the corridor. Heard the scraping again and then a clunk. Turning the handle of the autopsy suite door as quietly as possible, she inched it open – and saw something in one of the frosted-glass windows set high up in the outer wall.

The head and shoulders of a figure silhouetted against the night sky.

'Hey!' shouted Cassie, flicking on the light switch. She closed her eyes, blinded by the sudden assault of fluorescent light, and heard a loud *scrape-thump*.

With her heart tap-dancing in her chest she raced out of the main entrance, pulling the door closed behind her. Sprinted around the mortuary to the side where the windows gave onto a narrow strip of concrete path and a line of trees. Only then did she slow her pace, realising she might be in danger.

But all she found there was a ladder lying haphazardly on the concrete. Earlier that day two guys with chainsaws had been cutting back the dense leylandii that screened the mortuary from the hospital car park: they must have left the ladder here to finish up tomorrow.

Cassie stood there panting, feeling her heart jumping around. There was a soft breeze but the black-green of the leylandii foliage was eerily still and silent for a living thing.

She pulled out her phone and turned on the torch. Scoping the area ahead, she could see no sign of life but beyond the corner of the mortuary building, shaded from any lamplight, the rear wall stood in deep darkness. Was somebody hiding in the shadows?

Taking a deep breath, she killed the torch and stepped quietly closer, buoyed by a sense of outrage. If someone had tried to break into her mortuary, threatening her guests, she was going to catch them. *Stupid?* Maybe. But she'd always had a settled sense of confidence that she could handle herself.

Less than a metre from the corner, a dark figure sprung out.

She yelped in shock, raising her phone, as if that would be any use as a weapon.

'Cassie?' The face swam into focus.

'Oh Jesus Christ, Barney, you scared the shit out of me.' Barney was one of the hospital security guards.

'You and me both! I was having a cig in the car park and I see someone creeping around over here – turns out it was you.' Nodding down at her phone, which she still had half raised like a weapon, Barney gave a wheezing laugh. 'What were you going to do with that? Insta me to death?'

Cassie was still breathing hard. 'Did you see anyone else over here, before me?'

He shook his head 'No, it was the torch that alerted me.'

'Someone put a ladder up to one of the windows.' She lifted her chin. 'Could you keep an eye out? In case they come back?'

'I would do, but I'm going off shift. I could ask Davy when I hand over?'

They shared a sceptical look: Davy didn't stray far from the A & E waiting room with its array of vending machines selling crisps and chocolate.

'I'll do a proper look round now,' he told her. 'You go back in the mortuary.'

After closing the entrance door behind her she was tempted to call 999 but decided against it. If the cops even bothered to attend, which was unlikely, the prospect of talking to some patronising uniform who would probably doubt her story, filled her with gloom. She'd tell Doug about it in the morning and tell the tree-butchers not to leave ladders lying around.

Going back inside, she went looking for the long-handled hook they used to open and close the high windows: although she could barely recall the last time they'd been opened. Then she remembered that Jason had prepped a decomp the previous day: an old gent who'd died in his sleep and laid in his bed undiscovered for three or four weeks. He must have opened it to clear the smell and then failed to close it properly.

As she clunked it shut, she wondered who the intruder could have been. The obvious candidate was surely one of the true crime sleuths from Insta or TikTok who'd been hanging round since Bronte's death; maybe, spotting an open window, they'd hoped to sneak an image of the place where 'Tragic Bronte' had undergone her post-mortem.

Ghouls.

After pulling on her jacket she went back into the body store to turn the lights off.

The vibe in here was usually tranquil, but now she picked up a kind of jangling in the air, as if the attempted intrusion had left her agitated. Fanciful? *Probably*. But something drew her to the drawer marked 'Sophia Angelopoulos aka Bronte'. She went to set her hand flat on the steel – and got an electric shock.

Don't leave me!

The words clear, in Bronte's slightly harsh tones, and undercut by a note of desperate appeal.

Chapter Ten

It was 7 a.m. the next morning by the time she climbed aboard *Dreamcatcher* clutching two takeaway coffees and feeling exhausted. Thank Christ she was rostered off.

Archie stuck his head out of the cabin and she held out his coffee, saying, 'Peace offering?' He took it wordlessly, not returning her smile, before heading back down below. In the cabin she found him shaving in the tiny mirror hung over the kitchen sink. On another day she might have told him to use the one in the bathroom but this morning she was on the back foot.

'Look, I went for a drink after work with Jax and it got messy.' Trying not to sound rehearsed. 'I didn't fancy walking along the towpath pissed . . . so I kipped down on her sofa.'

Nada. Archie just splashed his razor in the sink and drew the blade up under his chin.

'Oh, come on, Archie, don't be like that.'

Taking a towel, he dried off his face before turning to her, his grey eyes serious. 'I was worried sick about you.'

Cassie grimaced: she could kick herself. *How could she have forgotten to call him?*

'I'm really sorry I forgot to text you till this morning. Like I say, I was wasted.'

'I'm just starting to wonder if you really want me here,' said Archie, pulling on his Barbour jacket.

'Of course, I do,' said Cassie, but she knew she didn't sound very convincing.

'I agreed to come live on this stupid ... floating coffin' – throwing a dark look at the ceiling an inch above his head. 'When we could be living in a nice warm flat with a washing machine and a TV. And *space*. The last few weeks you've been out every other night, and when you are here you're bad-tempered or monosyllabic half the time. I already feel like I'm here on sufferance – and now this?'

She bit her lip. Why didn't she just tell him the truth? That someone had tried to get into the mortuary and she'd felt she had no alternative but to stay there overnight. *To protect Bronte.* But it would just sound mad, and she'd have to get into what had happened at school that day to make Bronte leave and how bad she still felt about it.

She sent Archie an imploring look. 'Look if you're worried that I'm seeing someone else, I swear—'

'I'm worried you're not seeing *me*,' he said, zipping up his Barbour. 'I'm not really part of your life. More of a tolerated lodger.'

And before she could find the words to disagree, he was off, the boat rocking as he jumped down onto the towpath.

Her relationships always came to this. She took a kind of bitter comfort from the thought.

Within a heartbeat of her grandmother opening her front door those beady eyes had noticed something was amiss. But then the person who raised you from the age of four to seventeen was going to have certain insights.

Her gran didn't say anything, just kissed Cassie on each cheek, once, twice, three times in the Polish way, before ushering her inside. Cassie sniffed the air, detecting a steamy, savoury smell coming out of the kitchen.

'*Golabki?*' she asked.

'*Czesc.*' She nodded, steering her granddaughter into the living room. 'Just cooked. Sit down, I'll get you a plate.'

Ignoring Cassie's faint protests, she came back with two of the cabbage dumplings called *golabki* – literally, 'pigeons' – because of their shape rather than their contents, ladled into a soup plate with some of their cooking broth, which shimmered with goodness.

Cassie realised that after a night passed trying to sleep on the bench in the mortuary changing room she was hungry.

Her gran watched her eat, smiling but silent. *This one you had to give the space to speak, if and when she wanted.*

The simple savoury goodness of the meal – together with the warm fug of the living room, the gas fire *pop popping*, the hum of Polish spices and the sweet scent of her gran's face powder – catapulted Cassie back to her childhood. 'Have you put something different in these?' she asked, sensing some extra layer of umami beneath the wild mushrooms, buckwheat kasha, and obligatory fistful of garlic.

'You can't guess?' Babcia clapped her hands together with glee. 'It's soy sauce – just a dash.'

Babcia experimenting with culinary fusion? Cassie was surprised to find herself scandalised but she had to admit it worked.

After she'd finished, and made coffee for them both, she came and sat opposite her grandmother. 'It must have been tough for you, Babcia, bringing me up after Mum died and Dad went to prison.'

From the age of four Cassie had been brought up believing that she'd been orphaned when a car accident killed both her parents, and it was barely a year since she'd discovered what really happened. Her mother Katherine had been murdered, with her father Callum being convicted and sentenced to life for the crime – the car crash simply a fiction invented by Babcia to protect her granddaughter from the ugly truth. After his release from prison, Callum had turned up out of the blue to claim his innocence and Cassie had got drawn into investigating the case, finally helping to find the real murderer.

Now, he'd been officially cleared and was back in her life, and living locally, although he was currently on an extended visit to his home town of Belfast and beyond to see his family. *Their family*. Cassie hadn't just acquired an unexpected father but a clutch of aunts, uncles, and cousins – a discovery she was still getting to grips with.

Cassie pictured Archie's expression that morning: hurt and angry at her thoughtlessness. It was only recently that she had begun to understand the shadow that growing up without either parent had cast over her life – above all how difficult she found it making and sustaining relationships.

'How old were you when I came to live here, Babcia?' she asked. 'In your late fifties?' She had only recently started to appreciate how tough it must have been for her grandmother, taking on a hyperactive four-year-old so late in life.

Weronika nodded, glancing at the photo of Cassie on the mantelpiece alongside the one of her daughter who she called Katerina, and everyone else called Kath. 'When you were little you weren't too much trouble, but later, at fourteen, fifteen' – she waved an expressive hand – 'it was a little bit more difficult.'

'I'm sorry, Babcia,' said Cassie, awkwardly. She wasn't much good at apologies either. 'At that age you literally don't even think about other people, what they might be going through. You spend every minute just trying to work yourself out.' She could remember it still, the agonised self-questioning: *Am I pretty? Am I smart? Do people* like *me?*

Babcia nodded. 'It must have been even harder for you, the only girl at school without a mama and papa. Having your old granny coming to pick you up' – this with a wry but loving smile.

Cassie looked away. *It was true.* In her early teens she *had* been embarrassed by her gran, with her old lady clothes and uncool perm – while at the same time feeling hot shame for her disloyalty. The other girls' mums were so cool, with their on-trend outfits, ripped jeans and edgy haircuts. Especially Natasha's mum, *obviously*. Natasha was top dog, the *capo di capo* of the girls at the school, who, even in the dowdy-brown school uniform, still managed to signal her status. Her hair was dyed a dark glossy chestnut and cut in a severe fringe in homage to Katy Perry's retro style, nails manicured and varnished in a just-this-side of regulation natural, eyelashes dyed, blazer sleeves pushed up to show off her sunbed tan. The fourteen-year-old Cassie had studied her covertly in assembly, or while playing netball, like you might try to catch a glimpse of a celeb. She'd nursed a crush on her, *of course she had*, but that aside, she could still remember the intense need to be *accepted* by Natasha and her crew.

Now Cassie could see that her idol was an airhead and a bully. She'd put that horrible year or two behind her long ago, rarely thinking about it, but now she found herself wishing that she could go back and have the chance to play things differently. Especially around Sophia. *Sorry*, Bronte.

'What was it like for you at school in Poland, Babcia?' – realising that she'd never asked her before.

'Oh it was great fun!' – becoming animated. 'We were always boycotting lessons. We all refused to learn Russian, of course. And we loved to bait our history teachers, asking about how Stalin had invaded Poland alongside Hitler. And then there were the demonstrations! When you're young you don't consider the risks – the boys would get beaten up by riot cops and a few of us got snatched by the secret police.'

Cassie knew that as a student activist Weronika had herself been imprisoned for helping to organise a demo against the Soviet-backed regime. But it occurred to her that the oppression might have had an upside. 'You were all in it together, right? So I'm guessing you didn't get all the backbiting, the bitching about who was cool or uncool – you know the way girls can be together.'

Babcia narrowed her eyes. 'I've never really thought of it that way but you're right, *tygrysek*. We were united against a common enemy.' After a pause she went on, 'Was it bad for you then, at school? You never said anything.'

What would have been the point? School was a war zone in which adults were unarmed civilians.

'Oh, it wasn't that bad,' she said, getting a vivid image of how Kylie, one of the rough girls, used to grab her lunch box, and pretend to throw up at its contents – Polish sausage and giant gherkins instead of the regulation cheese strings and Wispa bars – making her little gang titter. Sophia came off even worse, like the time Kylie picked up a dolmades, a stuffed vine leaf, out of her box and waved it about in disgust. 'Oh my God! Look at the disgusting shit Dobby puts in her mouth!' Kylie had nicknamed Sophia 'Dobby' after the house elf in *Harry Potter* because she was the shortest girl in the class. 'It looks like an alien dick!' – positioning it between her legs to demonstrate.

If you were writing the Hollywood movie, Cassie and Sophia – the two outsiders – would make an alliance against the bullies. But in real life it was every teenage girl for herself. And she had to admit that Sophia could be annoying – always giving the teachers fancy boxes of chocs, and acting like she was superior to everyone because her dad was loaded. Cassie could picture her now, nose in the air, getting into his Mercedes outside school.

That's no excuse for what you did.

'Leave me alone,' Cassie muttered. The shrink she'd seen briefly last year had called them intrusive thoughts.

'Is everything all right, *tygrysek*?' Babcia looked worried.

After a moment of hesitation, Cassie told her about Sophia, aka Bronte, killing herself and how they'd been in the same class for a bit at school.

'God rest her soul,' said her gran, crossing herself. 'I saw about that poor child dying on the news but I didn't pick up on the name.' She paused, thinking. 'Angelopoulos you say? I have met her mother, Chrysanthi.'

'Seriously? Was this when I was at school?'

'*Nie, nie*. Just last year. Three or four times we chatted at church coffee mornings. That poor woman!'

Camden had several Catholic churches which had served the Irish community for decades – their congregations swelled by more recent arrivals from Poland – while the borough's Greek-origin population had four Orthodox churches to choose from. It turned out that Chrysanthi's church, St Ioannis, and Babcia's, St Bartholomew's, had a programme designed to foster interfaith relations, running social events to bring the two communities closer together.

'What was she like? Did she ever talk about her daughter?'

A troubled look crossed Babcia's face. 'Ah the poor thing hardly talked about anything else. Those two had a very difficult relationship. She didn't approve of her daughter's singing career – blamed it for the drink and drugs, the bad men. According to her, it was all the fault of her husband.' She shrugged resignedly. 'She married him far too young – when she was still a teenager. I gather the marriage went bad very soon afterwards.'

'But she didn't divorce him?'

'Oh, her religion wouldn't allow that. She is very devout.'

Which would help to explain Chrysanthi's bitterness against George: for her, marriage was a life sentence with no chance of parole.

'Did she say what went wrong between them?'

'I got the impression he was a Lothario' – pronouncing it with a long 'a' in the Mediterranean way. 'I felt so sorry for her. She was already a bitter woman, the kind who finds it difficult to move on. And now to lose her daughter. I must ask her for coffee, to condole with her.'

Cassie pictured Chrysanthi's raw grief as she cradled her daughter's body, her old-young face contorting with fury as she blamed her ex-husband for the death. One thing was certain: the chances of her 'moving on' now were zero.

Chapter Eleven

Cassie had gone straight from Babcia's flat to Camden Coroner's Court, relieved to have something to distract her from the situation with Archie, and the emotional turmoil that Bronte's death had stirred up.

Now she shuffled sideways on the back row of the public seating area so she was half hidden behind a pillar. She wanted to be able to see and hear the inquest proceedings without being seen herself. Dr Curzon was already here, sitting where witnesses waited to be called, ready to give his expert testimony, and she didn't want to risk him spotting her: he already thought she was an uppity minion and although it wasn't exactly forbidden for a mortuary tech to attend an inquest it would definitely be considered weird behaviour.

She was here because the case about to be heard – the unexplained death of twenty-six-year-old Felix Zuberi – had got under her skin. In the front row sat a professional-looking couple wearing dark suits, their shoulders touching – clearly his mum and dad. Mr and Mrs Zuberi hadn't viewed Felix's body at the mortuary, so there was no risk of them recognising Cassie.

The coroner, an intelligent-looking woman of middle years – appeared behind the bench and everybody stood. Taking her seat she introduced herself as Judy Ginsberg, and Cassie saw Felix's dad reach out and fumble for his wife's hand. Seeing the way they supported each other made her think about Chrysanthi and George, also facing questions about their daughter's death but unable to share the burden of grief.

The policeman, a young traffic PC with a razor cut under his chin, was the first into the witness box. He'd also been first on the scene in Forty Hill – a surprisingly rural area just inside the M25 – responding to the report of a body lying on the grass verge of a quiet road at seven in the morning. As the local mortuary was closed for maintenance Felix had been brought to Camden. Cassie could still see his dark eyes fixed open in shock above his battered body when she'd unzipped the body bag that day. He still wore his running gear, the front caked in mud from where he'd fallen, after supposedly being hit from behind by a vehicle on his regular morning run.

When the uniformed cop said that all the evidence pointed to a hit and run Mrs Zuberi leaned against her husband, who put his arm around her. Seven years working with the dead had taught Cassie one thing above all: the worst thing for a bereaved family was not knowing what had caused their loved one's death. Coping with the loss of a child was dreadful enough, but enduring a lifetime of doubts and questions – the endless *Why*? and *How*? – would be intolerable. She could only pray that her hunch had been right and that Mr and Mrs Z might get the closure they desperately needed.

Next into the witness box was Philip Curzon. He was wearing his 'court' suit – the one made by his tailor in Savile Row, as he never tired of mentioning – and now he turned his most ingratiating smile on the coroner. Her returning smile was cooler and more businesslike.

She had him walk her through the day of the post-mortem, which was still pin-sharp to Cassie.

Felix was one of five bodies on the list that day and Cassie recalled Curzon being in his usual hurry – lunch at Rules being next on his schedule. After his cursory external examination he'd bought the police theory of a car or van hitting Felix and failing to stop.

Cassie remembered eviscerating Felix. Certainly there was plenty of evidence of blunt force trauma – six ribs caved in at the rear, a hairline fracture of the skull, and his radius and ulna were broken, just like Bronte's, a classic defensive injury during a fall.

But.

Something had niggled her about the vehicle versus pedestrian story, although she wouldn't have been able to verbalise her doubts – not at that point.

Now, Curzon was saying, 'The injuries were entirely consistent with a vehicular impact from the rear. Blunt force impact to the ribs, skull fracture on landing. Death was the result of catastrophic injuries to the ribcage.' He smiled his best 'dear lady' smile at the coroner. 'Complex fractures of the posterior ribs pierced the lungs and caused a pneumothorax – that is, a collapsed lung – as well as pulmonary contusions.'

'What effect would that have had on Felix?' asked the coroner, sending the parents a sympathetic look.

'He was alive at this point, but would have died from respiratory distress within, oh, fifteen or twenty minutes?'

Seeing Felix's mum drop her head, clearly weeping, Cassie winced. Sure, the job of an inquest was to establish the facts around death, but did Curzon have to act like he was enjoying his moment in the limelight?

'So if this was a collision with a vehicle, and the driver had stopped, he or she might have been able to call for help,' asked the coroner, sounding sombre. 'Even possibly to save his life?'

Belatedly, Curzon made a stab at a 'sad' expression. 'I'm afraid so.'

Cassie couldn't look at Mr and Mrs Z, who were having to face the terrible thought that somebody would crash into their son and just drive off leaving him to die alone on a roadside verge.

The coroner referred to a file in front of her on the bench. 'And how do you account for the laceration on Felix's shoulder blade?'

He gave an expressive shrug. 'It was minor, and could have been caused by a broken wing mirror or something else on the vehicle.'

After Curzon left, Cassie saw a guy come in and take a seat on the bench where witnesses sat. She felt her heart starting to go *tap-tap* in her chest. He was plain clothes but obviously a cop. Was it the guy she had spoken to when she'd called CID anonymously?

The coroner stood Curzon down and the detective went into the box, introducing himself as DC Josh Brookwood. *Bollocks*. She did recognise his voice from the phone call but he looked all of fourteen. Would some newbie detective constable have gone the extra mile investigating some mixed-race kid killed in an RTC?

'DC Brookwood, talk us through your investigation of Felix's death?'

'Yes, ma'am. Our first line of enquiry was that Felix was hit by a driver who left the scene. His housemates say he ran along that stretch of road every day at 6 a.m. The roadside verge narrows just ahead of the collision site so our working hypothesis was that he had strayed into the road and been struck by a driver going too fast. It's a fairly quiet back road but that only encourages drivers to break the speed limit. We released a media appeal and put up roadside boards asking for information or any dashcam footage of Felix and vehicles on the route that day.'

'Did anyone report seeing anything?'

'No, ma'am.'

'And did you find any evidence of a vehicular impact – tyre marks, a broken light, that sort of thing?

'No, ma'am.' But Cassie had been watching him intently, and DC Brookwood's body language struck her as too ... *perky* to chime with someone whose investigation had hit a regrettable dead end.

The coroner must have picked up the same vibe because now she frowned at him. 'So do you accept the finding of the pathologist that the cause of death was "entirely consistent" with a vehicular collision?'

'No, ma'am.'

Cassie held her breath.

'Enlighten us, DC Brookwood?' said the coroner with a touch of testiness.

He looked over at Felix's mum and dad. 'We didn't want to release any information until we were certain, but we now have evidence that Felix took a short cut across the field adjoining the road. A field with a nine-hundred-kilo bull in it.'

Felix's mum gave a soft gasp, reaching out to grip her husband's forearm.

Cassie remembered the look of shock etched on Felix's face and the niggling feeling that he was trying to tell her something.

'You believe this animal attacked Felix?!' asked the coroner.

'Yes, ma'am. We believe that the bull charged Felix, striking him from the rear, and threw him over the fence onto the verge, causing his fatal injuries.'

The parents were sitting up straight, gazing at DC Brookwood.

'Whatever gave you this idea?' asked the coroner.

'I got an anonymous phone call. A woman saying that Felix might have been attacked by a cow or a bull.'

Cassie recalled how dismissive he'd been when she'd finally got hold of him, treating her like some kind of nutjob. But when she'd suggested the family might run their own tests on Felix's clothing – which they would be entitled to do – she had sensed him changing his tune.

'How extraordinary,' said the coroner. 'But a phone call isn't "evidence".'

'No, ma'am.' Brookwood pulled a piece of paper out of his pocket. 'We did have Felix's clothing sent to the lab for testing, and I only received the results this morning.' Unfolding it, he read from the printout. 'It confirmed that there were "multiple hairs" found on the rear of his hoodie which were "bovine in origin".'

Chapter Twelve

She cooked dinner that evening, trying to make amends for her screw-up the previous night, so that by the time Archie got home the cabin was warm and smelling of cooked tomatoes and peppers. It was her one-and-only party piece – a veggie lasagne – plus a steak for Archie which was resting in the oven. Despite going vegetarian after her very first post-mortem she had no issues with other people eating meat.

He raised an eyebrow. 'Good day?' But she was relieved to sense that his anger of earlier – *justified anger* – had dissipated.

As they ate she told him what had happened at the inquest, and on reaching the bit about the anonymous phone call, he shook his head, torn between admiration and disapproval. 'You're going to get yourself sacked one of these days.'

'Curzon never saw me.' She topped up their glasses with wine – corner-shop Shiraz but totally drinkable.

'When he hears about the coroner's finding he'll be apoplectic. And he's bound to wonder why the cops suddenly asked for an analysis of the clothing.' He washed down a mouthful of steak with his wine. 'What on earth made you think about a bull attack, of all things?'

Cassie shrugged, remembering wheeling Felix's reconstituted body back into the body store after his PM. The look of shock on his face had dulled, but as she'd gone to zip the body bag closed over his face she'd frozen, gripped by the feeling that foreshadowed her moments of connection with the dead: a slip-sliding sensation, a humming in the air, her senses gone into overdrive.

Run! A single word that seemed to rise from his unmoving lips in a whispered shout. And then silence.

When she'd resurfaced from the moment, it had made her think.

You couldn't run from a car.

She had gone straight back to the plastic sealed bag in which his running gear had been stored. Opened the ziplock and put her face into the opening. A faint smell wafted out. *Animal, not human.* Of course, she couldn't identify what kind, but outside a zoo there was only one animal strong enough to throw Felix far enough to cause fatal injuries.

'I dunno,' she told Archie. 'Maybe I smelled something on his clothes when he came in.'

She dropped her gaze, feeling uneasy about telling him a half-truth. It was something she'd never shared, this feeling that the dead sometimes 'spoke' to her. Was that wrong? Shouldn't she be able to talk to him, of all people, about it? But trying to imagine the conversation she found it never ended well. He was a scientist, a stone rationalist, and he would think she was batshit crazy. Anyway, as she always told herself, what she picked up from her guests was probably no more than a combination of her subconscious observations and a vivid imagination.

Probably.

Whatever the source of her hunch, the outcome would hopefully bring Felix's parents some closure and even comfort. Their son hadn't been struck by a driver who left him to die without even dialling 999; it had simply been a terrible freak accident.

Archie was looking at her with a half-smile on his face. 'You're not actually a witch are you?'

'Uh-huh.' She nodded. 'Can't you taste it in the lasagne?'

'What?' He frowned, his forkful paused halfway to his mouth.

'Toe of newt.'

He laughed but there was something dutiful about it.

'What's up?' she asked him, pushing her plate away.

'You are a witch,' he said wryly.

'And you'd make a terrible spy.'

He set his knife and fork together on his empty plate. 'That was delicious.'

She just raised her eyebrows but she felt a sense of vertigo. *Was he about to dump her?*

'Look what it is, I've been offered a special attachment with Prof Farmilow in Gloucester. He's *the* man to study hematopathology with so it's a big honour to be asked.'

'Wow. That's great.'

Archie wanted to specialise in the study of diseases of the blood, bone marrow and lymph system so it would be a big break for him.

'Yeah, his assistant has gone off sick so he'd like me to start tomorrow.' His long-lashed grey eyes scanned her face.

Tomorrow?!

'How long would it be for?' asked Cassie.

'Three months.' He eyed her tentatively, trying to gauge her reaction. 'Obviously, it's way too far to commute so I would need to stay down there for the duration. But we could meet up some weekends when we're both free, obvs.'

'It's a great opportunity, you should do it,' she told him.

His face grew a frown, and after a pause he said, 'You *want* me to go, don't you?'

'No! Of course not,' she said, quickly. 'It's just you shouldn't turn it down. I'll miss you, obviously, but I'll survive.'

He didn't appear entirely convinced by her protestations. As he stood to take the dishes to the sink he whacked his head on the ceiling for the 109th time since coming to live on the boat.

Honestly? Her instant reaction to the prospect of having the place to herself again could be summed up in one word.

Hallelujah.

Chapter Thirteen

Spring was stirring as Cassie strode along the towpath the following morning: foliage starting to erupt over the canal banks, and here and there, the buds of early crocus flamed like gas jets. The sun against her face felt as soft and warm as a lover's touch. Archie had left for his attachment in Gloucester that morning and as he'd climbed off the boat carrying his scuffed rugby holdall she'd definitely felt a tug of emotion.

But could she give up boat life just because it wasn't really working for Archie? She pulled a wry smile: maybe she just needed a shorter boyfriend – or girlfriend.

'I had it made by a silversmith in Hatton Garden for her tenth birthday,' Chrysanthi was telling her, the two women sitting side by side in the empty reception area. Just after Archie had left she had called Cassie to ask if she could see her daughter again. It was a Saturday and since she was really only on call for check-ins Cassie should have put her off until Monday, but she had never yet refused a viewing request from a grieving family member.

Chrysanthi was smiling down at the open locket, immersed in the memory of a time when her daughter was still alive.

It was elaborate, silver filigree, with a Christian crucifix woven into the design, and opened to reveal two locks of hair.

'It's identical, isn't it, your hair and hers,' exclaimed Cassie. In fact, mother and daughter had looked strikingly alike: the same wide cheekbones, winged eyebrows and those slightly hooded eyes which gave that seemingly haughty look she remembered in the fourteen-year-old Sophia. The look that had been a red rag to the bullies.

Chrysanthi nodded before closing the locket and pressing it to her lips. 'The morning after she died I went to her flat to pick up some mementos. I would like her to wear it.'

'You know once she is at the undertakers' she can wear her own clothes and anything else you like?'

'I want her to have it now,' said Chrysanthi. 'So that I can feel somehow I am with her.'

'It's not really allowed,' said Cassie, feeling torn. Mortuary rules were clear: no valuables were to be left on a body in case they went walkabout, leaving mortuary staff open to accusations of theft.

Chrysanthi turned her dark eyes on Cassie. 'Were you there when the doctor . . . examined my Sophia?'

Cassie just nodded: no need to mention that in a routine PM it was the mortuary technician who performed the evisceration.

'Because I don't believe what the police are saying, that she . . . destroyed herself.'

The violence of the old-fashioned term took Cassie aback. She remembered Babcia saying that Chrysanthi was devout Greek Orthodox, a faith which probably took a dim view of suicide.

'It must be unbearable to think that,' she said, quietly. 'But . . . if Sophia had been taking drugs, she wouldn't be responsible for her actions.'

Chrysanthi shook her head. 'She wasn't doing that filth anymore. She promised me.'

Oh Lord. The promises of an ex-junkie.

Chrysanthi pulled out her phone. 'Look,' she said, showing Cassie a video posted on social media. It came from @Charly_Detective – the woman who had stitched her up on TikTok a few days back. 'This girl doesn't think it was suicide. She says the police should have treated it as a possible murder.'

Cassie had an instinctive distrust of the police, but the video was another mash-up of rumour and outright factual error which hinted – without offering a shred of evidence – that foul play was involved. Death by suicide was the hardest thing for loved ones to accept – the ultimate abandonment – and she understood Chrysanthi's desperate need to find an alternative narrative, even if that was murder.

'You know these social media people, they call themselves detectives, Chrysanthi, but they aren't experts – they're not even proper journalists. I'm afraid they're just making money out of a tragedy.'

Chrysanthi pursed her lips. 'This Charly girl says it was a "Category-2 death"! So it should have been investigated.' Banging the flat of one hand on her knee.

The half-digested understanding of these keyboard detectives did nobody any favours.

'The police should have explained to you. A Category-2 death just means a sudden unexpected death. It doesn't imply foul play or suspicious circumstances.'

'The police didn't even interview her so-called ex-boyfriend, the one who got her into drugs in the first place,' said Chrysanthi bitterly.

'Ethan Fox?' The guy who'd been all over the press as Bronte's love interest in the months before her death: tall, dark, skinny, and good-looking in a dissolute way. The classic rock-star waster boyfriend, he had bad news written all over him. Ethan was lead guitarist in his own rock band, and the couple had sometimes shared a stage, but any fame – or notoriety – he enjoyed was really down to his relationship with Bronte.

'How long were they together?'

'Oh, not more than a year – on and off. And whenever it was on, she would go back on the drugs.' She waved a despairing hand.

According to the media, Ethan and Bronte had spent his-and-hers spells in rehab for heroin and cocaine dependency, but neither of them seemed to stay clean for long – and the tabloids were always there, waiting like hyenas for their next meltdown.

'Clean Break', the breakout hit that had got three million plays and won Bronte the recording deal with Melodik, suggested she had put dodgy men and Class As behind her. But just a few months into her record deal she'd got back with Ethan, gone back on the drugs, and the paparazzi were back in business.

'What makes you think he might be involved?'

'She broke it off with him so that she could stay off the drugs for good. But like I told the police, he wanted her back.' Chrysanthi looked contemptuous. 'Of course he did, with all that money. But she promised me she wouldn't, said it was more important to her to stay clean and healthy.'

Maybe, thought Cassie.

'Do you have any reason to suspect him?' Cassie asked gently. 'Was he ever violent to her, or controlling? Anything like that?'

Chrysanthi shook her head, her lips forming a rebellious pout, before pocketing her phone.

'Where are you having the funeral service?' asked Cassie to change the subject.

Chrysanthi hesitated. 'We're burying her in the church where she was christened, Agios Ioannis.' This with a defiant lift of her chin that reminded Cassie of the fourteen-year-old Bronte.

St Iaonnis was one of several Greek Orthodox churches in the borough. Cassie dimly remembered that cremation was forbidden by the Orthodox religion.

'Let the undertakers know and they can do all the liaising with the church,' said Cassie. Then she nodded at the locket loosely clasped in Chrysanthi's hands.' She could face a disciplinary for allowing it but what the hell. 'Let's go and put this on Sophia. Just don't tell anyone, OK?"

FLYTE

While Cassie and Chrysanthi were at the mortuary, Phyllida Flyte's boss and mentor William called her, apologising for disturbing her weekend.

The parents of singer-songwriter Bronte – whose suicide had been all over the media for the last few days – had brought a complaint against Camden police regarding their investigation of the death. They claimed it had been cursory and sloppy, and that foul play had been ruled out too quickly. The official complaint via a solicitor had been signed by both parents, but it was the mother who had sent all the emails, clearly taking the lead.

'You've heard of the case?' asked William.

'It's impossible to avoid,' said Flyte drily. The press were running non-stop 'updates', many cut and pasted from social media sleuths who were claiming 'new evidence' in what they called the singer's 'mysterious death'. From what she'd seen, her dear old pops would have called it 'thin gruel', but the media's hunger for clickbait seemed insatiable.

'I must say the investigation does appear to have been somewhat . . . basic,' he went on. 'The young woman's mother is also questioning the veracity of the suicide note sent from her daughter's phone.' He sent her a meaningful look. 'This was the unexpected and violent death of a young female celebrity.'

'Did they not anticipate the attention her death would attract?' Flyte didn't seek to hide her exasperation.

William gave a rueful shake of his head. 'The attending officer was a uniformed sergeant in his fifties. He didn't connect the name Sophia Angelopoulos with her performing name, Bronte, and to be honest, I'm not sure he – or I for that matter – are in the demographic that would have heard of her.'

Flyte took that on board – until a few days earlier she'd only vaguely heard of Bronte herself – and that was just from seeing the odd story in the *Evening Standard*. 'So you want me to go in to Camden CID and decide if any of their officers have a case to answer?'

'If you feel able to, yes. Starting Monday. The fact that you know your way round the set-up there and the borough politics would be an asset, although I would completely understand if you were to say no, given your history in the borough.'

She suppressed a shiver. It was bad enough that she still had to live in Camden, the lease on her flat having months to run. But working with the police there? Her last posting, at the borough's Major Crimes unit, had dramatically imploded, ending with her leaving the force, and the entire unit being disbanded. All the same, more than three months into her new career as an IOPC investigator she had to admit she was finding the processes slow and frustrating. And although there was some satisfaction to be had in bringing maverick officers to book, she did miss putting villains behind bars.

So the thought of a fall from height which might just turn out to be fishy set her pulse beating a little faster.

'OK,' she said. 'I'll do it.'

Flyte pushed open the door of the church and felt the cool air of the centuries envelop her. One of her reasons for accepting the IOPC job had been the proximity of their Holborn offices to St Pancras Old Church which allowed her to visit most days. It was here that her only child, Poppy, the baby daughter who had arrived stillborn, had recently been named in a ceremony performed by the vicar.

Flyte traced her fingers over the little brass plaque on the back of the pew which said simply *Poppy Flyte-Howard, beloved daughter* and the single date that marked both her birth and death. She should be three and half years old by now, going to nursery, making friends – her personality flourishing. Flyte had such a vivid inner picture of how Poppy would look as the months and years passed that she found it difficult glimpsing children of the same age in the street or supermarket.

'Hello, Poppy darling,' she murmured. 'Am I doing the right thing, do you think? Going back to Camden?' She pictured Poppy's wise little face, captured on her iPhone before the nurses had taken her away. Odd that she thought of a baby who hadn't even lived to draw breath as her touchstone – or perhaps she was really more of an internal sounding board. *My better self*. Whatever it was, the feeling that she got back was that all would be well.

The last few months had been the most dramatic of her life. She had narrowly escaped getting shot, left the police force in which she'd spent her adult working life, got her first tattoo – a poppy to commemorate her daughter – and after a lifetime of lying to herself, had come out as gay. She was making up for lost time on the last front: thinking about the newly opened club she was going to in Camden later brought a secret smile to her lips.

Seeing Toby, the reverend, emerge from the vestry, she felt a guilty pang. *Was it bad form, thinking about sex in a church?*

With a welcoming smile, he came and sat down next to her in the pew, and after a moment's silence, said, 'Matt was here last week. He sat here for nearly an hour.'

'Did you speak to him?'

Toby shook his head. 'He didn't invite that, if you know what I mean. I'd been wondering whether to mention it to you but, knowing how disappointed you were that he didn't come to Poppy's naming ceremony, I thought you should know.'

Flyte made a sceptical face. 'Even my mother came!' she said bitterly. That had been something of a miracle. A ceasefire in mother–daughter hostilities that had seen Sylvia fly in from her retirement bolthole in the Med, where she lived with her new husband, to honour her granddaughter. And relations had stayed, if not exactly warm, then certainly more cordial.

She and Matt had married just before she'd turned thirty – her mental deadline – getting wed in a picture-postcard church in the Hampshire countryside. Since boarding school days Flyte had been aware she was attracted to women but she'd shut those feelings down – totally focused on the goal of a 'traditional' family life: mummy, daddy, and children.

They were a good fit in many ways, and when Flyte fell pregnant nearly four years into the marriage, Matt was as delighted as she had been. But unbeknown to them, a rare defect in the umbilical cord lay undiscovered – *like an unexploded bomb.*

When Flyte went into labour prematurely, the cord had ruptured and their little girl had bled to death.

With Flyte half mad with grief and sedated to the eyeballs, it had fallen to Matt to handle the official business. By the time she'd resurfaced, her little girl had already been cremated and her ashes scattered in the hospital memorial garden, and it had been too late officially to name her on the stillborn birth certificate.

Flyte experienced a hot surge of fury against Matt. 'He couldn't be bothered to recognise his daughter's existence in the world,' she said through thinned lips.

Toby left a pause. 'Perhaps he still needs more time to come to terms with it.'

The gaze she turned on the priest was unbending. 'Don't ask me to forgive him, Father. It's beyond me.'

Chapter Fourteen

Cassie had wondered how she would feel, coming home to an empty boat. But opening the cabin door she just felt excited to have the space to herself again. No longer needing to worry about sorting what Archie called 'a proper supper', she scoured the fridge and made up a random plate of hummus, sardines, gherkins, and tortilla chips – giving Macavity half the fish. 'It's a treat,' she told him sternly.

Then, as dusk began to fall, she decided to make use of her newly minted freedom by going out. There was a new queer venue in the market she wanted to check out.

Not, she told herself, that she was looking to pick anyone up.

It was only 7 p.m. and the mood in the bar was still low-key, which suited her. Queer bars could sometimes feel oppressive – the drag queens, the 'come as Britney/Wham' nights, the fire breathers ... Exhortations to 'Have FUN!' usually had the opposite effect on her. She had come out to people-watch, her favourite pastime.

Tucking herself into a corner with a large Grey Goose, she let her gaze drift. And it snagged on a tall slender figure who'd just pitched up at the bar, her wheat-blonde hair now styled into a tight undercut at the back, her spine still straight as a broom handle. Cassie felt her stomach swoop: no need to see the rest of that razor-sharp jawline to know who it was.

Phyllida Flyte. She might not be a detective anymore but there was still something in her upright body language, the air of watchful authority that screamed cop. Not that an air of authority was necessarily unattractive . . . As Cassie watched, a young girl with curly hair she'd flirted with in the past, a bit of an airhead but super-pretty, slipped herself alongside Flyte at the bar and turned liquid eyes up at her.

Seeing Flyte shy like a skittish racehorse, Cassie grinned. *Good luck with that*, she thought, taking a slug of her vodka. But when she looked back, Flyte had leaned in and was laughing at something the girl – Mia, that was her name – must have said.

Cassie felt a frisson of what . . . *jealousy*? Her relationship with DS Phyllida Flyte had always been complicated. What had started out as naked mutual dislike had morphed first into wary cooperation and then respect, friendship even, after they'd been thrown together in the course of more than one investigation. There had always been an undercurrent of something more between them, but it seemed destined to go unexplored: Cassie was convinced almost from the off that the uptight Flyte was gay, but after spending her adult life barricaded in the closet it had looked likely she'd stay there . . . at least until the previous year.

After the devastating events at Flyte's old unit, which had destroyed her faith in the Met and put her life in danger, she had undergone a double metamorphosis. She had handed in her police badge, and come out to Cassie – tentatively, delicately, but also in a way that had hinted at her romantic interest.

Talk about bad timing. Only a day earlier Cassie had agreed to live with Archie on the boat, to see if their on-off relationship had long-term legs. A question on which the jury was still out.

At that moment Flyte glanced around the bar, and seeing Cassie, did a double-take. When Cassie raised her glass in ironic salute, Flyte said something to Mia and headed over, leaving the younger woman pouting in their direction.

'Fancy seeing you here,' said Cassie as Flyte set her glass of white wine down and took a seat.

Flyte smiled a private smile. 'I'm broadening my horizons.'

Their gaze met for a moment before breaking apart. Cassie had always been struck by Flyte's curious-looking eyes – irises of the palest ice blue, with a darker limbic ring, like a wild animal – or a super-hot extraterrestrial.

'She's a bit young for you, though.' Cassie nodded over at Mia, who was chatting to the barman.

'*Everyone's* a bit young for me,' said Flyte with a wry grin.

Curses.

Cassie didn't want her to think that their age gap – around ten years – had been any kind of factor against them getting together. To Cassie, the fact she was a cop had always been far more of an obstacle. 'Of course they're not – but Mia is still a stude for Chrissake. She thinks Magna Carta is a posh ice cream.'

Flyte's smile lit her face, turning her prettiness into a disturbing beauty. And there was a new edge to her look – as well as the darker undercut beneath her blonde top layer at the back, she'd had a second piercing in one ear – *daring*!

'How's boat life with Bertie?' she asked.

'Archie,' said Cassie, before seeing from Flyte's dry look that she'd been taking the piss. She made a face. 'He'd really prefer a nice normal flat, y'know.'

'Finding it a bit of a squeeze?'

Cassie just shrugged, feeling suddenly disloyal. 'So how's guarding the guardians working out?' she asked.

'Oh fine,' said Flyte, eyes hooding as she reverted to default cop mode.

'A bit boring after murder squad?'

Flyte just gave a tight smile. 'How's life at the mortuary?'

'Fine.' *Two could play at that game.*

'Any interesting cases lately?'

The too-casual way Flyte spoke got Cassie's antennae twitching ... *Did she mean Bronte?* Perhaps she'd seen the coverage – it was hard to avoid, after all – and was simply making conversation. Or had she heard something about the investigation via her old CID contacts?

'Same old, same old.' She shrugged.

Their eyes met, admitting an amused understanding between them.

Cassie took a drink of her vodka before asking, 'How's Matt?' Judging by Flyte's expression she wasn't being too intrusive, so she went on, 'Is he any closer to, you know, dealing with losing Poppy?'

'No,' said Flyte crisply.

Seeing anger flare across her face like a brushfire, Cassie wondered whether, subconsciously, she was fanning her fury against Matt, to keep it alive. Perhaps this unresolved conflict, with Flyte as 'good parent' and Matt 'bad parent', was keeping Poppy alive, or more present in some way.

She wished she could say something that might help, but they weren't close enough to talk about it.

After they'd exchanged farewells and Cassie had left the pub she was aware of feeling uneasy. Trying to locate the source, she realised that the charged atmosphere between her and Flyte made her feel guilty – and confused – about Archie.

Not because she fancied Phyllida Flyte, and had done since she'd first laid eyes on her. There was nothing wrong with her – or Archie – fancying other people. No, she was recalling all the times she could have talked to him about her moments of communion with the dead, regardless of how he might react.

Now it occurred to her: how could you have a meaningful relationship with someone while hiding such an important part of what made you tick?

Chapter Fifteen

Cassie's phone woke her at 7 a.m. on Monday. It was the mortuary.

WTF? She wasn't due in for another two hours.

'Doug?' She ran a hand over her face.

'I need you to come in straightaway. Something's happened.'

'What?' She pushed herself upright, her nerves jangling at the anxiety in his voice.

'I can't talk about it over the phone. Just look at the news.'

Levering herself upright she opened her newsfeed.

DEAD BRONTE PHOTO OUTRAGE, screamed the first tabloid headline she saw.

The piece led with an image of a head and shoulders shot of Bronte, her face pixelated but still recognisable, an edge of white body bag in frame. The report adopted a tone of faux outrage that an image of 'tragic Bronte' had been posted on TikTok while simultaneously milking it for all it was worth.

There was only one place the photo could have been taken – inside the body store.

Now, she and Doug were looking at the images on his computer at work. 'You told me about someone trying to get in the other night?' he said. 'Talk me through it again.'

'Someone put a ladder up against one of the windows in the autopsy suite. But when I put the light on they scarpered.'

'Well they got their photo somehow,' said Doug, looking beyond miserable. 'I've been onto Malcolm Bellwether at CID and he's promised to send over a detective. I've also informed the coroner and the HTA.' The Human Tissue Authority, the body who oversaw the handling of all bodies and samples in the mortuary system; a body with the power to initiate disciplinary action against staff or even to close a mortuary down.

Cassie decided against telling him that she'd spent the rest of that night at the mortuary to stand guard over Bronte. *Why add to his angst?* If the photo had come from a break-in it had to have happened some other night.

'This account they all say it came from @Charly_Detective – that's that . . . *woman* who filmed me without my permission.' At least the dead Bronte image had been taken offline now, possibly for offending platform guidelines. 'I suppose it could be faked?' she said. 'You know how sophisticated the tech is these days.'

Doug pointed to a faint red line, just visible through the pixelation. It ran from Bronte's left collarbone towards her sternum. 'That's the top of the Y-incision, isn't it?' he said glumly.

She scanned the image. He was right. It wasn't a detail anyone would be likely to fake.

The PM list was cancelled but when the promised detective arrived she wished she'd put her scrubs on anyway. That morning she'd just pulled on what she'd been wearing the previous evening: ripped jeans, and a black T-shirt emblazoned with a big image of Siouxsie looking at her most goth.

He looked like he'd just stepped off the set of some TV cop series from the eighties: sixty-plus years old, ginger sideburns, waistband of his past-its-best suit straining at his paunch, and what looked like ketchup on his tie. He looked at her chest before her face – *of course he did* – but when he went in for an old-school handshake she could hardly refuse.

'How do. DI Bacon.'

Bacon?! Suppressing a smirk, she took his outstretched hand. It felt warm and slightly damp, and she surreptitiously wiped it on her jeans.

After leading him to the autopsy suite, she talked him through the ladder-to-window incident – him taking no notes, she noticed.

'Who did you deal with at Camden?' he asked.

'I didn't report it.'

Seeing his frown, she said, 'Look, there was nothing to see, just the ladder outside where they'd dropped it.'

'That's not really your call though, is it?' he said mildly.

'Do you seriously think they'd have sent anyone?' she retorted. 'When we reported a missing body a couple of years back the nick had to be bullied even to send a uniform. The guy had barely started shaving.' Recalling how the spotty little twat had patronised her, doubting her report that a body was missing.

DI Bacon looked at her assessingly. 'This photo of Bronte, your boss reckons it's for real. In a case like this we'd usually start by looking for someone on the inside. Someone looking to make some money out of this poor girl's death.'

She dropped her gaze, recalling Jason's cringe-making excitement at having a celeb in the body store. He might be a sexist twat but he wouldn't . . . *would he . . .?*

'Yeah, well last time we had an intruder break in you lot wasted a ton of time hounding me for stealing a body instead of finding the real villains.' Cassie was getting testy. 'Why don't you start by asking this TikTok "detective" where she got the image?'

'Trouble is, since you didn't report we have nothing other than your word that it happened,' he mused, hitching his waistband up over his beer belly.

'For Chrissake, if I was going to invent an intruder story, then I would've made sure to call the cops to cover my back, wouldn't I?!' In the silence that followed she realised her voice had become quite heated.

DI Bacon seemed unperturbed by her outburst. He pulled out his notebook. 'Could you give me the names of everyone with access to the mortuary?'

Once that was done, she walked him to the front entrance in silence.

He paused with his hand on the half-open door and his gaze fell on Cassie's chest again.

Oh, for fuck's sake.

Cop or not, she was about to call him out when he nodded to her T-shirt. 'I saw her play once,' he said with a nostalgic smile, and she realised it was the image of Siouxsie he'd been looking at all along. 'The Roundhouse, 1978. Happy days.'

And with a beatific smile, he was gone, leaving Cassie blinking at his departing back.

FLYTE

It was an odd feeling, facing her old boss DCI Malcolm Bellwether across his desk. When she'd worked as a detective in Camden CID eighteen months back she'd often been sitting here in the position of a supplicant: asking to be given a more interesting case, or having to apologise for going off-piste. Despite his recent elevation to DCI rank, it was Bellwether who was on the back foot now. Flyte was here to put CID's actions in the Bronte case under the microscope and her report would make public any failings in their investigation, as well as deciding whether there should be any disciplinary proceedings.

'Obviously I'll need full access to the investigation team,' she said. 'Which detective attended the scene?'

He hesitated before admitting, 'None actually. Sergeant Hickey who attended found no suspicious circs, the neighbours heard nothing out of the ordinary, and there was no sign of forced entry.' He opened his hands. 'Add to which the deceased has a history of drug abuse and she had texted a suicide note to her mother.'

'When I was here it was policy for a detective to attend a Cat 2 death' – pinning him with an unforgiving gaze.

'I am aware of best practice, Phyllida,' he said with a hint of asperity. 'But we're a detective down and we have to prioritise. If the level of media and public interest had been anticipated then a detective would have attended as a precautionary measure. Unfortunately, Sergeant Hickey had no idea this young woman was a celebrity – to be fair she's not exactly a household name.'

'She is now,' said Flyte.

Bellwether grimaced. 'And now there's this mortuary photo of her splashed all over the media. I just had Sophia's father screaming down the phone at me.'

'I'm not surprised,' she said. 'I assume someone has questioned the mortuary staff?' – picturing Cassie Raven, who could be spiky when on the defensive.

Before he could answer there came a knock at the door followed by the entrance of a large shabby figure in a brown suit that looked like it had been bought for a wedding in the nineties. She eyed him. Was that . . . *tomato purée* on his tie?

'Speak of the devil.' Bellwether seemed relieved to see the new arrival.

'DI Bacon,' said the man, putting out his hand to Flyte. She looked down at it in confusion. 'I've been assigned to the Ange-pop-olous case from East London Major Crimes.' Mangling Bronte's name.

Hell's bells. The guy looked like a dinosaur in a bad suit: a cartoon rendering of the kind of cop who gave the Met a bad rep.

She shook his hand, which felt slightly sticky, and dredged up a smile. 'Phyllida Flyte,' she said, still not used to omitting the 'DS' rank that had defined her for so long.

Bellwether just smiled. 'I asked DI Bacon to come in as a fresh pair of eyes on the Bronte case, to see whether we should be recategorising the death as suspicious. Given that time is of the essence and you'll be going over the same ground it would be useful if he could sit in on your interviews. And he can also give assistance with anything you need for your investigation.'

Flyte gave a little nod. Her IOPC investigator status gave her the powers of a police constable, but Bacon's DI rank might prove useful.

'I was about to tell Phyllida that you attended the mortuary regarding this ghoulish photograph,' Bellwether told Bacon. 'So you can fill her in. And of course the team has been briefed to make themselves available to you both.' He looked at the wall clock. 'I've booked the meeting room so that you can start interviews.'

'Great,' said DI Bacon.

Time to establish some ground rules.

'That's thoughtful of you, Malcolm,' she said coolly, 'but I'd like more time to get across the details of the case first.' Getting to her feet, she buttoned her jacket and sent him her most charming smile. 'If someone could show me to my office I'll let you know when I'm ready to conduct interviews.'

It turned out that her 'office' would be shared with Bacon – although office was a somewhat grand term for the tiny box room that had evidently been hastily rigged with two desks facing each other and a giant photocopier of uncertain vintage filling the remaining space. The lino floor felt sticky underfoot, the air smelled like something had died in here and when she went to open the windows dead flies and dust bunnies fell from the blinds onto her shoes.

Bacon regarded her look of disgust with open amusement. 'I've seen worse.'

Ignoring him, she sat down at one of the desks and fired up the computer. 'I'm going to need a log-in – and an access code for the PNC and CRiS.' The two systems which between them held all UK criminal records, cautions, and reports of investigations.

'I'm afraid you're not allowed direct PNC access. But that's one of my jobs,' he chuckled, 'to help reach the parts other beers cannot reach.'

'What?' She stared at him.

'Just kidding. It was an ad for lager back when you were still wearing a school blazer. You're what, early thirties?'

'None of your business,' she snapped. *Christ, what a clown.* While also feeling a little buzz that he'd knocked five years off her age. 'Right, I'm going to need the report from the scene. The PM report and the deceased's phone records.'

'Aye, aye, ma'am,' he said.

Ma'am?

'How did you get on at the mortuary?' she asked. *No need to mention she and Cassie knew each other.*

'Fine. I'd say almost certainly an inside job. The girl – sorry, *woman* – I spoke to had some story about someone trying to get in, but there's no evidence of a forced entry.'

Picturing the pixelated image she'd seen splashed online Flyte thought of what poor Chrysanthi was going through, followed by a surge of pure rage. If anyone had shared a picture of her daughter she'd . . .

'Obviously we need to get onto this TikTok . . . *creature* – the one who first aired the photograph?'

A rumbling sound came from DI Bacon's belly. 'Down, boy,' he said, before getting to his feet. 'I'd better pop to Maccy D's for some emergency sustenance before we start. Can I tempt you to an egg and bacon McMuffin?'

She shook her head. 'Oh, and feel free to call me Phyllida.'

'Will do. I'm Alvin. But everyone calls me Streaky.'

Everyone except me, she silently vowed.

Chapter Sixteen

When Cassie pitched up at the mortuary entrance the next morning her heart sank to see who was at the door.

But Bronte's father George Angelopoulos greeted her amicably enough. She took him into the family room and made him a cup of tea. Then, taking a seat opposite him she met his gaze. 'Mr Angelopoulos, I can't tell you how sorry I am – we all are – about the image in the press. We have no idea how it was obtained but the police are investigating, as you know.'

Her NHS Trust employers would go apeshit if they could hear her: their mantra was 'never apologise or admit liability in any way'. *Well, screw that.* To her, the policy wasn't just inhumane, it was stupidly short-sighted: for most people it was enough to hear the word 'sorry', and parroting an infuriating corporate response only made a lawsuit more likely.

'Thank you,' he said in a quiet voice. 'And please, call me George.'

After a pause, she asked, 'Have you come to see Sophia?'

He shook his head. 'I can't,' he said simply. 'But you were so kind to us last week, I wondered if you could talk me through the process. Sophia's mother is driving me crazy about things she sees on social media, things they say were missed by the police.' His accent was a pick and mix: mostly London but with long, transatlantic-sounding vowels – and unlike his wife, scarcely a trace of Greek lilt. 'She says that final text Sophia sent "didn't sound like her" and I . . . I don't know what to think.' He pulled a heartfelt shrug.

He was as well dressed as ever but she noticed with a pang of sympathy that he'd buttoned his shirt up wrong, so that one side sat higher than the other. Neither he nor Chrysanthi would be functioning at anything like a normal level for some time. The funeral would be the first staging post on their lifelong journey of grief towards – hopefully – some kind of acceptance.

'You are talking to one another then?' she asked gently, scanning his face.

'If you can call it talking.' He made a regretful face. 'She only phones me to scream and shout about the police being idiots. Why aren't I doing something about it? Why aren't they questioning Ethan?' He made a resigned gesture.

'Yes, I gathered she really doesn't like him,' said Cassie. 'But then if it was him who got Sophia into drugs . . .'

'In my experience, nobody "gets" anybody into drugs other than the person taking them,' he said, shaking his head. 'No, I'm afraid Sophia's mother took against him from the moment she found out he was Jewish.'

'Oh . . .'

'Yes, I'm sorry to say that her religious belief isn't exactly the charitable kind. The Orthodox Church has been slow to enter the modern world, but it's also down to the priest at her church. He's in his eighties and very conservative, very anti-women, which is why I tried to keep Sophia away from the place – and from him – as much as possible.'

Struck by how worldly, how liberal, George seemed compared to his ex-wife, Cassie had been reading up on his career. After they arrived in Camden in the early nineties, George had used his cruise ship experience – and savings – to go into the high-end restaurant business. His first solo venture, a resto set in a converted church in chichi Fitzrovia, won a Michelin star for its 'high concept' version of Mediterranean cuisine. Within a few years it had become a magnet for music biz types, and there were dozens of images online of George carousing with music stars, agents and producers – making contacts that probably helped his daughter's career. The flagship spawned a small West End chain, which he'd sold a couple of years earlier for nearly five million.

Chrysanthi was absent from the images of George's public life, and despite being a lot younger than him, it was her whose attitudes seemed to spring from a previous era. Was it the age gap that had finished them? Or the culture gap between churchy Chrysanthi, only in her forties but already embracing middle age, and this modern-minded man who hung out with cosmopolitan types? – and had multiple affairs with them, if what Chrysanthi had told Babcia was true.

'What would you like to know?' she asked him.

'How long do we have to wait before we know if Sophia took something that made her suicidal? Strange to say, but I think it would actually help if she had.'

Cassie nodded. 'That's an understandable feeling.'

'The police said they found drugs at her place – could she have had a bad reaction?'

'Some drugs can trigger a psychotic episode that might have made her act irrationally. The coroner will release Sophia's body to you shortly so you can have the funeral, but the inquest will have to await the toxicology results – and I'm afraid they can take a while, sometimes weeks.' Not liking to say 'months', which was more the norm on a routine PM these days.

'Weeks?!' He looked shocked. 'To think she would take herself away from us – deliberately. That is the hardest thing to bear.' He lifted red-rimmed eyes to Cassie. 'I know it's a terrible thing to say, but I think that's why Chrysanthi would actually prefer it to be murder.'

Cassie recalled Babcia saying that mother and daughter had had a difficult relationship. 'Were she and Sophia close?'

He tipped his head, a rueful look on his face. 'Sophia loved her mother, of course she did, but she's always been closer to me, ever since she was a little girl. And then I became her manager so we spent even more time together. Her mother smothered her, tried to control her, never really stopped treating her like a child.'

Cassie tried to picture how her relationship with her own mother might have developed had Kath lived to raise her, especially when she'd left home at seventeen for the vagabond allure of a Camden squat. Her grandmother had been wise enough to leave her be, to let her get it out of her system – something a mother might have found much tougher to do.

After George had left she felt the need to phone her own father, Callum. After twenty-plus years believing he was dead she still found it hard to think of him the way she knew other people viewed their parents – as a constant presence in her universe.

'Hey, Dad.' It still felt odd calling him that. 'How's Belfast?'

'Oh, it's grand – I'm seeing all the old crew, some of them I knew from when I was a wain. They take the piss out of my

"London" accent of course, and keep dragging me down the pub even though they know I'm teetotal these days. There's only so much lime and soda a man can drink.'

A sudden flare of anxiety. 'But are you resisting temptation?'

'Yes, Catkin, I am.' His tone as cheerful as ever but edged with a hint of warning. When he'd turned up last year, the prodigal father, Cassie had embarked on a clumsy campaign to mitigate the damage that seventeen years inside and a dependence on illicitly distilled alcohol and roll-ups had done to his body. He had been overprotective of her in turn, forever banging on about the dangers of living on the canal. But gradually they had reached an understanding: he didn't try to come the patriarch routine with her and she'd agreed to trust him to take care of himself.

'Siobhan has said that wee Orla can come over with me and stay at Weronika's for a few days when I come back. She's dying to see you.'

Cassie smiled. Meeting her five-year-old cousin Orla had been one of the unexpected bonuses of being reunited with her dad.

'How is the little monster? Still bossing all the grown-ups?'

'Ah she's a proper little firecracker,' chuckled Callum. 'She's been chewing my ear off ever since I got here, demanding a sleepover on "Cousin Cassie's" boat. I said you might let her visit but she has to sleep at Babcia's.'

Whether it was being raised as an orphan, or something in her genetic make-up, Cassie had always been a bit of a loner, so the bombshell discovery of an extended family had been exhilarating – and scary. Little Orla was one thing – but so far she'd ducked meeting the rest of Callum's sprawling Northern Ireland clan.

'Anyway,' he went on, 'I dare say that boyfriend of yours would be none too happy having an extra guest on board who wakes everyone up at dawn.' He paused. 'Everything good with him?'

'Yeah fine,' she lied, realising with a guilty jolt that the only contact she'd had with Archie since he'd gone to Gloucester was a few WhatsApp messages. Maybe they were both treating it as a trial separation.

FLYTE

Flyte gave the uniformed sergeant sitting opposite her in the conference room a hard stare.

'Please stop saying "we followed procedure",' she said. 'That is for me to judge. I need you to give me a step-by-step account of what happened from the moment you arrived on the scene. Let's go back to the start.'

He suppressed a sigh. 'So when we got there I went and looked at the bod—'

'Look at me, please, Sergeant Hickey, not DI Bacon.'

He raised an eyebrow, but trained a bored look on Flyte before continuing. 'I established that life was extinct at 0415 hours. Then I told PC Gill to rig a screen around the body until the undertakers collected it.'

'How did you establish Sophia was dead?'

'The couple of litres of claret on the path was a major hint,' he said, sending a micro-smirk in Bacon's direction. 'She had life-ending head injuries, her skin was cold, and I checked her pulse.'

'Your notes say that the body was found "on the canal towpath". That's not exactly precise. Did you measure the distance between the building and the site of impact?'

'No. Why would I?'

'Because if somebody jumps, their trajectory will take them further than if they fell accidentally or were pushed.' Flyte's tone was acid, failing to hide her irritation at Hickey's uncooperative attitude, encapsulated in his body language: arms crossed defensively, legs spread wide to signal his contempt for the proceedings – *and for her*. She remembered her IOPC mentor's warning: 'expect everyone to view you with fear and suspicion'.

Hickey shrugged. 'The front door of her flat was secure, there was nothing to suggest anyone else had been there, or any kind of struggle, and her phone and laptop were sat there along with a pile of wacky baccy aka no suspicious circumstances.'

'Oh I'm sorry.' Flyte frowned down at her notes. 'I didn't realise you had undergone detective training.'

His face darkened and he muttered, 'I can read a scene.'

'Did you call CID to ask them to send someone?'

'No point,' he huffed. 'They're short-staffed and anyway they wouldn't necessarily send a detective to a straightforward jumper, not if I called it as a Cat 2. They trust my judgement.' Hickey's face was getting redder and redder.

'Did you ask your supervisor to sign off on your decision?' she pressed. 'As per College of Policing guidelines on procedure at the scene of a violent and unexpected death?'

'I don't have to answer that,' he burst out. 'You're not even a police officer.'

Leaning across the table, DI Bacon said, 'Answer the question, Sergeant.'

Flyte raised a hand: translation: *I'll deal with this*. 'Allow me to remind you, Sergeant Hickey, that when identified as a witness in an IOPC investigation you have a duty of cooperation to participate openly and professionally in line with expectations.'

'Whose expectations?' muttered Hickey, but his demeanour said he'd rolled over.

'Mine,' she said sweetly.

Hickey went on to admit that he hadn't even referred it up to a senior officer.

Once he'd gone, she let rip to Bacon. 'What a clown! No detective involved, nothing you could call a thorough search of the place, and do you believe him when he said they all wore gloves and shoe covers at the scene? And they still haven't tracked down these people who were staying in the upstairs flat. It's *beyond* slack.'

The next-door neighbours had been interviewed, but on the night Bronte fell the upstairs penthouse apartment had apparently been let via Airbnb to a Chinese couple who'd flown back to Beijing the following morning.

DI Bacon grimaced. 'You know how it is – staffing issues, stupid workloads, these guys have got a lot on their plate.'

Flyte had to stifle a rude riposte. How typical that Bacon's knee-jerk instinct should be to defend his comrades. That was the fundamental obstacle to fixing the police service: in a job where you might one day have to rely on a fellow officer to save your life, loyalty was baked in. But as had been brought home to her in her final job in the Met, it also fostered groupthink and a profound reluctance to challenge toxic behaviour.

'Anyway,' she said. 'Set your alarm early tomorrow. We're going to be paying someone a 6 a.m. call.'

Chapter Seventeen

At the crack of dawn the next day Cassie was woken by a rapping at the cabin door: a knock with the unmistakable note of authority.

Her heart beating double time, she pulled on Archie's towelling robe.

'I'm coming!' she said testily to the repeated knocking. And opened the door onto the starkly beautiful features of Phyllida Flyte.

'What the . . .?' she managed, before seeing behind Flyte the ginger-haired cop who'd come to the mortuary to question her about the image of dead Bronte on socials.

'Nice boat,' he said, sounding genuinely impressed. 'How old is she?'

'We need to ask you some questions,' said Flyte, ignoring her colleague. 'Pursuant to a complaint by the family of Sophia Angelopoulos to the Independent Office for Police Conduct.'

Pursuant to . . .? Flyte's job change hadn't loosened up her vocabulary.

'What, now?! Half dressed?' – pulling the robe closer.

'You can get dressed, of course, or we can do this down the station later if you prefer?'

Cassie rolled her eyes. Flyte might only be a civilian now, but she had brought a real cop with her. As she led them downstairs, she did a quick mental inventory – no pills on board – not since Archie had moved in – and only a tiny bit of weed, which was effectively decriminalised in Camden these days.

After retreating to the forward cabin to pull on some clothes, she came and sat opposite them at the banquette-style dining table, Flyte looking uncomfortable pinned into the corner by DS Bacon's considerable bulk.

Her cat jumped up on the table: he was always nosy about guests.

'Macavity!' said Cassie, giving him a little push.

But Bacon was stroking his head admiringly. '"He's the bafflement of Scotland Yard, the Flying Squad's despair: For when they reach the scene of crime—Macavity's not there!"'

Unusually for him, Macavity was allowing Bacon to scratch him behind the ears. 'Are you "a fiend in feline shape"? Hmm? "A monster of depravity"?'

Flyte made an impatient face. 'Could we get on?'

'I'm not stopping you,' said Cassie, picking up the cat and putting him on the floor.

'DI Bacon here has already questioned you about the photograph of Sophia's body. But there's been another development.'

Oh great.

'Yes, the self-styled "detective" who first aired the pics on TikTok has now posted details which appear to come from the preliminary PM report.'

'Really,' Cassie drawled.

Flyte pulled a chilly smile. 'Also, an examination of the mortuary access system and your entry code usage shows that you spent the night there last Thursday. Why was that?'

A chill washed over Cassie. This had horrible echoes of the time she'd stayed overnight at the mortuary a couple of years ago. That time it had been because one of her guests, a nine-year-old boy, Oliver, had drowned swimming in the canal on a hot day. His mum had been utterly distraught, not wanting to leave – and kept saying over and over how scared Oliver was of the dark. So Cassie had promised to keep him company, sleeping beside him on the floor of the body store. When the body of an old gent had gone missing months later, Flyte had been assigned the case, leading to her first encounter with Cassie. Having discovered her unofficial overnight stay, Flyte had leaped to the wrong conclusion: that the weird-looking, tattooed and pierced morgue girl had something to do with the theft.

'Look, I stayed because as I already told your buddy here' – widening her eyes – 'someone tried to get into the mortuary that night – probably one of these social media nutjobs trying to get a photo of the autopsy suite.'

'There is no evidence of any break-in,' said Flyte flatly. 'We suspect an inside job. Who do you think might be tempted to take a cash bribe for a photo of a dead celebrity?'

Once again it was Jason's moon-like face that rose in her mind's eye. But he hadn't seemed shifty when they'd discussed how the pics had got out – and she wasn't about to drop him in it.

'It could be anyone.' She shrugged. 'The porters are always coming in and out via the tunnel from the hospital when they deliver bodies.'

'What about the undertakers?'

Cassie shook her head. 'They only have access to the clean side of the body store – the drawers are double-sided so they can check in a body out of hours.'

Flyte made a note in her neat schoolgirl handwriting.

'What about the PM report?' asked DI Bacon. 'Who might have seen that, aside from the pathologist?'

She frowned. 'The family, anyone in the coroner's office, anyone with access to the police computer . . .' – widening her eyes for emphasis. 'Look, why don't you ask this Charly character where she got it?'

Seeing a frown flit across Flyte's brow, Cassie guessed something. 'Is it even a crime, sharing this stuff?'

It was DI Bacon who answered. 'Without an actual break-in, or payment of a bribe to an official, probably not. But rest assured we'll still be paying her a visit.' He cracked his knuckles meaningfully, earning a frosty look from Flyte.

The Neanderthal and the Ice Maiden. Cassie had to suppress a smile: these two were going to have a barrel of laughs working together.

Flyte pulled out her phone. 'In her latest video she claims the PM report overlooked "clear evidence" of foul play.'

'Oh Jesus.' Cassie rolled her eyes. 'Let me see it.'

Flyte tapped her screen and handed the phone to Cassie.

Charly had filmed herself at night on the towpath outside Bronte's flat, an uplight casting spooky shadows on her face. She flourished some papers. 'I managed to get hold of the pathologist's *top-secret* autopsy report from my sources. What I found in here *shocked me*. The police are *lying* to us about Bronte's death,' she said. The vid cut to a close-up of a phrase, the words looming larger to fill the screen – 'fracture of the hyoid bone'. Charly went on in a doom-laden voice, 'The hyoid is a tiny bone in the throat. What does a fractured hyoid strongly suggest? That Bronte was *strangled*.'

Cassie made a scoffing sound. 'What a load of crap.'

'Go on,' said Flyte.

'What this halfwit doesn't mention is that Bronte had multiple broken bones large and small, all over her body,' said Cassie. 'Falling ten storeys will do that to your skeleton. The hyoid bone is often fractured in a fall from height.'

'Not evidence of strangulation then, in your view?' asked Flyte.

'No! Curzon would hardly mention a hyoid fracture in the report without further comment if it meant anything.' *Even* Curzon.

'And you saw nothing else to suggest that she might have been strangled?'

Cassie noticed Bacon's sideways glance at Flyte – probably wondering why she was asking a lowly mortuary tech this stuff instead of the pathologist. She obviously hadn't told him their history, the cases they'd collaborated on.

Cassie pictured Bronte's throat: the flesh unmarked, with no tell-tale bruising, and the whites of her eyes clear, with a bluish tinge, but no sign of the petechial haemorrhages that were a red flag for asphyxia of any kind.

She shook her head. 'Nothing that was visible. But you know that it takes a forensic PM to look at the underlying tissues for any hidden injuries.'

Flyte motioned to DI Bacon that it was time to go.

Cassie felt a flare of anger. 'So am I a suspect for this photo stunt? Or did you drag me out of bed just to pick my brains?'

Flyte had the grace to blush – two points of pink high on those wide cheekbones. 'Your insights are always appreciated. Thank you for your time.'

FLYTE

After leaving Cassie Raven, DI Bacon wanted to stop at a greasy spoon for breakfast. He'd ordered an egg and bacon bap – making Flyte wonder if nominative determinism extended to food preferences – and having dispatched a good third of it in one messy bite, he wiped his mouth and asked, 'So I'm gathering you and this Cassie Raven have previous?'

'What do you mean by that?' she snapped. All her working life in the Job she'd had to deal with snide insinuations about her sexuality from male colleagues.

He shrugged. 'Only that your paths appeared to have crossed in the past, professionally I assume?'

She gave a curt nod.

'I assume this was when you were at Major Crimes?'

'Yes, and CID before that,' she said, taking a sip of her tea and grimacing. The café didn't have Earl Grey and even the slice of lemon they'd drummed up couldn't rescue it, the tannin fierce enough to strip tooth enamel.

'That business on her narrowboat, that was just a fishing expedition, right?' He inserted a finger into his back molar to dislodge some food fragment – a sight from which she averted her eyes – before continuing. 'Fair enough – I've seen technicians spot stuff the pathologists missed on a routine PM, in a hurry to get to the golf club,' he chuckled.

Flyte just pulled a frosty smile.

Bacon clattered his knife and fork onto his empty plate and sat back. 'Do you think she had anything to do with the dead girl's photos or leaking the PM report? Just for the record' – resting his eyes on hers. *Intelligent eyes.*

'No,' said Flyte, 'not in a million years.' Reaching for her bag, she said, 'Anyway, I've got to do some stuff at the bank, so I'll see you back at the office.'

Chrysanthi Angelopoulos's imposing detached house stood in a large leafy plot a few minutes' walk from Hampstead Heath, the kind of house built for the wealthy that had sprung up on London's fringes in the thirties. Today it was probably worth ten million. Flyte had learned from the case notes that Sophia's parents were barely on speaking terms, but the husband, George, had clearly left her in good financial standing.

As she made her way through the well-tended front garden she saw a big man in work gear up a ladder at roof level, apparently clearing the gutters.

Flyte didn't feel guilty about fibbing to DI Bacon: she'd get more out of Bronte's mother woman to woman, she told herself. While Chrysanthi disappeared to make tea, Flyte took the opportunity to check out the living room. It felt like something from an earlier era: a large brass carriage clock ticked discreetly on the mantelpiece, lace antimacassars guarded the backs of sofa and armchairs, and a glass display cabinet crouched in the corner was stuffed with china figurines, silver-framed photographs, and a darkly varnished icon of a cross-looking Jesus.

As Chrysanthi poured their tea from a silver pot, Flyte discreetly looked her over. She was probably only eight or nine years older than Flyte – in her mid-forties – but her tweedy skirt and oversized cardigan, the way she held herself, gave off the air of someone older. Almost as though Chrysanthi had made a deliberate decision to make herself unattractive.

After offering her condolences, Flyte got down to business. 'Mrs Angelopoulos, why don't you tell me in your own words why you made the complaint?'

'The police made up their minds straightaway that Sophia had . . . done a terrible thing to herself – and I knew she would never, *ever* do that.' Chrysanthi pulled out her phone and handed it over to Flyte. 'Look. You have seen the final text message I received, sent from her phone?'

Flyte had already seen a transcript of the message, which Bronte had sent just after 1 a.m., which had been a key factor in Sergeant Hickey concluding Bronte committed suicide.

Dear Mum, it read. *I am so sorry to do this to you and Dad but I can't go on. I hate Melodik, I hate what they are trying to do to my music, and I can't see any future. Just blackness and despair. Everyone will be better off without me. Look after Peppa. I love you, and Dad. S.*

Flyte got a sudden image of Poppy's little newborn face, the tiny hand curled under her chin as if in thought. 'I'm so sorry, Chrysanthi. You woke up to this on that morning?'

Chrysanthi's hand shot to cover her mouth and she nodded.

'You must have been devastated.'

'When I saw it at six o'clock that morning, I went straight around to the flat, of course, but they had already taken my baby away.' Anger entering her voice.

Flyte left a respectful pause. 'So you said on the phone that it was the mention of Peppa didn't sit right with you? Who is Peppa?'

'It's just a fish, an angel fish.'

A fish?

'From when she was a little girl Sophia always had a fish tank. I keep it in my bedroom. It's all I have left of her.' She took a shaky breath. 'It was only later that I realised.' She opened a file lying on the coffee table – the kind with plastic sleeves inside – and pulled out a greetings card. 'Look here.'

It was a birthday card, and inside, beneath the greeting '*To Mum*' in a large expressive hand was the message '*Love from Sophia and Pepper.*'

'You see?'

'The spelling of Pepper.'

'Exactly. She's had that fish since she first left home, oh nine years ago? She would never spell his name wrong.'

But someone in an overwrought state might not notice an overzealous auto-correction.

'And your conclusion?'

'That it was sent by somebody else. The man who killed her. To mislead everyone.'

'And do you have a view as to who that might be?'

'Ethan Fox, of course, her ex-boyfriend' – her eyes narrowing. 'I always told her he was a bad man.' Chrysanthi embarked on a three-minute character assassination, while offering no evidence or any real motive for why he might murder his ex.

Flyte had seen the transcript of Sophia's text messages in the days before her death and had been struck by the fact that the conversation with her mother had been very one-sided.

Chrysanthi sent her three or four messages a day, most of which went unanswered.

'When was it you last saw Sophia?' she asked gently.

'Not for a while,' said Chrysanthi, waving a hand, 'but we talked on the phone. She would decide sometimes that I was interfering – when I was only trying to look out for her – and for a while that would be that.'

'You used to message her about what she was eating – was there an issue there?'

Chrysanthi nodded. 'Since she was a little girl Sophia had problems with her stomach and I worried about her diet. She would say that I was nagging her. You know how can it be between mothers and their daughters.'

Flyte nodded sympathetically: she and her mother could go weeks without contact and their occasional conversations often felt dutiful on Flyte's side and chilly on Sylvia's.

Chrysanthi's face darkened. 'All the time *her father* told her she could eat whatever she liked – things like ice cream, chocolate ... far too rich for her.' The venom she packed into the reference to George was almost impressive. Then she pinned Flyte with an intense look. 'You mustn't think that Sophia and I weren't close you know. We couldn't have been any closer.'

Suddenly, a figure in workmen's clothes filled the living-room doorway and started speaking Greek in a deep voice. A hulking, broad-chested man whom Flyte had seen up the ladder outside, he fell silent when he caught sight of her and put a hand on his heart. 'Forgive me, Chrysanthi, I didn't know you had company.'

'Don't worry, Themi, this is the lady dealing with my complaint against the police.'

Was it Flyte's imagination or did Themi's eyes grow watchful at the word 'police'?

'I've cleared all the gutters front and back,' he went on in heavily accented English. 'You shouldn't have any more trouble.' Themi looked to be around the same age as Chrysanthi, but Flyte noted approvingly the way he addressed her – with the traditional courtesy of a man addressing an older lady. 'I noticed one of the downpipes is cracked so I'll get a new one and come back tomorrow to fit it.'

The pair of them lapsed into musical-sounding Greek. Before Themi left he sent Flyte a little bow of farewell – his politesse somewhat at odds with the old scimitar-shaped scar down one side of his face that made him look like a pirate.

As the front door closed, Chrysanthi told Flyte, 'Themi isn't just my builder, he's my oldest friend. We met when we were thirteen in the children's home in Cyprus' – a rare smile inverted the usual downward cast of her face, giving a glimpse of her relative youthfulness. 'I don't know what I'd do if I didn't have him looking out for me.'

Flyte wondered if there was any romance on the cards, but from the unembarrassed way Chrysanthi spoke, and her determinedly sexless aura, she decided it was unlikely.

She spent the next ten minutes reassuring Chrysanthi that she would be poring over every aspect of the police investigation to date, along with a new detective from another borough. Reading people wasn't her strongest suit, so she could only hope that her reassurances had worked.

As Flyte followed Chrysanthi out of the living room, her eye fell on the glass cabinet which held a faded colour photograph in an ornate silver photo frame: two tiny little children, a boy and a girl, holding hands. The picture brought her up short: the girl looked about three – around the same age as Poppy would have been had she lived.

Indicating it, she asked, 'Is that Sophia?' A nod. 'And the little boy . . .?'

'Sophia's twin brother, Alexander.' Chrysanthi crossed herself. 'God took him from me two days after his third birthday.'

'Oh no, dear God.' Flyte couldn't stop herself reaching out to touch Chrysanthi's upper arm. 'I'm so very sorry.'

'He and Sophia were both sickly children, but of the two of them she was the fighter,' said Chrysanthi, appearing to welcome the consoling touch.

Flyte had to bite her lip to hold back the threat of unprofessional tears.

The two women's eyes met in a moment of shared feeling and Flyte gave Chrysanthi's arm a little squeeze before withdrawing her hand. 'Do you have any family, here or back in Cyprus?'

'My mother died of complications after giving birth to me. As for my father . . .' Chrysanthi dropped her gaze and made a contemptuous sound. 'It would be better if I had never laid eyes on *him*.'

'Did Sophia ever go back? To Cyprus?'

Chrysanthi stared at her. 'Never. Why would she do that?'

As Flyte reached the end of the path through the front garden she turned and saw Chrysanthi still standing on the doorstep, looking old and . . . defeated.

Two children who had died before their time. Let down by the man in her life and without any family to turn to. And her closest friend an odd-job man. It was no wonder that Chrysanthi Angelopoulos seemed like a woman who had given up on life.

Chapter Eighteen

Phyllida Flyte's early morning visit left Cassie fuming. It felt as if their relationship had rewound to a time before they'd overcome their mutual suspicion to cooperate on cases and become almost-friends. *Almost-lovers* even.

After work she took a bag of washing down to the laundrette and went over the morning's encounter again as she loaded the machine. It dawned on her that Flyte had simply been putting on the tough cop act. It must be difficult for her being a freshly minted civilian after all those years in the police and she could hardly act chummy in front of her minder, the ginger gorilla in the brown suit.

She'd brought along some acetone and a bottle of nail varnish and once her clothes were lazily churning in a machine, cleaned off her old chipped polish and started to apply a fresh coat with practised strokes. Replaying Flyte's questions about whether there were any signs of violence on Bronte's body she wondered whether she was just going through the motions as part of her IOPC remit. Or did she suspect there was something off about the suicide conclusion?

The laundrette was empty, and as Cassie focused on each long stroke of varnish, the only sound the chug-chug of the washer, she drifted into a meditative state. Bored with her go-to black she was trying a new shade called Hades, the darkest red – the colour of long-dried blood. She pictured Bronte's nails, which had been painted black.

After finishing the second coat she was waving her hands about to speed up the drying process when she caught a movement in her peripheral vision. A face, reflected in the half-open glass porthole of one of the machines. Bronte, one side of her face a livid purple, her lips moving angrily.

What the . . .?!

She jumped up, twisting to check behind her. *Nothing*. Her heart going like a drum machine, she looked back at the glass porthole. The face had gone. But the image was still imprinted on her retina: Bronte had looked furious. Furious with *her*.

She must have clenched her fists in shock because on her right palm she saw a scatter of dark-red varnish, like the dried blood of a bad graze.

Like the abrasion on Bronte's palm, which Curzon had dismissed as an injury sustained in the fall.

Cassie knocked on the door of the lady who did the service washes. 'Sorry, Bella, I need to leave my stuff. There's something I forgot to do.'

It was dusk by the time she reached the mortuary, and making straight for Bronte's drawer in the body store Cassie unzipped her body bag to the waist. She half expected her to be wearing the expression she'd glimpsed in the glass – not fury, perhaps, but definitely exasperation, like Cassie was being unbelievably stupid. But her still, waxwork features looked neutral above the locket with the filigree cross which Chrysanthi had put around her daughter's neck.

'Look, Bronte, I need to check you over again, OK?' After pulling on some gloves, Cassie took her right hand – cold as sin but pliable again now that rigor had long passed – and turned it over. The black-red abrasion on the right palm and extending up the inside of the fingers was just as she remembered. Reaching for the left hand she turned it palm upwards, and angling it into the harsh fluorescent light, she thought she could make out some lighter grazing there, too.

What had come to her in the laundrette after 'seeing' Bronte was the idea that these injuries weren't as Curzon had suggested – sustained by chance during the fall – but the result of Bronte deliberately grabbing hold of something to save herself, however briefly.

Cassie turned the hand palm down and examined the black-painted fingernails: the varnish had largely survived the fall. Soaking a hank of cotton wool with some nail polish remover, she started to clean the middle fingernail of Bronte's right hand.

Her breathing grew faster as the layers of black gradually started to surrender, revealing the natural nail beneath.

Thirty seconds later, staring down at the varnish-free nail, she felt suddenly light-headed.

The pear-drop reek of the acetone clawed at her throat, the gurgle of the fridge grew oppressively loud, and she felt herself free-falling into the familiar state that was both dreamy yet hyper-real. She looked down at Bronte's face.

'*I don't want to die.*'

The words seemed to shimmer off the still, waxen face – sounding plaintive but not desperate. And anything but suicidal.

FLYTE

In his white forensic suit DI 'Streaky' Bacon resembled a large and dissolute snowman. At least he wouldn't be able to access his trouser pockets, thought Flyte sourly.

Dusk was gathering outside by the time Flyte and Streaky reached Bronte's flat: its previous life as a warehouse still evident in the vintage steel columns, stripped brick walls, and what looked like the original oak floorboards. A baby grand piano sat in the centre of the open-plan living room and framed posters of bands and artists lined the walls, some of whom Flyte had never even heard of. Like the black-and-white image of some moustachioed guy above the name *Django Reinhardt* in a jaunty retro font.

Seeing her frown, Bacon said, 'Gypsy jazz musician from the forties.'

Was 'gypsy' even an acceptable term these days?

'The girl had taste,' he went on admiringly as he browsed the images. 'Miriam Makeba . . . Etta James . . . that's Nina Simone.'

'I know who Nina Simone is,' said Flyte tartly, reading the inscription beneath Simone's uncompromising stare: *An artist's duty is to reflect the times*.

Bronte's place struck her as surprisingly neat and orderly for the home of a druggie music star. Maybe her mother had been right when she said Bronte was staying clean – literally. It always struck Flyte how every home had a unique and distinct smell: here she picked up the scent of recently burned candle or incense – a spruce-like, Christmassy fragrance. *Myrrh, at a guess.*

'Who's been in here since the death?' she asked.

'Just her mum and dad, to take some items of sentimental value,' he said. Then his face lit up. 'Hello, gorgeous!' he exclaimed. This was directed at the woman in the forensic suit with dyed blonde hair and lavender ombre rinse who'd just come in from the balcony.

'Well, look what the cat dragged in!' she exclaimed on seeing him, her London tones sounding as though they'd been kippered by decades of cigarette smoke.

Bacon introduced the woman, who appeared to be around his vintage, as Tina Verity, the crime scene manager who'd attended right after Bronte's death. Flyte noted the wary – and increasingly familiar – look that came into her eyes at the dread initials IOPC.

'Best CSM north of the Thames,' said Bacon beaming, before introducing Flyte. 'So, Tina, we need to take another look at the scene with fresh eyes.'

'Thank you, DI Bacon,' said Flyte meaningfully, before turning her gaze on Tina. 'Let's start with the balcony shall we.' This was still her investigation and she wouldn't stand for being demoted to the role of passive spectator.

The balcony was edged by a glass panel topped with a rail, and at only a couple of metres long by less than a metre deep, too small for any furniture.

Flyte indicated the steel balcony rail. 'Was this dusted for prints and swabbed for DNA?'

'It wasn't requested,' said Tina – a construction that avoided mentioning the name of Hickey, the uniformed sergeant who'd decided off his own bat that the death was non-suspicious.

'Well let's do it now,' she said.

With a flicker of her heavily mascaraed eyes towards Bacon, Tina replied, 'I can do, but after over a week of rain, pigeons et al, the chances of getting any results are close to zero.'

'I'm quite aware of that,' said Flyte sharply. 'We'd have had a far better chance had it been printed and swabbed straightaway.'

Bacon dropped to his haunches with an audible 'Oof', and examined the gap between the concrete base and the bottom edge of the glass panel. After whipping out a tape measure he measured the base and gap above before running the tape up to the top rail.

'One hundred and fifteen centimetres high,' he said. 'And the victim was only one hundred and fifty-seven centimetres, barely five foot three in old money, so even if she stood on the base, the rail would still be at chest height on her. Hard to see how a short-arse could have got herself over without anything to stand on – or a helping hand.'

Flyte nodded. Despite the questionable language his meaning was spot on.

Just inside the balcony doors she recognised the coffee table where the 'synthetic cannabis' had been found after Bronte's death. She and Bacon took a seat on the sofa which looked out over the canal and he handed her printouts of the scene photos, including those showing the tabletop with its psychedelic packaging and turquoise Rizla papers, which had prompted Sergeant Hickey to mention drug use in his report as a possible contributory factor in Bronte's supposed suicide.

'No remains of a joint, no ashtray?' huffed Flyte, gesturing at the photo. 'What was Hickey thinking? That she smoked a joint and then what, flushed the stub down the toilet, washed the ashtray and put it away?!'

Bacon gave a headshake, his expression making it clear that he agreed with her. 'I've told the toxicology lab to bump her samples to the top of the queue, given the public interest in the case.'

They went into the kitchen, where Flyte opened the built-in fridge-freezer. She called Tina in from the balcony and asked, 'I assume it wasn't empty before? What was in it?'

'It was pretty full, actually.'

'Here,' said Bacon, handing her another photo. Leaning in, Tina pointed out the fridge contents, which had been snapped lined up on the worktop.

'Bag of salad, fruit, tofu, yoghurt, a jar of mustard, vegan ice cream.'

It sounded more like the fridge of a health nut than a druggie.

Flyte tried to keep her expression neutral. It wouldn't be fair to blame Tina for the failure to properly analyse the scene: the blame for that lay squarely with Sergeant Hickey.

Suicidal people didn't tend to fill their fridge before topping themselves. And it would have been a challenge for a woman of Bronte's height to scale the balcony unaided. All of which would have raised a big fat red flag with any trained detective, had Sergeant Hickey bothered to request one.

Chapter Nineteen

Early the next morning, wearing her full PPE, Cassie was once again unzipping Bronte's body bag.

'Here,' she said, lifting free Bronte's right hand, all the nails now cleaned of varnish, before angling it into the light for the benefit of Phyllida Flyte and DI Bacon who stood the other side of the open drawer. 'See?'

The forefinger and middle fingernails were indigo, darkening to deepest purple towards the cuticle, while the third nail was a paler blue.

'And they couldn't have been bruised in the fall?' asked Flyte, frowning.

'Hard to see how,' said Cassie. 'All the other injuries are consistent with her falling on her left side.'

Flyte's gaze swung to Bacon. 'There was that gap at the bottom of the balcony, between the concrete and the glass, wasn't there?'

Bacon nodded. 'After she fell she must have grabbed hold of the ledge, if only for a moment. Until some bastard stamped on her fingers.'

Flyte and Bacon looked at one another for a moment, before Flyte swivelled her gaze back to Cassie. 'So why did you only remove her nail varnish now and not at the PM?'

Cassie tried to hide her irritation. 'We never remove nail varnish at a routine PM. Why don't you ask the cops why *they* didn't order a forensic?'

'Around four thousand reasons,' said DI Bacon drily.

'There you go,' said Cassie. A forensic PM, which could only be conducted by a pathologist on the Home Office register, took several hours and cost three or four grand – more if any specialist tests were needed. It was the cops who picked up the bill for a forensic and if they didn't suspect foul play then a body got the cheap and cheerful routine version, just like Bronte's had. Cassie had often thought the system was deeply flawed: discouraging the police from ordering a full bells-and-whistles PM in borderline cases.

Flyte told Cassie, 'You need to bag her hands and move her to the forensic fridge. You have her clothing still?'

'Of course. Already bagged and labelled.'

As Cassie closed Bronte's drawer, Bacon told her, 'Nice work. You lot do a good job.'

She shot him a look but he seemed genuine. 'Thank you.'

Flyte said, 'I'm just going to call my office to report the ... developments' – before stepping in to the corridor.

'I'm curious,' Bacon asked Cassie. 'What made you think to take off her nail polish?'

She pictured her 'vision' in the laundrette, and the words she'd heard rising from Bronte's dead lips later.

I don't want to die.

She shrugged before flashing her own nails at him, which she had repaired while waiting for them to turn up.

'Just intuition, I guess.'

He nodded, apparently accepting this. 'You APTs do spend more time with the bodies than anybody.'

'Uh-huh.'

'And you meet the family.'

'Yup.'

'What do you make of the mother?' he asked. 'Bit of a religious nutter by all accounts?'

Wow, this guy hadn't got the memo. But iffy language aside, she couldn't disagree with the underlying sentiment. She remembered Chrysanthi claiming her daughter would never 'destroy herself' – proper Old Testament shit – and the cross-embellished locket holding the locks of their hair which she'd brought in for Bronte to wear.

Flyte came back in. 'Right, this development is being reported back to DCI Bellwether.'

'Righto,' said Bacon, jingling the contents of his pocket as if in celebration. 'I'd better get back to the nick.'

'Alvin, I just have a few more questions here re the original complaint.' Flyte bestowed her most dazzling smile on him, making him blink in confusion. 'Shall we catch up back at the office?'

'Sure,' he said, beaming. 'See you there.'

Sucker, thought Cassie.

Once he'd gone, Flyte pinned her gaze on Cassie 'What's wrong?'

'Nothing,' but Cassie felt herself blush, a rarity for her.

'Come off it, I know you. A couple of minutes ago you realised something.'

Cassie felt a spurt of irritation. 'Don't talk to me like we're friends after that stunt you pulled yesterday, banging on my door with the ginger gorilla at six in the freaking morning.'

'Well, look' – sounding defensive.

'No, you look. I used to think you trusted me. Accusing me of selling photos of Bronte! As if!! Basically you were just picking my brains.'

Flyte rolled her lower lip between her teeth. 'All right, guilty as charged. But you have to understand that I can't simply ... freelance these days. I have to be professional, and keep DI Bacon on board.' Not quite able to hide a note of irritation at her loss of authority.

Cassie paused: still annoyed but also suddenly aware of the tightrope that Flyte must need to walk. '"DI Bacon", though? Seriously?' she deadpanned.

'And everyone calls him Streaky,' said Flyte. They both broke into broad grins.

'Of course they do.'

The exchange thawed some of the frost between them.

'Listen, have you interviewed this Charly woman yet?' Cassie asked. 'About who gave her the pics of Bronte – and details from the PM report?'

'Not yet. Why?'

'I need to tell you something.'

'Go on,' said Flyte.

Cassie pulled a face. 'It was Bronte's mother.'

Chapter Twenty

DI Bacon calling Bronte's mum a 'religious nutter' had reminded Cassie of Chrysanthi's last visit, and Bronte's silver locket.

Now she told Flyte that Chrysanthi had wanted to put the necklace round Bronte's neck herself.

'And you left her alone with the body.'

'Not exactly,' said Cassie. After opening Bronte's drawer and unzipping the body bag to her chest she had deliberately busied herself with some paperwork at the other end of the body store. 'I didn't leave the room but I gave her some space, not wanting to intrude on the moment, you know?'

Flyte nodded but her expression remained sceptical. 'You think she took the photo then?'

'It would have taken seconds to whip out her phone and do it.' Cassie shrugged. 'The photo went public two days after that.'

'But why on earth would she share something so . . . intimate with some social media clown?'

Cassie resisted the temptation to roll her eyes. 'Because she didn't buy the idea that Bronte killed herself and thought the police had done a sloppy job investigating it.'

'She was hoping that the coverage would bounce the police into a murder investigation' – Flyte sounded thoughtful.

Cassie nodded. 'That, plus the official complaint to you lot. And fair enough, it totally worked.'

'Well, that's one less crime to investigate,' said Flyte. 'There's no law against sharing an image of your own daughter, even if she is lying dead in a mortuary.' She shook her head. 'It's just beyond me, how anyone could want to see their dead child splashed across every news and social media outlet in the world.'

Cassie paused, understanding how Flyte's own loss would make that hard to comprehend. Softening her tone, she said, 'Suicide is the toughest thing for a parent or partner to accept, but I think she might have another reason for wanting it to be murder, weird as that sounds.'

'Go on.'

Cassie had done a bit of research on St Ioannis, the church Chrysanthi attended. 'You know she's devout Greek Orthodox, right? So apparently, her priest is in his eighties and very old school. Suicide is still a cardinal sin in Orthodox theology so if Bronte had killed herself he could have refused to hold a funeral service for her.'

Flyte's lips rounded into a pretty 'O'. She looked at Cassie with something of their previous intimacy, before saying, 'You know, if you hadn't had the idea of checking for bruising on the fingernails the police would probably have remained convinced that it was suicide.' She fixed Cassie with a look. 'No point asking you what on earth made you think of it, I suppose?'

Cassie pulled a half-grin. 'No point at all.'

She had half expected her discovery to bring her some kind of closure over Bronte's death but the initial buzz faded fast. As she wheeled her old schoolmate's body down the corridor to the dedicated forensic suite out back, she found guilt still hanging over her like a bad pills-and-vodka hangover. Bronte's bruised fingers might be clear evidence of foul play but it was still a long way from finding out who'd killed her.

'Look, I'm doing everything I can,' she told the shrouded figure as she rolled the tray holding her over to the open drawer into the forensic body store. 'And Flyte is a good detective. She'll make sure the cops do the business.'

Bronte's silence felt charged with scepticism.

After prepping the suite with all the tools and sample pots needed for the PM, she changed into civvies, and made a call to book Maddy, the locum she trusted most, to come in and cover Bronte's forensic PM, which would be happening the next day. Cassie had put in for the day off. After all, now the body was effectively an exhibit, the role of the APT was severely limited – no more than handmaiden to the pathologist. At least that was what she told herself.

Sunk in these thoughts she was pulling open the front door to leave – when she reeled back. A man stood there, his arm raised as if to strike her.

Her hand flew up to defend herself before she realised that he'd only been about to knock on the door. 'You scared the shit out of me!' she barked.

'Sorry, sorry,' said the guy, wide-eyed, both hands up in the air in surrender.

'The mortuary is closed,' she said, surveying him through narrowed eyes.

'Oh, right. I was hoping to see someone.'

He was tall and lean, all in black, with dark hair long enough to frame a clean-sculpted jaw and even darker eyes, the kind of guy who would shatter your heart into a thousand pieces and leave you to sweep up the mess.

No prizes for guessing who he was. Ethan Fox, Bronte's ex.

'Do you mean one of our guests?'

'Bronte. Sophia Angelopoulos.' He looked past her into the corridor, as if he might catch a glimpse of her.

Closing the door behind her, Cassie spoke gently. 'I'm afraid you would need permission from the family to view a body.' Not that Bronte could be viewed by anyone now, not until after her forensic PM.

That prompted a bitter laugh. 'Like that's ever going to happen,' he said.

Cassie started walking, steering him away from the mortuary.

He threw a last glance at the place before saying, 'I'm Ethan Fox, by the way.'

'Hey, Ethan. I'm Cassie Raven, one of the mortuary staff.'

He looked at her with molasses eyes, a wry smile lifting one corner of his mouth. 'I know. I saw your fifteen minutes of fame on social. Or more like fifteen seconds these days.'

'You saw that?' Cassie grimaced.

He grinned. 'Yeah. I punched the air when you told her to go fuck herself. They've been hounding me too, as you can imagine. The dodgy boyfriend who got poor Bronte into gear.' He snorted. 'That comes straight from her mother.'

She noted that he didn't say 'ex-boyfriend'.

'Is there really no way I can see her?' he asked.

'I'm really sorry, Ethan, not without her parents' say-so.'

He blew out a breath. 'It's so shit being out of the loop. You know the first time I heard about what happened was on social? The Feds haven't even called me.'

They'll be calling you now, she thought wryly.

She let him chat on about Bronte's death, understanding how it helped the bereaved to talk.

Ten minutes later, she drifted to a halt next to the stairway down to her section of towpath. 'This is me.' Although she felt sorry for him, she didn't want him knowing where she lived. Was she finally learning caution in her old age?

He nodded towards the 'Spoons next to the lock. 'Can I buy you a drink?' Seeing she was about to say no he pushed a hand through his hair. 'It might sound a bit . . . weird but, talking to you . . . it's the next best thing to seeing her?'

Seeing the look of embarrassed entreaty in his eyes, she nodded. The newly bereaved sometimes experienced a sense of accelerated intimacy with the person looking after the body of their dead loved one. And there was another reason: Ethan might let something useful slip, something he wouldn't say to Flyte and the cops, who'd be bound to treat him as a suspect. When it came to murder, lovers and exes were always top of the list.

Chapter Twenty-One

She sipped at the vodka-free tonic she'd requested – determined to keep her wits about her – before asking, 'It must be upsetting, all this coverage in the press and on social?'

He nodded, taking a drink of his JD and Coke. 'It's not nice being portrayed as the bad guy by a bunch of dickheads who don't even know me.' She noted that even though they were sitting inside he had put on shades and chosen a table in a corner with his back to the room. 'I mean this business about me getting Bronte into gear. It's factitious. Pure fantasy. Bronte had already done pills – and even smack – when I met her. One of her band members was a bit of a junkie.'

Factitious. Cassie liked an educated guy, and he used the word without any pretension.

'Her mother thinks she got into it cos she was "fragile"?' she said.

He considered the idea, a frown line between his near-black eyebrows. 'Bronte was a tough cookie but also really vulnerable at the same time, if you know what I mean?'

Oh, I know, thought Cassie, remembering how her own nickname in her squatting days had been 'Teflon' – when most of the time she'd felt like she was made of sugar glass. Casting her mind back to school, fragile was the last word anyone would use to describe Bronte, at least not until the events that saw her suddenly leaving. Maybe she and Bronte had been more alike than she'd thought at the time.

'Drugs and booze *are* a great way to take the edge off,' she said with a wry look. 'In the short term, anyway.'

'Yeah, exactly that.' Ethan looked into her eyes, a moment of shared understanding. 'We're all fucked up, one way or another, right? Especially musicians, writers, etc. You gotta have a screw loose to be creative, to have a gift.'

It struck Cassie that what she thought of as *her* gift – her bond with the dead – might also have come at a price: an inability to let the living get too close. Pushing away the image of Archie's uncomplicated smile.

'You know Bronte had a twin brother who died when he was small?' asked Ethan.

'Wow.' Cassie tried to imagine what it would be like to lose a twin – like having a shadow walking alongside you through life.

'Bronte had health problems, too. There was a ton of things she couldn't eat – bread, pasta, any kind of curry. Which meant her mother was always turning up with home-made dishes or a bottle of some old wives' remedy . . .' He rolled his eyes. 'Kind of sweet, but it drove her nuts.'

Cassie remembered Bronte's lunch box at school, strictly curated by her mother. Having lost one child, with another child sickly, no wonder Chrysanthi had been so overprotective – or controlling?

'Bronte loved her mum, don't get me wrong, but she tried to keep her at arm's length. Chrysanthi just wouldn't let her *be*, you know?'

'What about George?' It had crossed Cassie's mind that Bronte's mental health problems could be a sign of childhood abuse.

'Oh, she adored her daddy. He was the total opposite of her mum – adventurous, party-animal type of guy. She said that from the time she could talk, he told her she could do whatever she set her mind to. Apparently, George is a total pussy-hound, but I got on all right with him.'

He pulled out a packet of Camels. 'Is it OK if we pop out? I'm dying here.'

'I thought you'd never ask,' she said.

Again, Ethan chose the least public table – on the edge of the terrace, facing a wall. He lit her cigarette first, his fingers brushing hers as he cupped the flame, which sent a little frisson through her. *Watch out*, she told herself.

'Bronte used to say that her childhood was like growing up in a war zone,' he said, blowing out a plume of smoke. 'Her mum and dad always had separate bedrooms but they stayed under the same roof until Bronte went to uni. Even then you know they never actually got divorced?'

'Because of Chrysanthi's religion? – she would probably think marriage is for life.'

Cassie had barely smoked since Archie moved in and the cigarette was making her dizzy – in a good way. On impulse, she asked him, 'Bronte went to school in Camden didn't she? Did she ever talk about it?'

He squinted through the smoke, making the laughter lines scrunch around his eyes. 'She described it as a "pit of vipers".'

That was like a slap. *One you deserve.*

'She begged her dad to take her out,' he went on. 'Eventually, he did. She said that after that place even the convent boarding school she went to was a picnic.'

A female member of the pub staff came over and cleared Cassie's empty glass. Pulling an apologetic expression, she said, 'I'm sorry but you can't smoke anywhere on the premises.'

'Oh sorry,' said Cassie, immediately dropped her fag end and ground it underfoot but Ethan's face contorted with anger.

'You're joking right?! We're in the *open air*!' he snapped at the girl, whose eyes widened as she made herself scarce.

Cassie was taken aback by how easily he'd lost his rag, but after a moment staring at the girl's departing back, Ethan sent her an apologetic look. 'Sorry, about that. I'm not usually such an arsehole.'

'Listen,' she ventured, 'feel free to tell me it's none of my business, but were you and Bronte . . . back together before she died?'

He pulled an 'It's complicated' face. 'Yes, no, off and on.' He sent her a cheeky look. 'Break-up sex is the best, isn't it? But it does makes things . . . confusing.'

She broke the gaze. *True.*

'She was clean, by the way,' he went on. 'Although the last time I saw her she was in a bad way about something, but she wouldn't say what. So when I heard the news, I could see her doing it, you know.' Dropping his head, he took a savage drag on his cig.

She let the silence simmer: years of dealing with the bereaved had proven it a useful way of finding out what was really on someone's mind.

'So do the police think there's anything funny about it?' asked Ethan at last, his tone offhand.

She made a blank face.

'I mean have they found anything to suggest she didn't top herself?'

'I'm just a technician, Ethan,' she said, apologetic. 'That kind of thing is above my pay grade.'

FLYTE

Bronte's forensic PM took place at 2 p.m. the next day, and Flyte and Bacon arranged to meet the Home Office pathologist at the mortuary after he'd finished.

Dr Purdy was a balding guy in his forties, bespectacled, and with the manner of someone who had mislaid his keys and was perpetually trying to recall where he'd put them.

'So ummm. The haematoma on the deceased's right hand are consistent with somebody pressing down hard on the upper digits,' he said. It annoyed but no longer surprised Flyte that Purdy directed his attention exclusively towards DI Bacon. 'In my judgement, the force required implies pressure from a foot with someone's weight behind it, thus' – he demonstrated by pressing his foot on the floor and leaning in.

'So she was hanging on and somebody stamped on her fingers to make her let go?' Flyte asked, seeking his gaze.

'Yes, I think that's a reasonable conclusion given the circumstances of her death.' His eyes slid back to Bacon. Hard to know if he was a sexist dickhead or just one of those nerdy guys who were allergic to eye contact when it came to the opposite sex. 'Abrasions to the palm of her left hand suggest she hung on with both hands initially but once she was down to one . . .'

'Game over,' said Bacon crisply.

'Any other injuries?' asked Flyte. 'I know bruises can carry on developing after death.'

His gaze turned reluctantly to her. 'There's a bruise here, on the back of her right thigh, that has emerged since the routine PM,' he said.

'Could that be from her attacker manhandling her over the balcony?' asked Bacon.

'It's possible,' he agreed. 'I can find nothing else to suggest that she fought back. Nothing under the fingernails, nor any of the defensive injuries we usually see when someone is fighting for their life.'

Flyte frowned. 'It sounds like somebody . . . just tipped her over? Why didn't she put up a fight?'

The pathologist shrugged. 'She weighed less than eight stone: it wouldn't even take somebody especially strong.' He demonstrated hefting someone over an invisible balcony. 'Oh and her samples came back from the lab. Negative for drugs and only a negligible amount of alcohol.' He checked his watch. 'I've got to . . .'

'Who was the APT at the PM?' asked Flyte casually. She'd glimpsed a woman in scrubs whom she didn't recognise coming out of the forensic suite.

'I don't recall her name,' said Purdy with a frown. 'I think she's a locum.'

She caught Bacon's curious look.

So Cassie had ducked Bronte's second PM. That was odd, given the interest she'd taken in the case. Going by past experience, once the morgue girl had got her teeth into something, her bite was harder to dislodge than a pit bull's.

As she and Bacon headed towards the exit, she wondered whether to share Cassie's intuition that it was Chrysanthi who'd taken and leaked the photo of Bronte, but decided against. There was no proof after all.

Bacon appeared competent enough, but given that he was a Met Police lifer, Flyte couldn't bring herself to trust him. The events of the previous year had shattered her deeply rooted faith in the police service, and exposed a code of *omertà* between officers that seemed unbreakable. She had seen for herself how even the good cops kept their heads down rather than rat on a colleague, and her gut feeling about Bacon was that if push came to shove he'd probably do the same.

Chapter Twenty-Two

Through the train window, Cassie watched the suburbs dwindle, handing over to trees and meadows, the vivid limeade foliage of spring flashing past as they picked up speed. She found all this *greenery* mesmerising – and discombobulating. When had she last ventured out of town into deepest countryside? Probably not since she was a kid, on a day trip to Southend.

Cassie wasn't on call that weekend so when Archie had called to suggest spending a couple of nights in a country pub in his home county of Wiltshire – his treat – she'd jumped at the idea. Yesterday's meeting with Ethan Fox had left her feeling unsettled because – despite him losing his rag with the bar worker – she'd felt the unmistakable spark of attraction between them. She wasn't a total moron: he'd probably turned that deep brown gaze on dozens of women, Bronte included, but still . . . The way he'd looked at her had made her feel like the only person on the planet.

What, now you want my boyfriend? – those slightly grating tones from schooldays.

'I'm trying to find out who killed you,' she murmured, before catching the alarmed look of the student-looking guy opposite. 'Sorry,' she said, 'just thinking out loud.'

In any case she needed to find out where she and Archie were at, and a couple of nights of rural bliss away from the daily routine could be just the reset they needed. After she'd climbed off the train at Swindon and saw his coppery head looming over everyone else at the platform end she was relieved to find she still felt a buzz.

'Did you miss me?' he asked after giving her a bear hug.

'Yes,' she said, smiling up at him. Thinking that, weirdly, she missed him now, in retrospect, rather than at the time.

A cab took them through Marlborough and a couple of miles into the countryside where it pulled up outside a picture-postcard village pub called The Goose and Crumpet. But inside the vibe was fancy hotel and the woman behind the reception desk was so posh that Cassie only caught half of what she was saying. 'You have a table for dinner at eight,' she said to Archie. 'You're in luck, the chef has just refreshed the tasting menu.'

The *what*? Cassie was feeling increasingly out of place and not just because of her jeans and leather jacket.

Up in their room Archie stretched out on the crisp white linen of the sumptuous king-sized bed, beaming. 'This is the life!'

Meanwhile Cassie prowled the room like a wild animal exploring its new cage. The furniture looked properly antique, the silk curtains and cushions like something out of one of those interior design mags you saw at the dentist's. Gorgeous – *but unsettlingly alien*. Lifting the stopper on a glass carafe of red-brown liquid she sniffed suspiciously 'What's this? It smells like port but looks brown, like sherry.'

'It's tawny port,' he said with a grin. 'Help yourself – it's free.'

'Now you're talking,' she said, filling two tumblers and taking them over to the bed.

She handed him one before lying down. Sending him a sideways look she said mock-innocently, 'So, what shall we do till dinner time?'

An hour or so later they were onto pre-dinner drinks in the guests' snug – Grey Goose vodka martini for her, Campari and soda for Archie. Several other guests, a bit older than them, occupied the chic sofas and armchairs, and there was a burble of well-bred chatter. The women were dolled up in what she knew were called cocktail dresses, their hair freshly flounced and styled. Thank Christ she'd remembered at the last minute to pack her only frock, a floaty grey goth-esque affair with a black insect pattern. But she still caught one of the women giving her a head-to-toe once-over, either because of her piercings, or perhaps thinking high heels would be more 'appropriate footwear' than her DMs. Taking her piercings out to respect the raw feelings of grieving relatives was one thing, but sheltered rich folks? They'd just have to get over themselves.

Her sense of discomfort didn't fade over the meal. As she should've guessed from the stupid name alone the place was no longer a pub in any proper sense of the word: every table in what had once been the main bar was laid for dinner without even a single bar stool for a thirsty passer-by.

Archie seemed completely at home, *of course he did*.

'So, your old school in Marlborough,' she said, picturing the imposing Georgian building set in verdant grounds they'd passed in the cab. 'You were a boarder, right?'

He nodded. 'Yup, from thirteen, but I'd already been boarding at prep school for five years.'

'Wow.' *Eight years old.* 'But your mum and dad only worked in the City, didn't they?'

'Yup, corporate lawyers.'

'So why didn't you live at home?' – realising with a guilty jolt that she'd never asked before.

He shrugged. 'Both of them had boarded from the same age. I loved it. And I used to go home for the school holidays.'

'Right.' Cassie thought of her own childhood, both parents missing, presumed dead – until a few months ago. Although she'd been brought up as an orphan at least she'd had her grandmother's undivided attention.

She dissected the single spear of asparagus on a pool of green which formed their third course. Their serving gal – 'call me Tabby' – presumably short for Tabitha rather than named after the family moggy – had described the pond-coloured liquid as 'essence of nettle foraged from local hedgerows'. Cassie only ate the asparagus, unable to expel an image of the scabby clumps of nettle on the verge of the canal towpath, which were enthusiastically watered by passing dogs. 'The countryside round here is absolutely stunning,' she said, not wanting to come across as critical or negative.

'It's wonderful, isn't it? – even better from the back of a hunter,' Archie said. 'The Savernake Forest just south of here is just glorious.'

'You sound homesick ...' She paused before asking, 'So do you see yourself living here, eventually?'

He shrugged his big rugby player shoulders. 'Perhaps. The Cotswolds is pretty nice, too. I think the countryside is the only place to raise kids.' He met her eye. 'Don't you?'

Oh fuck. Luckily Tabby-cat came to clear their plates at that moment, giving her time to regroup.

Cassie couldn't imagine living anywhere except Camden, or some other inner-London borough. Here, every person in the room was white, middle class and so ... *homogeneous* – immaculately groomed, and radiating the terrifying confidence of long-held wealth. She'd counted four men wearing chinos in varying shades of red, which must be like the posh-guy uniform round here.

'I suppose I just feel more at home in London,' she admitted. 'All the different folks and accents and looks, it means that nobody can feel out of place?'

They paused to smile up at Tabby bearing course number four: Wiltshire roast vegetables – one purple heritage carrot, a strip of celeriac and a scrawny wedge of parsnip – Archie's portion garnished with bone marrow butter.

'What about kids?' he asked, pretending to study his food.

Cassie realised this was the first time the subject had come up in their eight or nine months together – at least in a way she hadn't been able to sidestep. It wasn't that she'd definitively ruled out the idea, but she had never felt even a trace of the urge to procreate that many – most? – women seemed to experience. Add in the inescapable fact that it was women who made the lion's share of the sacrifices, and she wasn't sure she ever would.

'I don't know, Archie. I like my job, and my freedom, I guess.' A pause. 'I'm guessing you do, though? Want kids?'

He met her gaze, his dark grey eyes looking serious. 'Oh yes, a brace of them at least.'

They both went to speak but were interrupted, not by their server, but a blonde woman almost six foot tall and not much more than a foot wide at her broadest point, with a face like a startled fawn.

'Arch?' she asked. 'It *is* you!' Before turning to Cassie and saying, 'I am *so* sorry to interrupt, but I was at school with Arch here.'

She smiled, showing her perfect teeth. 'It's Lætitia – with a diphthong.' Her look doubting that Cassie would have a clue what that meant. 'But everyone calls me Letty.'

'Di' from the Latin for two; 'phthongos' meaning sound or voice, thought Cassie to herself.

Letty and 'Arch' saddled up for a ride down Hooray memory lane: the night Letty got 'totally squiffy' on scrumpy . . . a mutual chum who'd just got a job at a Japanese bank . . . someone's upcoming weekend house party . . . *yada yada*. The exchange probably only lasted two or three minutes but Cassie was grateful when Tabby-cat arrived with the next course, as it saved her from having to extract her own eyes with a spoon.

After Letty had gone, trailing a cloud of vetiver, Cassie raised an eyebrow. 'Old squeeze?'

Archie's cheeks went pomegranate red: he blushed easily, like most ginger-haired people. 'A brief dalliance, years ago. No torches carried on either side – she just got engaged actually.' He dispatched half of his lozenge of sous-vide turbot, served on fermented kohlrabi, in one modest bite before taking a gulp of wine. 'I might go to the house party she mentioned. Harry's got a proper country pile with beautiful grounds. Hey, why don't you come with?!'

Her face must have betrayed her blank horror at the prospect of hanging out with Letty and her chums because Archie's face fell. Like, literally fell, as though the strings that gave him his default-cheerful expression had been cut.

They got through the rest of the meal on work chat, and when Tabby-cat asked if they'd like a digestif they both went for large brandies which they took up to the room.

There they lay side by side on the bed, fully clothed and not touching: the half metre of pristine white linen between them might as well have been the Himalayas.

'When Tabby said dessert was "banana three ways" I nearly made a bad joke,' said Cassie, trying to lighten the mood.

It didn't dispel Archie's brooding silence. Her stomach felt like it had been filled with quick-setting cement. 'Well, this is fun,' she said, about to pick a fight, her default method when an ending was inevitable to get it over with.

'You know I love you, don't you?' He spoke with what was clearly great effort.

But.

'But I sometimes feel as though my life is on hold.'

Cassie felt a sudden heat behind the eyes; her childish impulse to engineer a row gone.

He levelled his gaze at her. 'Could you meet me halfway? Not now, but in a few years, say, we could get somewhere outside London but still easily commutable? Like, I don't know, Surrey?'

Surrey? He might as well have said Mogadishu.

'I'm not trying to get you to give up your job,' he went on. 'I know you love it. But there are mortuaries everywhere.'

'What about the . . . kids thing though?' she asked, twisting her glass on the bedcover. 'I just don't see myself . . .'

'You're only twenty-seven!' he said. 'You might change your mind, a few years down the line?'

No chance. The realisation made her stomach plunge.

Meeting his hopeful, hopeless gaze she said, 'And if I get to thirty-five and still feel the same? What then?'

Chapter Twenty-Three

The cab/train/Tube schlep back from deepest Wiltshire the following day took Cassie nearly three hours and felt like twice that. When she finally climbed aboard *Dreamcatcher* Macavity cantered down from the deck where he'd been sunning himself to greet her. Following her below deck he jumped up onto the banquette, arching his back.

'So you missed me? Even though Uncle Gaz gives you bigger rations than I do?' Gaz was her neighbour on the next-door mooring. She sat down beside him. He gazed up at her lovingly, his purr as loud as a two-stroke engine, but when he set his paw on her thigh she felt something break inside. Burying her face in his hot black fur, smelling of canal and his own dusty mustiness she murmured, 'Have I fucked up?'

The scene in the hotel bedroom that morning kept playing on a loop behind her eyes: she and Archie getting dressed like two polite strangers, and then the phone ringing to say her cab had arrived. They'd hugged each other hard then, the first time they'd touched since the previous evening, before it all went tits up, cutting short their little holiday.

'I do love you, you know,' she had told him, her words muffled by his big shoulder.

She felt him nod.

'It's just...'

'I know,' he had murmured.

'Can we be friends?' – pulling her face back to see his.

He had blinked rapidly before kissing her on the top of her head. 'I don't think I could handle that.'

On the boat, after a cup of black coffee with an outsize vodka chaser, she was starting to feel a bit better. She would miss him horribly, but she couldn't see any alternative. Archie deserved a future that fitted his dreams: marriage to some gorgeous toff like Lætitia, a gaff in the countryside, a couple of strawberry-blonde kids, Pimm's on the patio, the whole deal. Ever since the kids-and-countryside conversation she had tried a hundred times to insert herself into that picture – and failed every time. Imagined herself doing the school run in a Chelsea tractor, the other mums at the school gates eyeing her tatts and piercings, asking, *What do you do? I work in a mortuary.* Yeah, right.

Cassie hadn't slept much alongside an equally restless Archie the previous night and after her unaccustomed lunchtime vodka she felt her eyes drift closed.

She had no idea how long had passed before they snapped open. 'Uhh?'

'I said, why the fuck didn't you come to my PM?'

Opposite her sat Bronte, her elbows on the table, the left side of her face a livid purple, one eye half closed. She was wearing her body bag like a hoodie, and through the half-open zip Cassie could see the black-red Y of stitches on her chest used to close the midline incision.

'I...uh...' Cassie stuttered.

Bronte dropped her head to gesture at the stitches visible through her hair – mending the ear-to-ear incision that allowed the scalp to be peeled back. 'Your locum did a crap job: here feel!' – reaching for her hand.

Crack! Cassie jumped but it was only the cat flap in the cabin door banging shut as Macavity legged it.

WTF? The seat opposite was empty, but Cassie's heart was still flopping round in her chest like a landed fish.

It took her a moment to calm herself. 'Just a dream, it was just a dream,' she murmured. A dream born out of a subconscious guilt that instead of swanning off to Wiltshire for port and posh eats she should have been at Bronte's forensic PM.

She opened her laptop and started to research Bronte's rise to fame – how she'd gone from the skinny but charismatic girl with the unruly curls who Cassie had seen playing niche Greek-influenced blues/jazz at local haunt Dingwalls, to Bronte – the polished-looking dance-pop phenomenon who could fill the Shepherd's Bush Empire. She was astonished to discover the sheer graft it had involved. In the three years before 'Clean Break' went triple-platinum Bronte had played more than forty gigs a year and not just in the UK but Amsterdam, Berlin, Oslo, Serbia, Sofia . . . a brutal schedule. But it was only *after* her mega-hit and signing by Melodik that she'd spiralled into a drink and drugs meltdown, regularly snapped by the paparazzi looking messed up, usually hanging on the arm of Ethan, who looked handsome but equally wasted.

She read the two longest interviews Bronte had given the music press. In the first one in *NME* right on the heels of her recording deal, Bronte sounded wide-eyed at her sudden success, 'thrilled' to be working with Melodik, and planning an album inspired by genres Cassie had barely heard of, like rebetika, gypsy jazz and klezmer. After a delve into Spotify she'd discovered it was roots music – non-Western and about as far as you could get from the clubland banger that had won her the big deal.

The second interview was on YouTube, just a couple of months before her death – and it felt strikingly different. Bronte looked drawn and distracted, sounding lukewarm about her first project for Melodik – another EDM single. Now and again her real feelings punched through. When the interviewer asked if the roots-influenced album she'd hinted at in the past would ever happen she snapped, 'You're damn right it's going to happen.'

The flash of defiance on her face took Cassie back to a moment in school. While waiting for the teacher to arrive in class, one of the girls who periodically baited the then-Sophia had snatched the sketchbook she was always drawing in. Waving one of the sketches around, she hooted, 'Look, at what Dobby's been drawing! Hang on, is this supposed to be Raven? Are you a *dirty lezza*, Dobby?'

Cassie had been totally mortified, of course. At that age she'd only had one aim: to keep her head down and get through the school day without attracting attention. Thankfully the exchange had been cut short when Sophia, looking furious, jumped up to snatch back the book, just as Mrs Hooper had sailed in. 'Settle down, girls!' she said in her distinctive honk and that had been that, for the time being anyway.

The memory flooded back ... *The awful sound of a girl's keening, the thread of vermilion in the shower tray.*

Cassie couldn't undo the past but there was something she could do. Just leaving things to the cops wasn't an option: she owed it to Bronte to find out who had killed her.

Turning to TikTok, she found Bronte still trending and started to wade through the latest outpouring of rumour dressed up as informed comment, a contest in which her enemy @Charly_Detective still led the field. Her latest vid was a mash-up of unflattering stills and footage of Ethan – stoned and playing his guitar badly at some gig to scattered boos ... drunk and snarling at a photographer, Bronte at his side, dwarfed by his height and looking vulnerable ... an old tabloid headline about him being arrested for threatening behaviour in a pub (which never reached court) and so on. Charly described him as a 'failed pop star' and 'the boyfriend Bronte dumped just before her death' and the piece ended with her outside Ethan's flat, laying on the fake concern. 'There have been no sightings of Ethan Fox since Bronte's tragic death.'

The inference viewers were meant to draw was obvious – that Ethan was a prime suspect in his girlfriend's death and had done a runner. If he'd been wealthy and powerful he could sue her for libel, but these armchair sleuths never aimed their outflow of septic innuendo at anyone who could afford to hit back. She replayed her own encounter with Ethan, trying to imagine him struggling with Bronte, pitching her over the balcony, perhaps in the heat of a row? He might be a wayward type with an impulsive streak, but capable of serious violence? She couldn't see it. *You've been wrong before*, said her caustic inner voice.

She closed down TikTok with a sigh. Once the police went public with the news that they were treating Bronte's death as suspicious, people like Charly would no doubt be crowing over 'their victory'. It made her want to throw up.

FLYTE

Flyte was on the phone to her mentor William at the IOPC.

'So you're saying that now Bronte's death is a murder case, DI Bacon is the lead investigator running the show day to day?'

'That's right. He will be deputy SIO to Malcolm Bellwether's SIO.'

'So where does that leave me?' Trying to repress her irrational fury.

'You will continue to shadow the murder inquiry since it is inevitably entangled with the original IOPC investigation. You'll be kept informed of all developments but DI Bacon will be in the driving seat. Your role from here on in is as an observer.'

'Right,' she said. 'I'm going to be kept out of the loop, aren't I?'

'Phyllida, now that it's a criminal matter clearly the police must take primacy,' said William, sounding testy.

'After they made a total hash of the initial investigation.'

'That was down to a uniformed sergeant from Camden. DI Bacon is a murder detective with a solid record at Canning Town and the incident room will be staffed with a team of detectives from outside the borough.' He paused to clear his throat. 'There has been a suggestion that you haven't been entirely ... candid about your contacts with the mortuary technician in the case?'

What the . . . ? So Bacon had been squealing. How appropriate.

'It's imperative that you share anything with any bearing on the ongoing investigation with DI Bacon. That would be the best way to ensure you stay *in* the loop.'

Flyte hung up fuming. She was already sensing a shift in the dynamic between her and Bacon: she would be tolerated, but would have little to no influence over the direction of the murder investigation.

It was Saturday, and she had the weekend off, but at 5 p.m. she opened the BBC News app to watch the live coverage of the Camden police press conference. It was fronted by Bellwether and Bacon, her old boss displaying the comms savvy that had seen him reach DCI rank by his mid-forties. He revealed what he would only describe as 'newly discovered' injuries to Sophia Angelopoulos's body which had emerged during the forensic PM. A journalist asked – reasonably enough – why a forensic PM hadn't been requested earlier. Bellwether said 'in this case, we should have done a better job exploring all possible scenarios' before pointing out that the IOPC investigation was ongoing and that 'their representative' would be given 'full access' to the murder inquiry.

Flyte made a scornful sound. It couldn't be clearer: from now on she'd be playing the role of fig leaf, a human shield to help deflect further criticism of the Met's screw-ups.

Bellwether finished by adopting his 'concerned' face: 'I want to assure the family and the public that we will not rest until the truth about Bronte's death is uncovered and any perpetrator brought to justice.'

Cut-and-paste corporate pap. Flyte knew that the chances of that happening were vanishingly small. The 'golden hour' at the start of any investigation was the critical moment in which evidence was found and leads established, and it had now been ten days since Bronte's broken body was discovered on the towpath. Ten days in which any useful forensics at the scene had been lost and potential witnesses' memories had long faded.

Opening the dating app which she'd recently signed up to she scrolled through her latest likes with a feeling of gloom. The experience of coming out – to everyone except her mother, that is – and dating women hadn't been the liberation she'd imagined it might be. She had already exhausted the possibilities of the only surviving bar in supposedly alternative Camden frequented by gay women. She didn't like the newly ubiquitous term 'queer' which, like the word 'lesbian', had only ever been used as an insult at her all-girls boarding school.

Clicking on the face of a freckled, red-haired woman, she skimmed her profile. KikiZee described herself as 'creative, passionate', but then ruined it with a flurry of cretinous emojis, hobbies that included 'climate activism, self-care, reiki, veganism', and a stern list of NOes – 'NO Tories, NO Brexiteers, NO meat-eaters, NO Terfs' ... What would KikiZee make of a former police officer? *Fascist pig*, probably. It had come as a shock, discovering how judgemental a long-marginalised minority could be.

Prejudice came in all shapes and sizes.

The next 'like' came from ... A leap of excitement. *Was it ...?*

Clicking on the image she realised her mistake: the Mediterranean colouring, the undercut and soot-black hair was similar to Cassie Raven's but without Cassie's heart-shaped face and generous lips.

She berated herself: that ship had sailed – or never even been launched – so why the hell couldn't she stop thinking about the morgue girl?

Chapter Twenty-Four

The next day Cassie pushed open the door of Honest Bob's vinyl store, and felt her stomach swoop. Her mother Kath had worked for Bob, the guy who owned the place, when she'd been just nineteen, before she'd met Callum and long before Cassie was born. Seven years later she was dead – murdered. The last time Cassie had been here she'd been trying to find out the truth about her mum's death; at least this time she was only here to get intel about the music industry.

In the café area she found Bob standing behind the coffee machine. 'Hello, stranger,' he said, giving her a lingering up-and-down look that made her feel like a prize cow getting sized up at market. *Creep*.

Anyone else would've got her death stare on full beam but since she was here to pick his brains, she pasted on a girly smile.

'I'm just making an espresso,' he said. 'Want one?'

'Thanks.' She smiled, going over to the corner table he indicated.

Guys of that generation seemed to think that women spent their lives craving the attentions of *any* male – even a fossilised old rocker like Bob, with his greasy-looking steel-grey hair scraped back in a ponytail. She'd read once that the euphemism for this unwanted attention was *gallantry*. It creeped her out.

In Camden's musical heyday, Bob's shop had been legendary: a magnet for punks, post-punks and goths, on the hunt for some rare import from New York, or even a glimpse of some famous musician. Her dad, who had once played in a band himself, never stopped boasting how he'd once chatted to Joe Strummer here in the nineties. The place had somehow survived the area's gentrification long enough to benefit from the resurgence of vinyl among a new generation.

Since she was last here a graffiti-style neon mural of Amy Winehouse had been painted on the wall – instantly recognisable from her trademark beehive and batwing eyeliner. As Cassie watched, a blonde-haired girl stepped in front of it with her boyfriend to snap a selfie – Scandinavians, going by their overheard chat. She understood the impulse to pay homage to a talent – but it was hard to escape the feeling that Amy the person was gone, leaving behind Amy the brand. A fate that no doubt awaited Bronte too.

As Bob arrived with their coffees, he followed her gaze. 'Up until the nineties we used to get a few tourists, but nine out of ten of the customers back then were hard core musos. Now thanks to Amy, it's the other way round.' He leaned towards her confidingly. 'I'm not complaining. The pilgrims will pay silly money for anything Amy-related. I can charge forty quid for a copy of *Back to Black* that goes for a tenner on eBay.'

She pulled a wry grin. 'Pilgrims' was spot on. The T-shirts, posters and even mugs featuring the singer's heavily lined eyes were the equivalent of the badges and icons once sold to the faithful visiting a medieval shrine, while her Camden haunts and the house where she died were practically stations of the cross.

'So business is good?' she asked.

'Uh-huh' – resting his eyes on her face, lazily flipping his amber worry beads over his knuckles. *Clack . . . clackety-clack*. 'But you're not here to talk business. What can I do for you, Kath's girl?'

'It's about Bronte,' she said quickly, to head off any talk of her mother.

'Ah.' His expression turning genuinely sad. 'What a waste. She was another real talent.' He tipped his head towards the mural. 'But they can't handle the pressure, these young girls.'

She took a sip of coffee to hide her expression. 'You know the police have decided she was murdered now?'

He nodded. 'I saw on the news. She wouldn't have made old bones anyway – like most proper artists she had a screw loose.' Spinning a finger at the side of his head. 'And she had a taste for smack, like that boyfriend of hers.'

'You know Ethan?' – picturing his sharp jawline and those big dark eyes.

A nod. 'He comes in here now and again. Bought a rare pressing of a Django Reinhardt album for her not long ago actually.'

'You could probably sell that story to some vlogger,' said Cassie darkly.

He frowned uncomprehendingly before saying, 'Oh, you mean those ambulance-chasers on social media. I wouldn't give that lot the shit off my shoe.'

She felt a little surge of warmth towards him: he might be a Jurassic-era sexist but on this topic they shared the same instincts.

'What did you make of him? Ethan.'

He shrugged. 'Bog-standard guitarist for a minor league band who trades off his pretty-boy looks and bad-boy reputation. Not like Bronte. She was the real deal.' He pulled a dry smile. 'And now she's dead she'll make everyone a lot more money.'

'How so?'

Clack-clack went his beads. 'Look, there was a good chance that Bronte's career would have crashed and burned. You know that EDM hit she had?' Seeing her uncomprehending look, he said, 'Electronic Dance Music. What was it called?' His forehead creased as he tried to retrieve the name.

'"Clean Break".'

'Yeah, that's it. So the word is that her record company wanted her to cut ten carbon copies of that, but her heart was set on an album inspired by her Greek heritage, something to showcase that voice of hers. But Melodik wasn't having any of it – and her contract stopped her releasing her own stuff. The result: an ugly stand-off and no album.' He shrugged. 'So, if she'd lived the chances were she'd have been a one-hit wonder and disappeared back into obscurity' – he waved a hand – 'gigs down the Dublin Castle, tiny world music festivals in some muddy field. But dead, she could turn out to be a gold mine.'

'How?'

'Melodik will have recordings of all the songs she's been laying down since they signed her. Now they can take her vocals into the studio, layer 'em up with electronically generated drums and synth, set the machine to a hundred and thirty beats per minute and bingo – release an EDM album she would hate but which will sell like a bastard now she's dead.' He sent her a cynical wink. 'And trust me, they won't be calling up any bouzouki artists.'

Seeing she wasn't convinced, he went on, '*Back to Black* was a big hit when it first came out, sure, but in the four weeks after

Amy died it became the biggest-selling album *of the century*. Sales before she died – about three million and steady. Sales today? *Sixteen* million and counting.'

'Wow.'

'Do you remember her posthumous album?'

'Yeah, *Lioness: Hidden Treasures*.'

He made a dismissive face. 'It was cobbled together out of unreleased demos and out-takes. Amy was a perfectionist, she'd've *hated* it. But here's the thing – it still went triple-platinum. I tell you, the suits at Melodik who are shedding crocodile tears over "poor Bronte" in public will be breaking open the champers in private.'

Chapter Twenty-Five

Monday morning Cassie was back in the mortuary – and from the look of the list it was going to be a mare of a day. The only bright spot: Prof Arculus, her favourite pathologist, was down to conduct the PMs.

Since seeing Bob, she'd spent hours going over what he'd said. He was right: asking the question *Cui bono?* – who benefits? – was always a good place to start. When she'd quizzed him on who exactly would profit from any post-mortem sales spike, he'd said that Bronte's A&R man – aka her handler at Melodik – might be on a sales bonus, and her manager, aka her father George, would presumably get commission. She could see no obvious way it would deliver a payout for Ethan, which brought her an unexpected gust of relief.

She texted George with an excuse: could they meet to discuss the arrangements for transferring Bronte's body to the funeral director's once the coroner released the body? He came straight back, suggesting lunchtime at the Costa Coffee overlooking the canal.

Jason was in a good mood, whistling happily to himself as they prepped the autopsy suite, and she felt guilty for ever suspecting him of selling the pics of Bronte's body.

'Good weekend?' she asked.

'Banging weekend. Went to a rave out near Basildon.' He eyed her. 'You're not going to ruin it by giving me the jumper are you?'

She grimaced. 'No, you take the asthma death, I'll take Mr P.'

'Good luck with that,' chuckled Jason. 'I never was any good at jigsaw puzzles.'

The remains of Mr P, aka Jack Perez, had arrived in a heavy-duty black body bag. Several witnesses had seen him throw himself off a footbridge into the path of a high-speed train. The effect of a 150 mph impact on the human body wasn't dissimilar to an explosion, and as sorry as she felt for poor Jack, she felt even worse for the Transport Police cop who'd got the gig of scouring the track to collect any surviving body parts.

She emptied the bag as gently as possible onto her work table, releasing the smell of blood and diesel. All that was recognisable was the head, or most of it, a bloodstained tie, and some longish sections of limb, which she could tell were legs from the scraps of the suit trousers he'd been wearing.

It was a challenge to feel any connection with the dead when they no longer resembled a human body, but she always tried. Jason had put his earbuds in and was working on his customer so she leaned into what was left of Mr P's head and said, 'I'm so sorry that you were so unhappy with your life. The police have been to see your wife and parents to break the news. They'll be put in touch with people, professionals, who can offer them support.' She made a mental note to check with the coroner's office to ensure this wasn't an empty promise.

The police report said that Jack Perez had recently lost not just his printing business, but his wife, who had left him for someone else.

Prof Arculus came in just as she'd finished arranging Mr P's remains into some sort of vague order. He shook his head sadly. 'Oh dear. Poor man. High-speed train?'

She nodded. A Tube train never reached sufficient speeds to wreak this level of carnage.

'Witnesses?'

'Yes, two people saw him jump. The train driver is in a bad way, as you can imagine.'

The Prof nodded. 'Righto. There would be zero point in dissecting the remains of this poor fellow. Cause of death *manifestissima est.*'

Aka blindingly obvious. In cases like this the coroner would be happy with an external exam and tox.

Having returned the bag containing Mr P to his drawer in the body store she went back to the autopsy suite, where Prof A already had Jason's guy – the one who'd apparently suffered a fatal asthma attack – on his dissecting bench. Since Mr P hadn't needed eviscerating it gave her time to observe the Prof in action.

He twinkled at her over his glasses. 'Aah, Cassandra, as a keen student of anatomy you will be interested in this relatively rare example of fatal asthma.' He indicated the outside of one lung which showed faint bar markings 'What do we see here?'

'Marks left by the lungs pressing the inside of his ribs.'

'Meaning?'

'His lungs were swollen: hyperexpanded' – remembering the proper terminology.

'Bravo.' After making a series of swift but precise strokes of his large-bladed scalpel in the tissue of one lung, he splayed the sections as if he was opening a book – which she'd heard called 'reading the organs'. Pointing out several areas with a bloodied gloved finger he said, 'Classic pulmonary lesions consistent with asphyxiation.'

Pulling the trachea and larynx towards him the Prof sliced that open too and beckoned Cassie to look. 'The upper airway has only minimal signs of inflammation though. Why might that be?'

She racked her brains. 'Post-mortem de-swelling?'

'Indeed.'

Cassie glanced over at the body lying on Jason's work table minus his viscera. The guy had been middle-aged but fit-looking, with a slim torso and well-defined thigh muscles and biceps. She picked up his notes. *Jake Ecclestone*. 'Christ, he was sixty-four! He looks a lot younger. And to be honest I always associate asthma deaths with children.'

'*Au contraire*,' said the Prof. 'The age of maximum danger arrives in one's sixties.'

'He was obviously super-fit,' said Cassie. 'He died while competing in an Iron Man event! His notes mention he suffered from asthma, but what triggered the attack? There's no mention of any allergies.'

Jason appeared at the bench. 'You done with the lungs, Prof?' and at his answering nod, started to scoop them into a pail for weighing.

'I'm afraid this chap's fitness regime killed him,' Prof Arculus went on. 'A phenomenon known as exercise-induced asthma.'

'Seriously?' said Cassie.

'It's a well-known issue among athletes. Exercise, especially endurance forms, in dry or cold conditions, can trigger perilous levels of broncho-constriction.'

'There you go! I've always said it's dangerous, this fitness lark,' said Jason, hefting the pail of lungs off the bench. 'When I kick the bucket I want to be sat on my sofa watching Formula 1, with a fag on, drinking Jack Daniel's.'

The Prof chuckled. 'Bravo, Jason. And I shall be on hand to confirm cause of death as "heroic disregard for life-lengthening measures".'

With four further PMs taking up the rest of the morning, Cassie had to rush to reach the rendezvous for her meeting with George Angelopoulos.

He was already there – downstairs in the basement of the Costa where they were the only customers – and intent on his phone.

Over his shoulder she saw that he was looking at a pic of Bronte, aged seven or eight, holding a double scoop of ice cream in a cone, a delighted grin splitting her face.

'Marine Ices!' said Cassie, recognising the electric-blue lettering of the shopfront in the background. 'My dad used to take me there.'

George stood up to greet her. 'She loved it there. It used to be our weekly treat, till she left home.'

She talked him through the timeframe of when the coroner might release Bronte's body for burial now that it was a criminal investigation. 'She will call for a second examination by a Home Office-approved pathologist – in case of any challenge by the defence if it comes to court.'

'*Another* post-mortem?!'

Seeing his alarmed look, she tried to reassure him. 'He might only need to do an external exam and double-check the original report.' Mentally crossing her fingers, since that couldn't be guaranteed.

'What about her blood samples and so on?'

'All the samples that were taken at the first PM are being held at the lab in case someone is charged and goes to trial.'

He looked down at his hands for a moment. 'You know the police won't even tell us what this new evidence is?' – his gaze raking her face.

She shrugged apologetically. 'It's not unusual for the police to withhold details in case it might help with their investigation.'

'But you know what these online detectives are saying? That the police are hiding the evidence simply to cover their backs.'

'Those people are idiots, George.'

He seemed jumpy today, his eyes red-rimmed, the whiff of ethanol coming through his pores, evidence of a heavy night on the booze. He was still dressed immaculately though: his dark suit twinned with a casual but pricey-looking merino V-neck underneath, and a Breitling wristwatch that didn't look like knock-off. The sale of his restaurant business had made him wealthy, but recalling what Honest Bob had said, she wondered whether, as Bronte's manager, her death stood to make him even richer?

Feeling a spurt of guilt at the thought, she sought his eyes and asked gently, 'How are you doing?'

He shook his head slowly, staring at the table, before looking up, his bloodshot eyes meeting Cassie's.

'I'm fine, for a man who just killed his daughter.'

Chapter Twenty-Six

Cassie was taken aback, but only for a moment. When someone died suddenly – especially by their own hand – family members often took the blame on themselves.

'Why do you say that, George?' she asked gently.

He was silent for a long moment, staring at the tabletop between them. 'Her mother was right. If only I hadn't encouraged her musical ambitions ... You see, Bronte, Sophia, she could seem tough, as if she was completely in control? When she was a little girl her mother would scold her for being bossy but even then I knew it was just a symptom of anxiety.'

'Do you have any idea what caused it? The anxiety?'

'I think she picked it up from her mother. When I met Chrysanthi I was a good deal older than her.' He pulled an embarrassed grimace. 'Too old. I realise that now. She was an orphan like me, and had been brought up in children's homes, so neither of us had any family. I'd been away from Cyprus for most of my adult life working on the cruise ships. We were both ... a little lost, rootless. When I first saw her she was working in a florist's shop in Larnaca.' He smiled at the memory. 'She was ... like a flower herself.'

'What is the age difference, can I ask?'

Another grimace. 'I was thirty-six – nearly twice her age.'

Wow. That was quite a gap – especially with Chrysanthi still only in her teens – but who was she to judge?

Fishing out his phone he tapped at it, before showing her an image. It looked antique, although that was more to do with its stagy set-up in an old-fashioned studio – silvery drapes hanging in the background, a random pot plant behind George's shoulder. George and Chrysanthi were formally dressed, him smiling straight into camera, her face half turned up towards him. Age-wise they might have been an older brother and a young sister, an effect magnified by them both having dark winged eyebrows, like gulls in flight.

'The age gap didn't feel like an issue at first, but it was a fatal flaw. After we came to England I was working all hours building the restaurant business. The bigger it got, the more I had to be out in the evenings, entertaining investors and so on. She was too young to understand, so she became jealous, possessive.'

Maybe she understood too well.

Cassie prompted him gently, 'And the source of Bronte's anxiety?'

'Not long after we got married Chrysanthi gave birth to Bronte – Sophia – and her twin brother, Alexander. We . . . lost him when he was just three.' George crossed himself, ending the gesture by touching his lips. 'Chrysanthi never recovered. And . . . she took her bitterness out on me.'

'I'm so sorry,' said Cassie. She'd seen it happen several times, how the death of a child could drive a wedge between parents, creating a faultline that could eventually split them apart.

'Her fear of losing Sophia too made her obsessively protective,' George went on. 'That fear transmitted itself to Sophia and made her anxiety worse. Even after she'd grown up and left home her mother wouldn't stop, turning up at her flat with food parcels!' His voice became hoarse. 'But I blame myself, not Chrysanthi. If I had realised how fragile Sophia was I would never have encouraged her to go professional. In the music business I've seen too many people soar, then crash.' He had raised a hand before letting it fall, in unconscious imitation of his daughter's fate.

'You were her manager, right?'

He nodded. 'I tried to look after her, really I did, but once she got the recording deal, the company edged me out of the picture. I shouldn't have let them. But she kept saying she could handle them, she could stand up for herself. She was good at pretending.'

Remembering her own *Teflon* nickname, Cassie nodded. She and Bronte really did have something in common: a talent for hiding inner turmoil.

'Is it true that she'd fallen out with Melodik over . . . musical direction?' – feeling a bit of a dick for using the term.

'Yes. Sophia was no fool, she wasn't planning some kind of *folk album*, but she was determined to get some Greek instrumentation in there.'

Cassie took a drink of her cooling coffee. 'Had she recorded the melody and her vocals? Enough material for them to release an album?'

'Yes, they leaned on her to record the basic tracks and told her there was "plenty of time to finalise the musical approach later".'

They shared a look. 'So . . .' said Cassie. 'Now they can do what they like with her voice and release an album which will make them a ton of money.' She met his gaze. 'And you too I assume?' *Risking the outright approach.*

'As her manager you mean? No, I never took a cut: I wasn't about to charge my own daughter commission.' He drew a deep sigh. 'Anyway, her mother and me, we might not see eye to eye but we agree about one thing: if Melodik do release an album any profits that come to us will go into a trust in Bronte's name, to help artists with drug and mental health problems.'

FLYTE

'Time of death is a guesstimate but given how long Bronte's body lay undiscovered she most likely fell before 0100 hours to give enough time for lividity to develop and become fixed.'

DI Streaky Bacon was running a case conference for the newly arrived team working on the Bronte murder investigation. Aware of curious eyes upon her, Flyte had arranged her face into what she hoped would pass as a neutral expression. But she was not enjoying the experience of being a passenger – *a civilian*.

'The lack of any forced entry suggests she knew her killer,' Bacon went on. 'The downstairs entryphone has a camera and there's a spyhole in her front door. We know from Bronte's phone records that on the day of her death she spoke with her father, her mother and her on-off boyfriend Ethan Fox – in that order. They all say there was nothing unusual in those conversations, and all deny being at the flat that day. And, of course, all three of them have legitimate reasons for their DNA to be present.'

He turned to a youngish guy with a sharp haircut and suit to match. 'Craig, did Ethan's alibi check out?'

'Yes, guv. He was doing band practice over in the Holloway Road and one of his bandmates has confirmed Ethan stayed at his flat on the night of the murder.' Along with most of the six other officers in the room, DS Craig Ellwood had been recruited from DI Bacon's regular base: East London Major Crimes in Canning Town. The sideways looks which Flyte caught were cautious, if not outright suspicious, but Craig, who seemed to act as Bacon's unofficial consigliere, made an almost-comic point of ignoring her. He reminded her of the detectives in her last, doomed posting, the breed whose casual sexism, racism and homophobia – the full house of antediluvian attitudes – had tarnished the Met's name so badly in recent years.

'CCTV update?' asked Bacon.

'Nothing in her block,' said Craig. 'We're on the hunt for any footage from the other cams nearby, but it's not looking good – the key council camera was vandalised, and the ones from outside clubs and so on, they only tend to keep the files a week or two.'

'What about door to door?' Bacon aimed the query at Becca, a DC in her twenties and the sole female on the team. Looking flustered, she opened her notebook, but before she could answer Craig jumped in.

Of course he did.

'Nothing useful, guv. The old dear next door said she might have heard "heavy breathing" but she wasn't sure it was that night or even whether it actually came from Bronte's place.' Craig's raised eyebrow indicated how reliable he found the account of an 'old dear'.

'In case she did hear something let's recheck all the block residents,' said Bacon. 'What about the Chinese couple who were in the penthouse upstairs – the Airbnb?'

'No reply yet from the email address we have.'

He frowned. 'They're party people aren't they? Communist Party I mean, not the fun kind.' Bringing a titter from his audience. 'That could be problematic.'

'What about the printing of Bronte's phone?' Flyte jumped in, drawing hostile looks.

'Thanks, Phyllida,' said Bacon, with a tight smile. 'I was just coming to that. Clearly it was Bronte's killer who sent the fake suicide message from her phone. And so it wasn't exactly a surprise to find the handset had been cleaned of all prints.'

'Which, had it been discovered at the outset, would immediately have prompted suspicion' – Flyte couldn't resist pointing out.

There was a silence you could eat with a spoon.

Ignoring the jibe, Bacon went on, 'Moving forward ... Obviously it tells us that the killer was known to Bronte. Close enough to know her phone passcode.'

'It tells us something else as well,' said Flyte, failing to hide her impatience.

'Enlighten us, Phyllida,' said Bacon, starting to sound irritated.

'Assuming that the killer arrived at her flat planning to murder her, he would surely have *expected* the phone to be fingerprinted. And knowing that a clean phone would look suspicious, he – or she – must have planned to put Bronte's prints on it *after* he'd sent the suicide text. He was hardly going to tip her over the balcony then take the lift down and do it on the towpath, was he? So he must have been planning to kill her inside the flat.'

'Maybe she was trying to get away from him and ended up going over accidentally,' said Bacon. 'But once she caught hold and was hanging there, he had to finish her off.'

'You said yourself that given the height of the balcony her killer would need to have lifted her to tip her over.'

'And if you're saying his initial idea was to kill her in the flat and make it look like suicide how exactly would he have pulled that off?'

Flyte made a face. 'I don't know. Get her stoned on the psychoactive cannabinoid, then make it look like a hanging, or slash her wrists?'

'Her tox screen came back negative for drugs,' Bacon pointed out.

Fair point. 'Maybe something went awry with his plan,' was all she could say.

After the meeting broke up he caught up with Flyte in the corridor, and leaning towards her said in a conversational tone, 'IOPC or not, if you try to fuck me over in front of the team again, I'll tear you a new one.'

Chapter Twenty-Seven

Slap! The wake of a passing boat hitting the wooden hull beside Cassie's ear jerked her from sleep and left *Dreamcatcher* rocking violently. *Going too fast* – especially this early in the morning. The warming weather was bringing out the amateur boaters who had zero grasp of canal etiquette.

Rolling over, she was about to moan to Archie before remembering with a scalpel stab under the ribs that they were done – for good this time. But already the sharp pain of separation was easing down into the settled ache that she knew from experience would pass – eventually. She counted off in her head the number of relationships she'd had as an adult that hadn't gone the distance. After reaching five she stopped and stretched out across the bed, luxuriating in her recovered space. Maybe it was just time to accept that she was a loner, by character and inclination.

Finding no sign of her fellow lone wolf Macavity, she pulled on some clothes and went into the cockpit. Gaz, her ex-roadie mate and neighbour, was already up on deck next door smoking his morning fag, intent on his phone.

'Hey, Gaz. You seen that disloyal beast of mine this morning?'

Ignoring the question, he nodded to the phone. 'You seen the latest?'

Shaking her head, she pulled up her own newsfeed. One of the fringe news sites was running the headline: ETHAN FOX ACCUSED OF BRONTE ABUSE. It didn't take many clicks to find the whole story: @Charly_Detective had posted a vid on TikTok. She had dug up an old selfie of Ethan and Bronte when they were still a couple, which she claimed showed 'clear bruising to Bronte's throat'. Zooming up the darker area, Cassie decided they were a long way short of clear-cut throttle marks.

Charly shared 'new and shocking information' suggesting that Ethan had a kink for strangling his girlfriends during sex. She went on to recycle the misleading 'evidence' that the hyoid bone in Bronte's throat had been broken. It was all framed piously as 'questions police need to get answers to: *now*'.

The post had gone viral, with @BinkyBinks96 summing up the calibre of comments with the insightful comment: '*Your telling me that someone with bone broken in throat wasn't strangulated? Poor Brontes druggie ex has a SHITLOAD of questions to answer.*'

Cassie snorted derisively.

'So was she strangled?' asked Gaz.

'No! it was the fall that killed her. The world's gone barking mad.'

'True,' said Gaz, pinching out his cig. 'By the way, I gave that cat of yours a tin of mackerel this morning,' he said with a cackle that revealed a gold molar.

'Oh thanks a bunch, Gaz.' She shook her head. 'He'll be demanding poached salmon next.'

Lost in her thoughts, she had almost reached the mortuary when a tall figure materialised at her side.

'*What the fu—!* You nearly gave me a heart attack.' And it was true that her heart did do funny things whenever she laid eyes on Phyllida Flyte. 'You coming to the mortuary?'

Flyte shook her head. 'I'm not a cop anymore, remember?' She sounded bitter. 'I wondered if you could spare time for a quick chat? I could buy you a coffee?'

Seeing that Flyte's cheeks had coloured a fetching pink, Cassie remembered how much she hated asking for a favour. 'What for?' she asked coolly. 'As you say, you're not a cop anymore.'

Flyte blinked rapidly. 'I . . . just had a few more questions about Bronte.'

Seeing her obvious discomfort, Cassie relented. 'I'm due on shift' – frowning down at her phone. 'But you could come and chat to me while I get ready?'

It was pretty weird, getting into her PPE with Flyte sitting there, although she studiously avoided looking at Cassie. Not that Cassie got down to her knickers and bra – she wore her scrubs tops and bottoms over her jeans and vest top – but there was something innately intimate in the act of even partially undressing in front of someone.

'Hmm. You saw the latest about Ethan?'

'Yeah.' Cassie sent her a dark look. 'The thing about the hyoid fracture is bollocks, but you know that, right?'

She nodded. 'But of course it got the top brass all twitchy – and sent everyone scurrying back to the PM report and looking again at Ethan. Officers who could be following up serious leads.'

Cassie made a face. 'And this claim he likes to strangle women, you know, during . . . ?' They broke eye contact, both suddenly embarrassed.

'It's probably just gossip but we'll have to question this *Charly Detective*,' Flyte sighed. 'Or risk being accused by all and sundry of ignoring an important tip-off. We've got the techies taking a look at the image of the bruised neck.'

'"We"?' asked Cassie, turning to the mirror she raised both arms to brush her hair up into a topknot, caught Flyte's gaze on her for a moment before it skittered away. The room felt suddenly too small and too warm.

'The police, I mean,' said Flyte, staring resolutely at the ceiling, walls, anywhere but at Cassie.

'I can't see him committing murder,' Cassie protested, picturing Ethan's dark eyes.

'You've met Ethan Fox?' Flyte's gaze suddenly piercing.

She turned back to her locker to hide her expression. 'Yeah, he came to the mortuary, wanting to see Bronte. I had to turn him away, obviously.'

'And that brief exchange convinced you he was innocent?' The arch of Flyte's perfectly shaped eyebrow seeming to say she wasn't born yesterday.

Curses.

Cassie looked up at the clock. 'I've got to go.' But catching Flyte's expression she relented. 'OK, five more minutes. What *is* it I can do for you exactly?'

Flyte frowned. 'Look, it's probably nothing, but one of the neighbours might have heard a noise from Bronte's flat before she fell.'

'What kind of noise?'

'Heavy breathing?' Flyte raised a hand and let it drop. 'I don't know, is it possible that her killer put her in a headlock, say? Before pitching her over the balcony?'

Cassie shook her head. 'Look, even if it was missed at the routine PM there's no way the Home Office pathologist would have missed any injuries to the neck structures.'

Flyte shrugged despairingly. 'I just feel so *powerless*. At least when I was a serving officer I could follow up leads. Now it's become a murder investigation I'm . . . *tolerated*.'

Cassie grimaced: she felt the same way when one of the more self-important pathologists ignored her opinion. It was the first time she'd seen Flyte so despondent. Surely leaving the misogyny and homophobia of her last posting and finally feeling able to come out should have brought her some peace? But then Cassie's own experience had been so different – she'd never felt the need to put a label on herself, having dated boys and girls from her late teens. The only person who she'd tried to keep it from was Babcia, although in the end it turned out she'd known about her granddaughter's sexuality all along.

'Have you looked into who stands to benefit from Bronte's death? Financially, I mean?' asked Cassie.

'Like who? Bronte hadn't made a will – who does at twenty-seven? – so the parents will inherit as next of kin but it's all going into some charitable trust.'

'I meant the record company people. I heard that she was refusing to make the album that they wanted. Now they can do what they like with the material and make seriously big bucks out of her death.'

'That hit track of hers *is* everywhere at the moment,' Flyte mused. 'But seriously? Some record company suit murdering an artist? It's just not plausible.'

It was hard to disagree.

'I'm afraid the chances of getting a fruitful lead two weeks after she died are close to zero,' said Flyte quietly.

'No!' The word came out louder than Cassie intended and Flyte blinked rapidly. 'Sorry. I mean, look, you have to keep trying. You'll find something.'

Flyte was looking at her with open curiosity. 'What is about Bronte's death that has got you so involved?'

Good question – but one she had no intention of answering.

'Christ, look at the time,' she said. 'I really do have to go. But, you know, call me if I can help with anything.' Their eyes met for a long moment and Flyte managed a wan smile.

FLYTE

Flyte spent the rest of the day in the Bronte incident room feeling like a spare part. But as she was heading home, DI Bacon caught up with her in the corridor. 'Ah, glad I caught you,' he said. 'We've finally got this "Charly Detective" – real name Charlotte Wiggins – in interview room one and it never hurts to have a female present.'

Flyte frowned. 'To get her to open up?'

'No, so that I can scare the bejesus out of her while you work the sisterhood angle,' said Bacon with a piratical grin.

'So let me get this straight, Charlotte.' Streaky was still smiling at this point. 'You didn't actually get this story about Ethan Fox strangling his lovers for kicks from one of his ex-girlfriends, did you?'

'It came from someone in the know,' said Charly, leaning back, combat-trouser-clad legs splayed, playing the defiant journalist. 'But obviously I'm not revealing my source.'

Bacon turned to Flyte with an exaggerated look of confusion. 'Did I ask anyone to reveal their source?' She shook her head. 'Oh good, I thought I was losing it for a moment there.' He levelled a neutral look at Charly. 'I'm asking you whether you spoke directly to someone who claimed he had strangled them during sex.'

Charly gave a sulky shrug/headshake. 'Not *directly*. But that doesn't make it any less true.'

After eighteen months living in Camden, Flyte was inured to the pink buzz-cut hair, the tunnel ear-piercing and tattoo reaching up her neck, but the girl's attitude made her itch to reach across the table and give her a slap.

'Here's the thing, Charlotte,' said Bacon with an insincere smile. 'I could walk out of here and say that you admitted to killing Bronte yourself. There's no tape recording because you aren't being interviewed under caution ... yet. So how would anyone know that I was lying?'

Charly sat up a little straighter. 'Obviously I'd say you misquoted me.'

'There you go. But without the testimony of Ethan's mystery ex-girlfriend, there's no opportunity to confirm or deny this so-called story either. In court, the unconfirmed testimony of a third party is called "hearsay". It's more commonly known as gossip.'

Picking up an invisible cue from Bacon, Flyte took over with a smile. 'Look, Charly, I realise that you were motivated by concerns that Ethan might have a history of abusing women.'

'Exactly!' she said, grasping gratefully at this offered straw.

'Talk me through how you came across the photo showing these supposed bruises on Bronte's neck would you?'

'It was on a tiny online site a while ago, but nobody else had spotted the bruising – least of all the cops.' Charly sent a look at Bacon, who didn't react, preoccupied with using his little finger to excavate the contents of one ear.

'I've seen a lot of domestic abuse cases,' Flyte told Charly, her tone confidential. 'So an image like that is obviously a red flag.'

'That's right!' said Charly, leaning forward.

'Could I see it again? Because the original doesn't appear to be online anymore.'

'I . . .'

'It's surely on your phone?' – indicating Charly's phone sitting in front of her on the table.

There was a yawning pause while Charly considered her options. In the end she tapped at the phone, before turning the image to show Flyte. Leaning across the desk, apparently to get a closer look, Flyte's hand shot out like a cobra to take it.

'That's better,' she said, before tapping the edit button.

'You can't . . .' Charly was open-mouthed.

'Oh, what have I done?' she asked Bacon.

'It's reverted to the original image,' he said, peering at the screen. 'Zoom it up?' He gave a disbelieving chuckle. 'I haven't seen one of those since the school disco in 1976.'

Flyte sent Charly a concerned look. 'It's a love bite, isn't it, Charly? Filtering and darkening the image makes it look like serious bruising.'

Charly had gone bright red.

Flyte handed the phone back.

'It *could* be fingermarks,' Charly protested. 'I was only trying to get you lot to investigate properly.'

Streaky leaned towards her, elbows on the table, his face like thunder. 'Shall I tell you what you've actually achieved? My officers have spent hours poring over other images of Bronte looking for signs of injury and reinterviewing all her close contacts to uncover any potential evidence of physical abuse. They found none. Nothing. *Nada*. Right now I should be out there' – pointing to the door – 'pursuing actual leads, not wasting my time investigating your ... chuffing clickbait.'

His tone had become quite heated so Flyte cut in again. 'I feel I should warn you that Ethan Fox's solicitor has been in touch to ask if we have any reason to support this allegation of physical abuse. We have told him there is none. So, you might find yourself being sued for libel.'

'And never mind a civil action,' said Streaky. Looking up at the ceiling, he quoted from memory: '"It is an offence to cause a wasteful employment of the police by knowingly making a false report that they have information relevant to a police enquiry." Criminal Law Act 1967.' Turning to Flyte he said, 'Remind me of the maximum penalty?'

'Six months imprisonment,' she said, making a sad face.

'But it was just social media,' Charly wailed. Her body language had gone from fearless to pathetic in the space of a minute. 'What can I do?' – opening her hands on the table in appeal.

'If I were you, I would delete the posts and admit you were wrong,' said Flyte. 'And publicly apologise to Ethan Fox.'

'Will I ... be charged?' – sending an appealing look to Bacon.

Ignoring her question, he stood up and said, 'We'll be in touch.' Telling the uniform stationed outside the door to see her out.

As they took the lift back to their floor, Bacon sent Flyte an admiring look. 'Has Ethan's solicitor really been in touch?'

'Oh, did I give that impression?' asked Flyte demurely.

Bacon chuckled. 'I'll brief the press office to put it out there that we've questioned her, and that we're considering pressing charges. With a bit of luck that might put the wind up the rest of these keyboard detective *wankers*.'

Flyte didn't like the use of bad language, especially in a professional context, but this time, she felt able to make an exception.

Walking back into the incident room, they saw a huddle around Craig's desk.

'What's all this then? A hen party?' asked Bacon, going over.

Craig turned to him, looking excited. 'Ethan Fox has been attacked by a couple of muppets in The Hawley Arms. It's all over social media. He's been taken to A & E.'

Chapter Twenty-Eight

Cassie was on *Dreamcatcher*, heating up some leftover pizza for her tea when she heard a shout and a commotion from the towpath. Racing up above deck she was met by a shocking sight: Gaz wrestling a younger guy onto his back on the path.

'What the fu—?' she said.

'Tea leaf,' said Gaz, who was surprisingly wiry for a guy in his sixties. He pinned the guy down by his shoulders. 'Caught him peering in through your windows' – sounding a bit breathless.

'Gaz, it's OK, I know him,' she said apologetically.

Gaz looked almost disappointed: maybe he missed the touring life when roadies would pile into the crowd to break up fights. Standing, he extended a hand to the lanky figure on the ground. 'Next time you come visiting someone on the canal, you hail the person by name,' he growled.

'No worries. Sorry, man,' said Ethan. Cassie noticed he was breathing heavily and had to lean a hand on one knee to lever himself upright.

After Gaz had gone they stood looking at each other a long moment.

'You'd better come inside,' she said and he clambered on board with some difficulty.

Below deck, she peered at his face 'What happened to you? That's not fresh enough to be Gaz's handiwork.'

He touched the flesh around his eye socket, swollen red but not yet bruising, then his cut lip. 'Couple of guys in the pub read about me strangling Bronte on social and decided I needed some Camden justice.' He looked more weary than angry. 'I've had blokes take a pop at me in pubs before but no one's ever called me a murderer before.'

'Oh Jesus, Ethan.' Her hand to her mouth.

He pulled up his T-shirt to examine several developing bruises on his stomach. She averted her eyes quickly, but not before registering his six-pack with a jolt of surprise – she'd have put Ethan down as a dedicated exercise-dodger.

'Sit down' she said, pointing to the banquette dining table. Going to her medicine box she pulled out some TCP and cotton wool and handed it to him. 'The skin is broken *here*.' Touching the side of her own temple.

'That's where I hit the sink going down,' he said ruefully.

'They jumped you in the gents'?' A wave of fury came over her. 'The fucking cowards. You should report them to the cops.'

He shook his head. 'What and see my mug all over the press *again*?' He pulled a grin that emphasised the long lean lines of his face before holding up the cotton wool with a helpless expression 'Would you . . .?'

As she leaned in to clean his wound she felt his breath warm on her cheek and it struck her this was the second time today she'd been in an intimate situation with somebody she was attracted to. Half undressing in front of Flyte, and now performing first aid on Bronte's undeniably hot boyfriend.

'You should have gone to hospital,' she told him. 'You could have a concussion, or even a skull fracture.'

'I did. Someone found me on the floor of the bogs and took me to A & E. But I changed my mind.' At her querying look he added, 'I caught people giving me the evil eye in the waiting room.'

'These *idiots* spreading crap on social media,' she fumed. 'Electing themselves judge and jury when they know fuck all. Why don't they leave it to the cops?!'

He sent her an amused look. 'Do you trust the Feds?' he asked lightly.

'No . . . Yes . . . Some of them?' – visualising Flyte's serious expression. 'Look, no question some of them are monsters, but we can't shut the whole thing down. That just ends up in . . . chaos.' She blinked, startled to find herself defending the police, picturing Flyte raising an ironic eyebrow.

She put two Steri-Strips across the cut on his temple. 'There. That should minimise the scar.'

He touched his busted lip. 'What about this, Nurse?'

'You can do that yourself' – passing him the TCP. *Too intimate*.

She got up to take the pizza out of the tiny oven. 'What are you doing here anyway? And how did you know where I lived?' – fixing him with a challenging look.

He shrugged 'You said you lived on a boat and there's only a few on this part of the towpath. I just looked through all the lit windows.'

'Why?'

He gave an embarrassed shrug. 'It was nearby and I guess I'm worried about going to my own place. Tomorrow I can go to my mate's over in Holloway Road.' The look in his liquid brown eyes was suddenly boyish, vulnerable. 'But tonight, I need shelter.'

Chapter Twenty-Nine

Cassie gave him the lion's share of the pizza, and after eating, they sat there drinking beer. The cooker had warmed the place up, the TCP had left a not-unpleasant medicinal sweetness in the air, and the fairy lights strung from the ceiling completed the cosy vibe. She'd had to take them down when Archie lived here: they kept getting tangled in his barnet.

She pictured the image he'd sent her earlier: a tranquil view over a wooded valley in Wiltshire, with the accompanying message: *We could have woken up to this every day*. And her reply: *Where's the kebab truck though?* Keeping it light to quell the vertiginous feeling that still gripped her now and again.

Have I done the right thing?

'You all right?' asked Ethan, scanning her face, his eyes crinkled with worry.

'Yeah fine' – shaking her head to dispel the melancholia. 'So have you been getting a lot of this kind of shit since . . .?'

He pulled a rueful smile but dropped his gaze. 'Yeah. And the band haven't had any bookings for a bit. They're playing with a stand-in guitarist this weekend. I can't blame them – there's too much heat around me. Nobody wants a bunch of paps turning up, annoying the punters.'

'Do you miss it?'

'Like you might miss breathing,' he said with a sudden flare of passion.

His Bronte connection aside, Ethan's band was just one of the dozens of indie rock bands scraping a living playing at pubs and Camden's smaller venues. Still, a passion was a passion. She stood to retrieve a bottle of Polish vodka from the freezer compartment and poured a couple of shots.

'Can I ask you something, about Bronte?' she asked.

'Sure.' But she'd picked up the guarded look that had flickered across his face.

'What was her relationship like with Melodik? Did she have any serious fallings-out with anyone specific there? Anyone who might have visited her at the flat?'

He took a swig of beer from the bottle, giving the question some thought. 'Not as far as I know. She had a few screaming rows with her A&R man, Jesse Harbinger, about the new album's direction but that was over the phone.'

'*Harbinger*? As in—'

'Harbinger of doom, right! That's what she called him. But as far as I know, he never came to the flat. For big meetings with the suits she'd always go to Melodik. She reckoned they thought the fancy Soho offices, the boardroom lined with platinum discs, would faze her.' He chuckled. 'Which showed they really didn't have a clue about her.' He paused to think. 'Funnily enough the person she really despised was another creative.'

'Really? Why?'

'You heard of SkAR?' He spelled it out for her.

'Is that a name?'

'Yeah. He's a club DJ who became a big deal producer. He produced that huge dance hit last summer, "Take Me Home"?'

She pulled an apologetic half-shrug, 'I'm allergic to dance music.'

'Anyway, Melodik were ecstatic they'd been able to hire him for her follow-up to "Clean Break". She had to go to Berlin and record it in some studio where he insisted on working – and she hated flying. But she was excited cos his parents were from Cyprus too, and she thought he'd be an ally, you know, to give her sound a Greek vibe.' He frowned, remembering. 'But it didn't work out like that.'

'So what did she say about this SkAR character?'

'Not much. Just that he started out all nicey-nicey but when she tried to discuss the sound he was giving the tracks he turned into a bully and a sexist twat. After she came back she told Melodik she would never work with him again, and that she was done being their rent-a-vocal artist. Which was the final nail in the coffin. After that they basically put the album on ice, and her contract meant she couldn't even release anything on her own. She said she felt like a wild animal with its paw in a trap.'

Something occurred to Cassie. 'You said she didn't like flying. Did she ever go back to Cyprus?'

'Never, as far as I know.' Ethan started scrolling on his phone so Cassie stood to clear the plates. It struck her as odd that someone as into traditional Greek music as Bronte should have had shown no interest in exploring her roots.

'Look at this,' said Ethan.

Cassie turned from the sink to see Bronte's face staring out at her from his phone screen.

'Oh!'

The video showed her sat cross-legged on the sofa at home, in a T-shirt, make-up free, dark curls still wet from the shower, a guitar across her lap – looking young and vulnerable. After strumming an opening chord, she said, 'It's called "Skeleton".'

Then Bronte broke into a half-spoken, half-sung refrain – that thrillingly deep voice of hers making the skin on Cassie's neck prickle. The lyrics were cryptic, but there was a lot about secrets. '*Nobody can know but everyone should know*' ... and '*there's a skeleton knocking on the cupboard door*'. The song ended chillingly, with the spoken line: '*Your secrets be the death of me.*' Then Bronte struck a final chord before using the flat of her hand to quell the sustain and looked up at camera, her expression suddenly fragile. 'Was that all right?'

'You filmed this?' Cassie asked Ethan. 'It's ... powerful. Would you send it to me?'

'Sure.' He nodded. 'It could have been a great track but by then Melodik had cut her dead.'

'This business about secrets – any idea what she's talking about?'

'She wouldn't tell me.' He shook his head. 'But just recently I did start wondering if that producer guy SkAR, did something to her when she was in Berlin?'

'You mean sexual assault?'

His brow crinkled. 'Maybe. She hinted on the phone that he was a bit ... handsy. But when she came back from Berlin she was ... different. Distant, jumpy, always losing her rag. And she refused to talk about him.'

It did sound suspicious. *Or was that what Ethan wanted her to believe?*

'*Something* happened there,' he said. 'She was never the same again. She went totally off sex, for one thing.'

Their eyes met for a little too long. Cassie stood up. 'OK, here's the deal.' Indicating the dining table, she said crisply, 'This turns into a bed. The top collapses like this. You can fix the bolts while I get the mattress.'

'OK, boss.' He grinned. When she came back from the forward cabin carrying the foam mattress he took it from her with a half-smile in those dark eyes.

'Are you sure you don't need a bed warmer?' he asked.

'Positive,' she said. 'And if I hear anyone creeping around in the night I'll shout for Gaz.' Seeing his forehead crinkle, she added, 'My personal minder, who you met earlier?'

He laughed at that and, taking her hand, kissed the back of it, but with a jokey flourish that saved it from being creepy.

As Cassie got into bed, her pulse was still bumping in her throat. She could hear Ethan turning over in bed barely two metres away through the plywood wall. She found herself replaying the night in the squat aged seventeen, the one and only time she'd done smack. *Why was she remembering that?* Because she recognised that just like the heroin, Ethan Fox could be fatally addictive; and just like the heroin, she really shouldn't go there.

FLYTE

The next morning Becca, the DC who struck Flyte as seeming a bit unsure of herself, came over to Bacon's desk in the incident room. Flyte overheard her saying that she'd got hold of the Chinese couple who'd been staying in the Airbnb above Bronte's flat the night she'd died.

'I booked a Zoom call for 10 a.m. our time – 6 p.m. over there. In the email the husband says he speaks English. I thought better to grab them quickly than wait till we've found a Mandarin interpreter?'

Bacon waved a hand. 'Courageous and correct,' he said. 'Do you want to sit in?'

Becca shook her head. 'Now we've got a warrant I need to trawl Bronte's emails.'

'Fair dos,' he said, getting to his feet and hitching his trousers up. Turning to Flyte he asked, 'Care to join me?'

'Sure.' She had to admit that despite his eighties throwback act, Bacon appeared genuinely to value the female angle.

Half an hour later, they were in the conference room facing a screen which showed a middle-aged Chinese guy and his wife seated at an island in a swanky kitchen. After the introductions, Bacon said, 'As you know, Mr and Mrs Chen, we are investigating the tragic death of a young woman who lived in the apartment directly beneath you, on the final night of your stay in London. Did you see or hear anything unusual that evening after coming back from the restaurant?'

Mr Chen did the talking, his wife smiling but silent beside him. He spoke like a man used to addressing minions – apparently he was a Party bigwig – but despite what he'd told Becca, his English was hit and miss to say the least. He was able to make one thing clear though: they had neither seen nor heard anything out of the ordinary that evening either when they returned from dinner or during the night.

Flyte thought she detected something a bit too definitive about his claims – no hesitation, no racking his memory, no asking his wife – as one might have expected. No doubt the Party wouldn't be ecstatic at the prospect of one of their officials getting entangled in a UK murder case.

Flyte could see Bacon's leg starting to jiggle under the table as he grew impatient, although his manner remained calm and polite. After a while, he turned to the wife. 'What about you, Mrs Chen?' But Mr Chen raised a hand. 'My wife doesn't speak English,' he said, sweetening it with a smile.

'No problem,' said Bacon – before launching into a stream of fluent Mandarin. Flyte couldn't stop herself from turning to stare at him.

Mrs Chen was talkative and seemed keen to help, despite her husband's increasingly meaningful sideways looks. Flyte couldn't understand a word, but it was clear from their back and forward that she was telling Bacon something of possible significance. Bacon asked a supplementary question and she nodded vehemently, and touching her neck, made a guttural sound as if she was trying to clear something stuck in her throat.

This brought a furious look from her husband who cut in, clearly trying to bring the conversation to a close. Bacon was laying on the charm when Mr Chen leaned forward and cut the connection.

He and Flyte looked at each other.

'You got the gist?' he asked.

'She heard someone coughing? Choking?'

He nodded. 'She got up in the night for some water, stepped out onto their balcony and heard someone – she couldn't say if it was a female – gasping for breath from the floor below. But the noise stopped quickly and she went back to bed.'

'Did she hear anything else? A scuffle? The fall?'

'Nothing. Just the gasping. We can't know whether it was just before Bronte fell or earlier of course.' He frowned. 'And as we know there was no post-mortem evidence of someone strangling her.'

'Suffocation? Plastic bag over the head?'

Bacon screwed up his face. 'That ought to leave physical signs.'

'Petechiae.' The pinprick haemorrhages found in cases of asphyxiation.

'Yeah. I'll double-check with the pathologist – if I can get hold of him. Why don't you talk to your chum at the mortuary?' He nodded to himself. 'She struck me as a smart cookie.'

After a pause, Flyte said, 'So you speak fluent Mandarin. Clearly.'

'Just enough to get by,' he demurred, before sending her a sly look. 'My Cantonese is pretty solid though.'

What the . . .? Flyte couldn't think of a question that wouldn't sound over-personal or intrusive. But after a pause Bacon put her out of her misery. 'My wife comes from Hong Kong. We've been married thirty years.'

Chapter Thirty

That morning, when Cassie had been woken by the chirruping of the moorhens, her first conscious thought had been of Ethan. Venturing into the main cabin in her dressing gown she'd discovered that he'd already left. *Of course he had.* No note. No text.

Bronte's face swum in to her mind. She was shaking her head. *I wouldn't if I were you.*

She was on late shift so on impulse she headed over to her grandmother's – feeling guilty about how long it had been since her last visit. She'd been putting it off, not looking forward to telling her about the split from Archie, who Babcia adored.

She used her key to let herself in, before halting at the sound of voices in the front room.

'Cassandra! What a lovely surprise,' her gran said, before gesturing towards her younger guest who sat in the upright armchair. 'I think you have already met Chrysanthi Angelopoulos' – looking a little embarrassed at this conjunction of visitors. 'And you know my granddaughter, of course.' Her careful tone recognising Chrysanthi's loss and the fact she would never now have grandchildren of her own.

'Of course. She's been very kind,' said Chrysanthi, managing a smile. 'It has meant a lot to me knowing my child is being looked after by someone who cares.'

After a bit of awkward small talk she got to her feet. 'I must be going. Thank you for the tea.'

When Babcia returned she was shaking her head. 'That poor woman. She says her life is over. And she's only in her mid-forties.'

Cassie did the maths: if Chrysanthi was say, forty-five, she could only have been eighteen when she'd had Bronte.

Cassie was concerned to see how the visit seemed to have extinguished her grandmother's usual spark. The way she lowered herself down carefully into the armchair, her inward look – it took Cassie back to her months of convalescence after she'd had a mini-stroke. But she was nearly eighty after all.

'I'm making you a strong coffee, with cream,' she said.

She returned with a tray carrying the coffee and two slices of poppyseed cake. Babcia hadn't moved or spoken. 'I found some *makowiec*. It looks delicious.' Knowing that if she ate some her grandmother would have to join in. 'So have you been seeing much of Chrysanthi?'

She nodded, absent-mindedly breaking off a morsel of cake. 'We have had coffee a few times. At the church and here. She is much younger than me, of course, but we understand each other.' She took a sip of coffee. 'We both lost our only daughter. But of course it is so much more raw for her.'

They both looked at the age-bleached photo of Cassie's mother – Kath – Babcia's beloved only child, aged about sixteen, which had always occupied pride of place on the mantelpiece. *Like an icon.* Cassie had been inoculated by two decades of exposure to her mother's hopeful, innocent look in the photo; and irritated too, during her teens, by the way her gran had held her daughter up as some kind of a saint. It was only recently that Cassie had discovered Kath's wild streak, her troubles at school and, after she'd become a mother, the bouts of depression which she had treated with alcohol.

'I remember being just where Chrysanthi is now,' said Babcia. 'The fury is all that sustains you. And hers is all directed against Sophia's father, for no good reason that I can see.'

'What does she say about him?'

'That he is "mired in sin".' They exchanged a raised eyebrow. 'When I ask why, she will only say that he's a pig, who has spent his life rutting with anything that moves.'

Cassie grimaced. 'But she doesn't suggest that he had ever hurt Bronte ... in any way?' That 'any way' code for sexual abuse.

'I asked her about that. Do you know what she said?' Babcia arranged her face into a mask of vengeful fury and pointed to the sky – '"I swear by the Almighty Father, if he had ever laid one finger on my child, I would have killed him. Mortal sin or not." And I believe her.'

Blimey.

'What about the ex-boyfriend, this guy Ethan Fox?' Cassie asked.

'Oh she hates him, even more, if that's possible. She's convinced he was involved in the death of her child.'

Pushing her *makowiec* around the plate, Cassie recalled Ethan losing his rag at the bargirl in the 'Spoons at the lock. But having a quick temper didn't make you a murderer.

'And of course the poor thing has no family to turn to,' Babcia went on. 'Her mother died right after having her, and she never even knew her father.'

'Does her faith give her any solace?' asked Cassie. Believers often seem to cope best with bereavement: the conviction that everything was part of God's plan, and the belief in an afterlife, bringing comfort.

'She worships her priest, Father Michaelides, but he is a very stern man.' Babcia gave a little shiver. 'Not a lot of love and forgiveness in that church. Still, she has asked me to go there to pray with her and I said yes.'

Yikes. Cassie felt torn between two competing emotions: desperately sorry for Chrysanthi, but also worried about the effect exposure to all that grief and fury might have on her grandmother.

'Will you tell me when you're going? I'd like to come along. I could take you both for coffee afterwards.' That way she could keep an eye on things.

She pulled on her jacket and bent to give her grandmother a kiss. 'Does Chrysanthi ever go back to Cyprus?' she asked.

That brought a grim chuckle. 'Cyprus? No. She calls it Satan's island.'

Half an hour later, she was climbing back on the boat, where she found a plastic bag standing beside the cabin door. It held a bottle of Wyborowa – her vodka of choice – and a scrawled Post-it note stuck to the label that made her smile despite herself. It read, 'Thanks for looking after me last night, Nurse Raven. E x.'

Macavity wound himself round her ankles as she prepped his food, encouraging her with a deep purr. But when she set it down he sniffed at it once and threw her a look that said, *What is this shit?!*

'It's Sheba for Christ's sake,' she told him. 'You used to love it.' Looking at the food again, his back twitched once in disgust, and he left the cabin, scooting through the cat flap with unnecessary force.

Should she hold her ground over Macavity's latest food fad? Or just roll over and bulk-buy tinned fish?

Her phone rang, making her heart do a little backflip. *Ethan?* But the sight of Flyte's name on the screen triggered equally complicated emotions.

As ever, Flyte wasted no breath on social niceties. 'A neighbour heard the sound of someone struggling for breath from Bronte's place the night she died. Could somebody have choked or suffocated her without it leaving any physical evidence?'

Cassie pictured Bronte's face, pale apart from the lividity on one side. 'Her face wasn't congested, although it's not always a feature in asphyxiation. There was no sign of petechiae but that's not—' She stopped abruptly.

'Cassie?'

Cassie had been bending down to pick up the cat's saucer of uneaten food. As she straightened to set it on the worktop, she heard a single, discordant guitar chord which stopped her breath in her throat.

It seemed to come from right behind her but also, somehow, from a yawning distance. She tried to breathe but her throat stayed closed. She tried to speak but only a choking sound came out.

'Cassie, what's wrong?!'

Starting to feel dizzy from lack of oxygen, Cassie made herself turn slowly, inch by inch, convinced that she'd find Bronte sat behind her, guitar on her lap.

The cabin was empty. She drew a gasping breath.

The fading jangle of that chord seemed to hang in the air still. Cassie's brain was whirring like a fruit machine.

'Sorry,' she told Flyte. 'Something just occurred to me. Meet me at the mortuary in half an hour.'

And ignoring Flyte's questions she cut the call.

FLYTE

'Are you going to tell me what the heck is going on?'

She was following Cassie down the corridor from the mortuary entrance.

'In here.' Cassie waved her into the body store, clearly impatient to show her something.

She tapped at a name marked on a drawer. Flyte squinted at it 'Jake Ecclestone?' she read. 'What has he got to do with Bronte?'

'He's got nothing to do with her – except for the way he died' – wearing a look of secret excitement that was starting to irritate Flyte.

She folded her arms. 'And?'

'You said a neighbour heard gasping. But there was no evidence of her having been strangled or suffocated. It got me thinking about this guy, Jake, who we PM-ed recently. He died of asthma induced by exercise.' Cassie's eyes were bright with excitement. 'His airways closed up and he basically self-suffocated.'

Flyte frowned. 'But Bronte didn't suffer from asthma, did she?'

'No, but we know she had to be careful about what she ate. And it occurred to me, what if she had an extreme allergic reaction to something?'

'Anaphylactic shock you mean?'

Cassie nodded. 'Which can close your upper airway within minutes of ingesting an allergen.'

'How come the Home Office pathologist didn't see any evidence of it?'

Cassie had to stop herself rolling her eyes. 'Because without witnesses, or a known history of allergy, anaphylaxis is notoriously difficult to identify. The main sign is swelling of the airway, but that often subsides post-mortem.'

Now Flyte was starting to share Cassie's excitement. Could this explain something that had always bothered her? Why, instead of killing Bronte in the flat, the killer had thrown her off the balcony, with the risk of being seen by a neighbour or passer-by? According to Chrysanthi, Bronte had to be super-careful about what she ate; if she'd also had a dangerous allergy, that would offer a way to make her death appear accidental. Her murderer could have administered the allergen, and then simply sat and watched as she choked to death. A plan that had gone awry.

'So how do we prove it?' she demanded. 'Reopen the body?'

Cassie shook her head. 'No point.'

'Are you saying we can't prove it?' asked Flyte, exasperated. *Had this infuriating girl dragged her here just to deliver an evidential dead end?*

'No, I'm not saying that. All her samples will still be in the fridge at the lab. If she died of anaphylactic shock there's a good chance it will show up in the bloods. When the immune system detects a substance it considers alien it produces tryptase, which stimulates the mast cell—'

'All right, Einstein, I don't need a biology lesson. So you're saying we can request testing for this tryptase?'

'Already done.' Cassie grinned modestly. 'Prof Arculus has agreed to sign off the lab requests in the light of new evidence. You just need to square it away your end.'

'OK.' Then Flyte's ever-present frown line deepened. 'I assume the tests won't tell us what she was allergic to?'

'No.'

'Was there anything in the PM report about her stomach contents?'

Cassie had already checked the original report. 'Nothing. Stomach contents aren't even noted at a routine PM unless there's a bunch of tablets.'

'So whatever she'd eaten would just have been washed away?'

''Fraid so.'

Flyte started pacing up and down. 'OK, we'll ask her parents – they would surely know if she were seriously allergic to something. And the ex-boyfriend, that Ethan guy. Although he's not exactly forthcoming.'

After a pause, Cassie said, 'I could ask him, if you like?' – trying to sound casual.

Flyte stared at the pink dots in Cassie's cheeks: she couldn't remember seeing her blush before. 'You're ... friendly with him are you?' Her expression signalling exactly what she meant by 'friendly'.

Cassie made a non-committal gesture.

Flyte hesitated. It was none of her business, but ... 'Look, we're friends, right?'

Meeting her eyes, Cassie nodded.

'I think you should be very careful around him.' Flyte didn't like to ask about her pathologist boyfriend, the one she'd been living with. *Was she being unfaithful?* Somehow she couldn't see it.

'Why? He's not a suspect is he?' Cassie's heated tone and lifted chin warned Flyte that there were limits to their friendship.

'Not officially, no. But think about it. Whoever killed Bronte had to be close enough to her to know what she was allergic to. Which means we can't rule out any close contacts including Ethan and her father.'

'Or her mother,' said Cassie.

Flyte made a sceptical face. 'What possible motive could she have?'

Cassie shrugged. 'Some women can't cope with their children growing up because they can no longer control them.'

Flyte thought of her difficult relationship with her own mother. But the problem there had been Sylvia's maternal coldness, an inability to show love or affection to her only child. It was a failing at least partly explained by Sylvia's recent revelation that her first baby – who would've been Flyte's older sister – had died in infancy. Which reminded Flyte that Chrysanthi, too, had already suffered the loss of a child before Bronte's death.

'You don't seriously think that having lost Bronte's twin brother she'd kill her only surviving child? Are you forgetting the way she pushed the police to investigate? According to you, she even released her dead daughter's image to pile on the pressure.'

But Cassie was wearing that mulish expression she got when she couldn't be budged. Flyte could tell she didn't really consider Chrysanthi a serious suspect; she was simply incapable of seeing Ethan as a murderer because she was infatuated with him. A thought that bothered Flyte more than she cared to admit.

FLYTE

Taking the short cut via the market back to the nick, Flyte navigated the crowded pavement like an old Camden hand. Spring had brought out the tourists and trippers keen to get their vicarious fix of 'alternative' London. They posed for selfies with the punks who hung around on the canal bridge, their towering neon-dyed Mohicans looking distinctly performative to Flyte's eyes.

Passing Camden Tube, she walked through a pungent cloud of skunk smoke that she traced to two guys leaning against the wall openly sharing a joint. She realised with a start that she no longer felt tempted to confront them, and not just because she wasn't a serving officer. She had lived and worked here long enough now to accept – albeit reluctantly – that arresting and processing random spliff smokers was a poor use of police resources already stretched to breaking point.

Back in the incident room, seeing no sign of Bacon, Flyte made a beeline for Craig's desk. The look that came over his face when he saw her was one to which she'd rapidly become accustomed: borderline surly with a streak of apprehensive.

'Hey, Craig. Where's DI Bacon?' she asked.

He frowned. 'Streaky? He's just popped to the caff for a late lunch.'

Concealing her impatience, she headed straight out again to the greasy spoon she knew he favoured. There she found him, sat at a Formica table, holding forth to the Turkish guy who owned the place.

Recalling the builder's tea they served here she politely declined a drink, before nodding to Bacon's plate. 'That's a bit healthy-looking, for you?'

He studied his omelette, with its tragic old-school 'salad' – a couple of limp lettuce leaves cradling sliced tomato and cucumber – with a mournful look. 'The wife read me the riot act yesterday, put me on a diet,' he admitted. But just then the café owner returned carrying a large plate of chips, which he plonked on the table saying, 'On the house.'

'Cemil, you spoil me!' said Bacon, beaming – before throwing Flyte a guilty look. 'I'll pay for them, obviously.' When she sent him a sceptical look, he leaned forward and added under his breath, 'Cemil is my CHIS. Unofficially.'

'I don't want to know,' she said, shaking her head. A CHIS was a Covert Human Intelligence Source, or informant. And these days there was no such thing as an 'unofficial' one: there were forms to fill out and official permission to be sought. But she told herself she wasn't here to nail anyone for procedural irregularities.

As he ate, she gave him the lowdown: that an anaphylactic reaction could have caused the gasping heard from Bronte's balcony. 'As you know, if she was hyper-allergic to something it would only take the tiniest trace to make her airways close.'

Bacon stopped eating to stare at her. 'Which would explain why she didn't fight her attacker or scream blue murder.'

'Too busy trying to breathe.' Flyte nodded.

Bacon went quiet, before setting down his knife and fork. 'When I was on the beat I attended a sudden death, a young fella who died of a nut allergy in a fast-food joint. No EpiPen. He choked to death before the ambo came.' She was shocked to see tears well in his eyes. 'Celebrating his GCSE results he was. I had to do the death knock.'

'Golly,' was all Flyte could say.

Collecting himself, he picked up a chip. 'This is a serious lead, Phyllida. If this tryptase stuff shows up in her bloods then there are clear questions that we need answers to. One, what was the allergen; two, who knew she was allergic to it; three, how was it administered.' Having used the chip to drive home his points he now dispatched it, before adding, 'So what do you think happened that night?'

Flyte narrowed her eyes, picturing it. 'I think someone turned up with a takeout, or made her a drink and slipped something in there. Plan A was simply to wait for Bronte to collapse and die before making themselves scarce. Perhaps placing a panicked 999 call once it was too late to save her.'

Bacon nodded. 'And if Plan A had come off no "suicide note" would have been needed. The death would go down as a tragic accident.'

'Precisely. But instead of collapsing inside she makes it out to the balcony, choking, desperate to get some air into her lungs.'

'The killer can't have that – the noise might wake the neighbours – so he simply tips her over. She hangs on so he has to finish the job.' Bacon folded two chips into his mouth and chewed thoughtfully before swallowing. 'The killer has to think fast. He taps out the suicide note on her phone before cleaning his prints off it.'

'Can we go back to Bronte's flat? Now we know what happened?'

'Let's do it. I'll go and pay.' He got to his feet and headed for the counter, saying loud enough for Flyte to hear, 'Now look here, Cemil, I don't want any argument about the chips.'

As the owner started to protest, she slipped out the front door, having realised something. She couldn't care less if Streaky got the occasional free plate of chips: it wasn't exactly major league corruption.

Chapter Thirty-One

Walking down the corridor of her old school, it wasn't so much the look of the place as the remembered smell that took Cassie back to her time here. Girl sweat and plimsoll rubber, the waft of vintage cooking oil and boiled veg from the canteen, and the high reek of teenage angst – a potent mix that made her anxiety levels spike. Incredibly, it had been more than a decade since she'd left Camden High, trailing a history of misdemeanours and an academic performance that had disappointed her grandmother and teachers alike.

A few minutes later, averting her eyes from the detention suite, she found the door that was still marked 'Althea M. Knowles. School Nurse' and after a moment of hesitation knocked softly.

When it was opened by the woman everyone had called Mrs K, Cassie – feeling flustered – put out a hand in greeting.

'Get here, girl!' she said laughing, folding Cassie in a warm bear hug that smelled of camomile and Pears soap, stirring up such a mix of memories it made Cassie's eyes burn. It had been weirdly comforting to discover on the school website that Mrs K was still here.

Inside, the smell of TCP reminded Cassie of her own bit of nursing on Ethan's cut face – a little flutter in her chest at the memory.

Mrs K sat her down in her tiny office, and putting her head on one side, frankly, smilingly surveyed her. 'Still got that alternative thing going on I see. Suits you.' Then her smile faded and she shook her head. 'How terrible what happened to Sophia. We were so proud of her, and for her life to be cut short, and in such a way...'

'I know,' said Cassie, feeling the weight of it pressing down on her again. 'She was twenty-seven, the same age as me.'

Mrs K reached out and clasped Cassie's hand, those kind eyes she remembered seeking hers. 'How are you doing? It's very tough, very upsetting, the first time you lose somebody your own age.'

Death had been Cassie's lifelong companion, not just the roll call of bodies at the mortuary, but people she had loved – *her mother ... her teacher ... her best friend*. But Mrs K was right: Bronte was the first person of her own age to die and the shock of it still reverberated through her like the echo of that guitar chord.

'Did you two stay in touch after leaving?' asked Mrs K.

Cassie shook her head. 'To tell you the truth, we weren't even friends at school.'

'No?' The gentle prompts she was always so good at. Cassie had suffered with her periods when she was fourteen, fifteen, and had spent many an hour in Mrs K's sanctuary – getting painkillers, sometimes being put to bed in the one-bed sick bay next door with a hot-water bottle. She might sometimes have exaggerated her symptoms just to get a break from the gladiatorial bitch-fest that was Year 10 – and she'd had a hunch that Mrs K knew it.

Cassie drew a deep breath and blew it out. 'I did something... bad.'

Mrs K just gave Cassie's hand a squeeze and waited for her to go on.

'We both got bullied in Year 10, Sophia and me, for being ... different.' Seeing her rueful look of understanding, Cassie remembered that back then Mrs K had been one of only two black women on the staff – the other being the geography teacher.

'Different how?'

'Oh you know, I didn't have a mum and dad, just a Polish granny who everyone made fun of. Sophia's family was Greek – and loaded – and sometimes she could come across as kind of stuck-up.'

'Young people can be very narrow-minded. At that age it's all about fitting in, isn't it?'

Cassie nodded miserably. Extracting her hand from Mrs Knowles's warm grasp she started to twist her lip ring through the piercing. 'So the two of us were always getting slagged off by the mean girls for the food in our lunch boxes – you know, Greek and Polish stuff. I got off more lightly than Sophia because she stood up to them and I didn't.' Twisting the piercing so hard it hurt. 'Anyway, one day we were in the showers after gym. You remember they used to have those cubicles with no doors?'

They shared a look. 'Ridiculous,' said Mrs K, drawing herself up. 'I used to tell the head, growing girls are self-conscious and they need *privacy*.'

'So, Sophia and I were the last two showering next door to each other.' She felt sick remembering it. 'I heard giggling and whispering in the changing room and I knew something was going on.' Closing her eyes, she pictured the scene, jerkily cut like a horror movie.

A thin but piercing scream. Cassie coming out, wrapping herself in her towel. Sophia staggering backwards, naked, out of her cubicle, hand to her mouth. Following her stare to the tiled floor. Taking a moment to work out what's lying there. A doner kebab, the pitta bread splayed, slices of grey meat, salad spilled onto the wet floor. The shower is still on and a thread of what looks like blood is running down the drain hole. Kylie, the ringleader of the bullies, jeers, 'What's wrong, Dobby? Too much chilli sauce?'

As Cassie related the story Mrs K's hand went to her mouth, her head shaking in disbelief.

'How dreadful.'

'Yeah, can you imagine going to all that trouble, buying a kebab and smuggling it in?'

'It was another jibe at her difference, her Greekness, right?'

A nod. 'Anyway, Sophia totally lost it, started making a weird noise and shaking all over. I saw that they'd hidden her towel so she had to stand there stark naked.'

Now Kylie's piggy gaze swivels towards Cassie. 'What's up with you Ca-Ca-Cassie? I didn't know you and Dobby were 'friends' – using the mocking sing-song everyone knew from The Inbetweeners. Are you a lezza too?'

Twisting her lip ring faster, Cassie blew out a harsh breath. 'I could've given her my towel, or gone to get another towel. Or just told that bitch Kylie to shut the fuck up ... But you know what I did? I just walked away.'

Chapter Thirty-Two

Mrs Knowles had taken something out of her desk drawer and handed it to her: 'Here, you're bleeding' – nodding at Cassie's lip, concern in her eyes.

Cassie dabbed at her piercing with the sterile wipe, tasting iron-rich blood on her tongue. After a moment she went on. 'That was it. Sophia didn't grass on Kylie, nobody got into trouble, and the next day she'd just . . . disappeared. She never came back to school.'

'So that was why her parents sent her off to that private Catholic school. I often wondered.'

Cassie nodded. 'Closest thing to Greek Orthodox, I suppose.'

'And you? How were you afterwards?' she asked.

'*Me*?! I wasn't the one publicly humiliated and . . . tortured by bullies.'

'No, but you carried this with you – the feeling that you should've done something different. Something you couldn't put right.'

Cassie gave a miserable nod. 'I was brought up to do the right thing – my grandmother went to *jail* for standing up to a communist regime for Chrissake! But I acted like a cowardly little bitch. And I didn't even get punished.'

'Are you sure about that?' asked Mrs K, raising her eyebrows. Leaning forward she said, 'Listen up. You were *a child*. You were *fourteen*! Half the time *adults* don't do the right thing – what child could be expected to have the emotional resources to deal with a situation like that?'

'But I should have—'

'Enough! You were a kind and thoughtful girl, without a mum and dad, going through puberty. And like everybody else at that age, just trying to fit in and get by.'

Cassie let out a breath. 'Funnily enough, I did stand up to Kylie in the end, but a couple of months after Sophia left. I caught her taking the piss out of my gran – she'd rolled her socks down to look like wrinkled stockings and was doing an "old lady" walk down the corridor.' Her face darkened at the memory. 'I lost it. I put her up against the wall and beat the crap out of her. Apparently they had to call a teacher to pull me off.' She pulled a rueful smile.

'Good for you!' said Mrs K, before adding, 'Although you were lucky not to get expelled.'

'Oh my gran got pretty good at playing the "poor little orphan" card with the head. Anyway, after that, I was suddenly one of the cool kids.' Remembering her crush, Natasha, the Katy Perry clone, making overtures to her. 'But I got my own little gang.' Tribe more like – an assortment of geeks, baby goths, and misfit loners.

Mrs K put her hand on Cassie's again. 'Listen to me, Cassie Raven. You're an adult now and it's time that you forgave your fourteen-year-old self. OK?' – looking at her expectantly.

'You mean . . . actually say the words?'

'Yes!' Giving her hand a little affirmative shake.

Closing her eyes, she pictured poor naked Sophia for about the thousandth time, heard the hiss of the shower and the malicious laughter ricocheting off the tiles, saw that thread of red in the water.

She shook her head slowly. 'I can't.'

The only meaningful way to make amends to Bronte was to find out who had killed her. And if Flyte and the cops were going to fixate on Ethan, even more reason for her to do her own digging.

'No need to do it right now, but think about it, mmm?' Mrs K gave Cassie's hand a final squeeze. 'Now I'm guessing you didn't come here just to reminisce about the joys of school days.'

Cassie made an apologetic face. 'Between you and me, it's possible that Bronte might have suffered an anaphylactic episode – before her killer tipped her over, I mean. There's nothing in her recent medical records, and I suspect that her family would have used a private doctor when she was living at home. So I was wondering if you were aware of her having any serious allergies?'

'Not that I can recall.' Mrs K frowned. 'She did have digestive problems – she would come to see me in the afternoon complaining of stomach ache and nausea. I put it down to anxiety. But if she was at risk of anaphylactic attack and carried an EpiPen I'd definitely remember.'

'There might be something in her school medical records though? If she did have a food allergy her parents must have alerted the school when she started here.'

Cassie could have simply called Bronte's parents and asked them, but Flyte had warned her off any 'freelance approaches' to George or Chrysanthi.

Mrs K was regarding her with a dry look. 'You're asking me to divulge confidential medical information?'

'Yes.' Seeing the doubt on Mrs K's face, she went on, 'Going through official NHS channels would waste precious time.' She paused. 'And time is the one thing Bronte doesn't have.'

Mrs K thought about it. Finally, she said 'Well, you are a fellow NHS professional. And if you're asking, I know you must have a good reason.' She regarded Cassie, her head on one side. 'You know, I'd forgotten how determined you could be.'

FLYTE

Any hopes that a second visit to Bronte's flat might turn up some clue as to the contents of her last meal – like a takeaway receipt – swiftly evaporated. Flyte and Streaky studied the photo taken of the fridge contents but the listed ingredients on the labels were too small to read. In any case, since the list of potential allergens ran into the hundreds it probably wouldn't have helped.

Flyte threw herself down on the sofa. 'And the parents say no allergies that they were aware of?'

'Right,' said Streaky, padding around the living room like a disconsolate bear. 'And there's no record of her having a GP – not an NHS one anyway.'

Flyte felt something digging in her back. Investigating, she found a book wedged between two cushions. A guidebook to Cyprus, new-looking, with a couple of pages turned down – a dreadful habit. The chapter that Bronte had marked this way was titled 'Villages of the Troodos Mountains'.

Flyte recalled how indifferent, hostile even, Chrysanthi had seemed to her home island: a lack of interest she insisted that her daughter shared. She showed Streaky the book. 'Did anyone say anything about Bronte planning a trip to Cyprus?' she asked.

Streaky shook his head. 'Not to my knowledge. But it's not exactly a smoking gun, is it?'

She shrugged. 'It's probably nothing, but maybe she was in contact with some extended family we don't know about? We should get one of the DCs trawling her online footprint to find out more? Becca would do a diligent job.' *Translation: not that self-important pipsqueak Craig.*

'Right you are, boss,' said Streaky, but his tone was jocular.

Spotting a bookshelf in the corner, Flyte found a row of self-help books, the kind that claimed to offer solutions to troubled adults – *Moving Beyond Trauma* . . . *The Mountain is You* . . . *How to Heal Your Inner Child* . . . Hippy-dippy nonsense. But there was also a fat medical tome titled *Diseases and Disorders in Early Childhood* and another called *Understanding IBD and Crohn's Disease*, which suggested that Bronte had been exploring her lifelong health issues – or perhaps an allergy?

Seeing *The 27 Club* along the spine of another book she pulled it out. The cover featured images of famous musicians – Janis Joplin, Kurt Cobain and Amy Winehouse among them. Reading the blurb reminded her of the unenviable entry requirement for the so-called 'club': you had to be a music star who died at the age of twenty-seven, preferably in tragic circumstances. *Just like Bronte.* Leafing through it she found the dedication 'To Bronte' spelled out in small neat type at the top of the title page and below it, a sprawling signature that began with a flamboyant 'E'. *Ethan Fox.* Riffling through the pages she made another discovery: the receipt, probably tucked inside by the bookseller.

'Streaky, could you come here a sec?'

Wordlessly, she showed him the receipt. Sending her a look, he pulled out his phone. 'Craig? Get hold of Ethan Fox. Make out it's just a routine review of the evidence *blah, blah*, but please could he come down the nick pronto to answer some questions.'

Two hours later, Ethan Fox was being ushered into the interview room by a female uniform. Her cheeks were pink and she was suppressing a smile – no doubt he'd been exercising his charm on her en route.

Flyte had been curious to see Ethan Fox in the flesh. Although she was personally immune, she recognised his appeal: it wasn't just his dark good looks, but something in the way he held himself – relaxed, self-possessed, but with just a hint of vulnerability that would be catnip to women. *Women like Cassie*, who it was clear had a major crush on him.

Folding his long body into the chair, he set a packet of Marlboro and a lighter on the table and sent Flyte an appealing smile. 'I don't suppose . . .?'

'You suppose correctly,' said Flyte, returning the smile with a serving of frost. She dropped her gaze to her notes, blinking away an unwelcome image: Ethan and Cassie having sex.

After starting the tape, Streaky read him the caution, and noted that he had declined the right have a solicitor present. Ethan lifted one shoulder, an unconcerned smile on his face. 'I'm not really a lawyer kind of guy.'

'So I've just been refreshing my memory of what you told DS Ellwood, the first time you were interviewed,' said Streaky, leafing through a printout with a distracted air. 'Oh where is it . . . ah, here we go. So you said that you and Bronte were no longer together and the last time you saw her was several days before her death.'

Ethan gave a shrug-nod in response.

'Sorry, Ethan, but could you answer for the tape?' Streaky sounded apologetic.

'No worries. Yeah, that's what I said.'

'To be specific, when DS Ellwood asked you to nail the timing, you said it was "at least five days" before she died.' Streaky blinked at him absent-mindedly. 'Sorry, but could you just confirm that was accurate?'

'I couldn't tell you what day exactly it was but yeah, five or six days earlier is about right.' Ethan picked up his lighter, his brow creased now.

Flyte slid *The 27 Club* book, opened and face down, in its clear evidence bag, onto the table between them. 'Do you recognise this?'

He craned forward. 'Ummm, not sure.'

She turned the book over, revealing the title page with its dedication.

'This *is* your signature, isn't it?'

Leaning forward, he said, 'Oh yeah, I remember now, I got it for Bronte.' He was still sounding unconcerned but the way he was fidgeting with the lighter, reflexively turning it over in his long fingers, told a different story.

'I know it's hard remembering what happened on any particular day more than two weeks ago,' said Streaky, still playing Mr Chummy. 'Sometimes I forget what I did yesterday! But how soon after getting Bronte the book did you give it to her? Just roughly.'

'I gave it to her pretty much straightaway, I think.'

'And that was when exactly?' Streaky asked.

'Uh, the last time I saw her, yeah.'

'"Five or six days before she died", according to your last interview?'

'Yeah, must have been.'

Picking up the book, Flyte pulled a face. 'It's a bit of a weird gift, isn't it? A book about troubled rock stars who died at the age of twenty-seven? When Bronte was the exact same age and pretty vulnerable herself?'

'I wouldn't expect you to understand,' he said, with a flash of aggression. *Momentary but revealing?*

Holding his gaze, Flyte set the receipt in its separate evidence bag in front of him. 'For the benefit of the tape would you kindly read out the date and time on the receipt for the book, Ethan?'

Frowning down at it, he bit his lip.

'It's for 6.20 p.m. on the fourth of March, isn't it, Ethan?' she went on. 'In other words, just a few hours before Bronte went over the balcony of her flat. Which means that you lied to us about the time you last saw her.'

He opened his mouth to speak before thinking better of it.

Flyte was enjoying herself now. 'Were you trying to get back with her? Did she turn you down?'

A headshake.

Streaky leaned forward, hands steepled like a priest-confessor. 'This is your chance to give us your side of what happened, Ethan. You were with Bronte when she died, weren't you?'

Ethan crossed his arms and stared at them. He didn't look so cool anymore. 'I'm not saying anything else until I speak to a lawyer.'

Chapter Thirty-Three

Althea Knowles came back re Bronte's school medical notes the next morning while Cassie was making her morning coffee.

'There's nothing on file about a serious allergy, or any allergy come to that. I always made a note of her stomach issues and kept her parents informed but I don't know what, if any, action they took: the notes say they used a private doctor for everything, even vaccinations.' Mrs K hesitated. 'There was something in there I'd completely forgotten though. But you really can't share this.'

'Absolutely not,' Cassie assured her.

'The previous nurse made a note right at the start of her Year 7 when she arrived here. She had a sibling, a twin brother who died at the age of three.'

Cassie remembered Bronte's father George telling her about Alexander. 'Did it say what of?'

'Beta thalassemia. It causes a haemoglobin deficiency that can be fatal in the early years.'

After hanging up Cassie went straight to her medical textbooks. An inherited genetic abnormality, beta thalassemia major was indeed a life-threatening condition requiring lifelong blood transfusions, and some children, like Alexander, didn't survive to their fifth birthday. But it wasn't much help in getting to the bottom of Bronte's death. Bronte had been a female, non-identical twin and clearly hadn't inherited the condition, and anyway there was no association between beta thalassemia and severe allergy.

An hour later, at work, she got an email from the tox lab at Imperial. They'd run the tests on the sample of Bronte's femoral blood stored in their fridge. The normal range of mast cell tryptase was between 3 and 5 nanograms per millilitre; Bronte's was off the scale at 41.4.

Cassie forwarded it to Flyte and less than two minutes later her phone rang.

'Is it reliable?' asked Flyte without preamble.

Cassie grinned. 'I'm fine, thanks, Phyllida, how are you?'

'Yes, OK, fine, how are you, etc. So, would it stand up in court as proof that she suffered anaphylactic shock?'

'I'm no expert, but it should do. Tryptase levels can increase post-mortem but this is so high it looks conclusive.'

'OK, good ... Of course, proving she had an anaphylactic reaction doesn't help unless we can prove someone fed it to her and then tipped her over the balcony when she started choking.' She paused. 'But how would the killer get Bronte to eat or drink something to which she was allergic?'

Flyte's old-school grammar made Cassie grin. 'Good question. Apparently the severity of reaction will be worse according to how big a dose of the allergen you're exposed to. But you do hear of cases where even the tiniest trace of peanut, say, picked up during food prep can kill you.'

'So even a tiny bit sneaked into her food or drink might be fatal,' Flyte mused. 'The key isn't so much finding out *what* she was allergic to but establishing who knew.'

'Yeah. Any progress on a suspect?' Cassie asked.

'You know I can't discuss that with you,' she said stiffly before saying, 'I will tell you this. You are not to discuss *any of this* with Ethan Fox. Is that understood?'

A few minutes later, Cassie called her dad, Callum, in Belfast. 'To what do I owe this honour?' he said, with that ever-present smile in his voice.

'I'm sorry, Dad,' she said. 'It's just been stupid busy at work, and . . . you know I'm not great on the phone. How's it going over there?'

'Good. Yeah.' The sounds of kids shouting excitedly in the background came over the line. 'It's been great seeing the wains, you know? We're about to take them to the seaside.'

'Really? Is it warm over there?' Northern Ireland wasn't known for its Mediterranean temperatures, especially in March.

'I'll have you know it's getting on for fifteen degrees. Roasting.' A soft chuckle.

'Do you remember taking me to Marine Ices?' she said, feeling suddenly nostalgic. When she'd been little, with her mother spending a lot of time in bed with depression – or a hangover – it was her dad who'd done the lion's share of the parenting.

'Of course.'

'What was my favourite flavour?' Testing him.

'Rum and raisin.' No hesitation.

'Aha, so you're to blame for giving me the taste for alcohol,' she told him.

'What was mine?' he asked, cunningly.

'Come on, I was four!' she protested. 'Umm . . . tutti-frutti?'

'Impressive! You always did notice every little thing.'

'It's . . . good to hear your voice,' she said, biting her lip – after so many years without a dad this stuff still didn't come easy to her.

'I love you, Catkin.'

A little surge of panic. But after a moment she found her voice. 'I love you too, Dad.'

Chapter Thirty-Four

Around ten that evening Cassie found herself freezing her arse off in a queue of excitable Gen Z-ers outside a dance music venue in Camden Lock. She had Ethan to thank for the unscheduled night out. As a stranger to social media she'd've had no clue that SkAR – the dance-pop producer Bronte had worked with in Berlin – was doing a guest-DJ spot that night.

'Maybe you can try to find out what happened over there to freak her out?' Ethan had said on the phone earlier. 'I'd ask him myself but he probably knows who I am.'

Picking up the anxiety in his voice, she remembered how arsey Flyte had been with her about not speaking to him. 'Has something happened, with the cops?'

'They think I was with her when she died,' said Ethan, sounding miserable.

'And were you?'

'No! Look I did see her that evening but it was much earlier.' A pause. 'You believe me, don't you?'

She made a non-committal sound. 'So if this SkAR was involved it'd get them off your back.'

'I know it's a big ask, Cassie. But you want to know what happened almost as much as me, right?'

'Why would he even speak to me?' she asked, playing for time.

'He has a rep for liking pretty girls,' said Ethan, having the grace to sound embarrassed.

Yecch.

But if the cops were homing in on Ethan then somebody had to check out this SkAR guy.

And so that evening she'd dug out her black spider's web tights, plus a short leather skirt she hadn't worn in an age and put on some make-up that wouldn't scare the normals. She had agonised over shoes – not possessing anything remotely girlie – and in the end had gone for her cherry-red patent leather Doc Martens. Now, catching sight of her red lips and bat-winged eyes reflected in a massive mirror in the club entrance, she pulled her skirt down, suddenly self-conscious: was she too old to pull it off?

Inside, a pumping dance track was playing but the stage was empty, just two guys setting up the decks. Skirting the edge of the gyrating crowd, she reached the front and caught the eye of one of them, a muscular guy in his forties wearing a T-shirt with 'CREW' on the front, obviously one of SkAR's roadies. He came to the front of the stage and dropped to a crouch. She pressed a little card with a note on it in his hand and after checking it out he just nodded.

Then she took up position to the side where she had a good view of the stage. But by the time SkAR appeared, suddenly spotlit at his decks, a dance track pumping, she had to peer past the forest of arms holding uplifted phones to get a look at him. Dressed in black, and older-looking than she'd expected – in his late thirties, maybe more. Not that she could see much of his face: beneath a beanie he wore wrap-around shades and a dark beard shaped into a goatee.

Had the roadie given SkAR her card? On it she'd asked for a brief interview for her TikTok channel, borrowing the identity of someone called @beatzbabe who covered dance music and had a sizeable but not ridiculous following. It had taken a while to find someone who never actually appeared on her reels and whose profile image was a dark-haired pierced avatar vaguely resembling Cassie.

During the first track, she stood still so that she'd be noticeable amid all the frenetic movement and after a moment he looked over to check her out. She felt a jolt of anxiety: *Would she pass*? *What if he'd met this TikTok person?* After a few more tracks – all sounding generically similar to her ears – she felt a tap on her upper arm. It was the roadie from earlier. Unsmiling, he handed her a black plastic card printed with the words 'VIP' and 'Backstage' before disappearing. When she looked up at SkAR, he tipped his head as if to say, *You're welcome*.

Twat. He must have a prearranged signal with his roadies. But she just smiled and gave him a little wave.

Twenty minutes later, he'd finished his set and announced the next act would be coming on after a short break. She left a decent interval so as not to seem overkeen before heading backstage. At the door, another unsmiling flunky nodded her through and pointed out SkAR's dressing room. The door was ajar.

'*Virtus Omnia Vincit*,' she murmured, before pushing it open. *Courage conquers all.*

'Hey there, hot stuff,' he said, spinning his chair round and splaying his legs. Stripped of the on-stage light show he looked ... ordinary, a slightly overweight sweaty guy you wouldn't look at twice in the street. The air was thick with some sickly cologne that he'd slapped on in a (failed) attempt to cover the smell of his sweat.

After closing the door behind her, he handed her a shot glass already filled with some clear liquid. She felt her heart start to thump, before picturing Bronte wearing a scornful look. *Don't be ridiculous,* you're *not allergic to anything.*

'Cool set,' she said, sipping the tequila – a drink she loathed. 'I'm going to post about it.'

'Oh yeah? You got a big following?' His eyes moving from her legs to her breasts.

'Eighty thousand,' she said modestly, hoping she'd remembered right. Still, she hoped he wouldn't go online to check: it would be just her luck if @beatzbabe was right now posting live from some club in Ibiza.

'You know, I usually go for black girls' – he put his head on one side, assessing her – 'but I like an edgy chick too.'

Lucky me.

'Thanks!' Time to change the subject. 'It's so great you've got a new residency here and I was thinking maybe we could do a little interview?'

Lust wrestled with narcissism on his face, and he shrugged. 'Why not?'

'I interviewed Bronte you know, just before you two worked together.' She crossed one leg over the other, a move he followed with dog-like attention. 'What was she like?'

Still looking at her legs, he said, 'She was high maintenance.' He gave 'high' two syllables, standard in urban street-speak but fake-sounding in a guy his age. Cassie remembered her grandmother's reaction the time she'd come home from school talking like that: *We might be poor, but we can still speak the Queen's English.*

'Really? High maintenance?' she asked, mirroring the long 'i' sound. 'I thought it would be *amazing* to work with someone that talented.'

'You're not recording this, right?' he said, frowning.

'What, no!' she lied, making a show of pocketing her phone. 'We'll do the interview in a minute. Go on, tell me about her, I was a bit of a fan-girl.' Putting her head on one side and playing with her hair like she'd seen silly women doing. 'She was soo beautiful.'

He leaned over and put his hand on her thigh, saying, 'She wasn't as pretty as you.'

Panic flared in Cassie's chest. She wasn't in any danger, was she? *Nah*. With a packed dance floor just metres away she only had to scream her lungs out for someone to hear.

So she just smiled and said, 'She must've been totally thrilled for the chance to cut a track with you.'

'You'd think, right?! But we didn't really see eye to eye.' The feel of his clammy palm through the spider's web tights was making her want to puke.

'Oh really?' Dropping her voice, she asked, 'Was she a diva?'

'She was a diva all right,' he said darkly. 'And she wasn't very . . . friendly' – taking his hand from her leg to pour them some more tequila.

Cassie could imagine how this creep defined 'friendliness' when it came to women.

His face darkened. 'I'm probably not allowed to say ball-breaker these days.'

Except you just did.

'Was it a case of too much fame too fast, d'you think?' she asked.

He took his fleshy lower lip in his teeth, a vulpine gesture. 'That's exactly what I told her. She was just a pretty girl with a half-decent voice who got lucky.' His voice rose in anger, lost in a memory. 'She thought she could lay the law down – to me! Lecturing *me* about "musical authenticity" and being true to her "roots". You know what I said to her?'

Cassie shook her head.

'I told her, you're a fucking nobody and your so-called "roots" are a one-donkey shithole down a dirt road in the Troodos where they don't marry outside the family.'

His voice was full of entitled rage. It was blindingly obvious to Cassie then that he'd tried it on with Bronte and when she'd fought back had thrown insults at her – and worse? She remembered Ethan saying that SkAR and Bronte shared Greek-Cypriot heritage – had their families come from the same area? Maybe even the same village?

'Did you know her hometown then?'

But just then the next set started up, the baying voice of the DJ and a frenzied electronic dance beat booming out. As if a switch had flipped, he reached over and slid his hand up her leg to her crotch, fumbling hotly at her knickers.

Cassie threw her tequila in his face and he leaped back with an angry shout, rubbing at his eyes. She scrambled to her feet and went for the door, but couldn't work the lock quickly enough. Then he was behind her, one hand on the back of her head, pressing her against the wood face first, so hard it made her cheekbone hurt. His body had her pinned against the door and his other hand had cranked her right arm painfully high up behind her back. She scrabbled to reach him with her free arm but she couldn't land a blow.

He said in her ear, 'You're just a fucking scammer, here to dig up dirt' – hot spittle landing on her cheek and his erection pressing against her lower back. She tried to scream but was horrified when nothing came out. But in any case the music was so loud the vibrations were using her skeleton like a tuning fork.

One hundred and thirty beats per minute.

Now he was pulling her skirt up over her butt with his free hand, sending waves of panic through her.

Fuck fuck fuck!

Tugging at her knickers, he murmured in her ear, 'You know what happens now, right?' – savouring the moment, enjoying the power he had over her.

This couldn't be happening.

Closing her eyes tight, Cassie saw Bronte's face, looking fierce, mouthing something – and knew what she had to do.

Forcing herself to go limp, to stop resisting, she felt him relax.

'See?' he crowed. 'This is what you all want, you bi— ' His words curdled into a half-scream. She had slammed her boot heel down with brutal force and found his foot. Pulling free, she spun round and kicked him full in the groin. He folded like a cheap deckchair onto the scuzzy carpet, curling into the foetal position, hands over his groin, emitting a high-pitched moan.

Bending down, her face was level with his, Cassie said, 'What's up? I thought you liked edgy chicks.'

But by the time she reached the street, the fierce rush of the adrenaline that had held her together was ebbing fast and, leaning against a lamp post, she threw up the tequila. As she wiped her mouth, a bouncer approached her and bent down so their heads were level. 'Are you OK? Can I get you an Uber?' The concern in his eyes seemed genuine. For a fraction of a second she almost said, 'I've been assaulted, call the cops.'

As if. Everyone knew how that went down. He said/she said. The flunkies who would say she went willingly to his dressing room. The unspoken *and look at what she was wearing* – the rapist's get-out-of-jail card. The cops would think just another encounter where a silly girl bit off more than she could chew. *Ha fucking ha.*

FLYTE

The next morning, Flyte was making coffee in her flat when the entryphone buzzed and she checked the video feed.

Streaky.

He came in, wearing a rain-soaked overcoat. 'It's caning it down out there.' He shook himself like a big dog, spraying water everywhere. 'So I thought I'd call by to give you a lift to the nick.'

'Where did you park?' she asked with a puzzled look: her flat – part of the first floor of a late-Georgian house – was on Delancey Street, which was end-to-end double yellow lines.

'Right outside,' he said, frowning, like it was a stupid question. 'Warrant card on the dash.'

Totally against the rules, of course.

She rolled her eyes. 'Coffee?'

'Do you have any herbal tea?' he asked, patting his paunch. 'I'm still fighting the flab.'

Streaky's smart new dark-blue suit was a major improvement on his vintage brown number even if the overall look was somewhat marred by the scrap of toilet tissue he'd stuck to a razor cut on his upper lip.

When she came back into the living room with his tea, they sat either side of the coffee table. One arm stretched along the back of her sofa, he cast an admiring look around. 'You got the *piano nobile*. Nice.'

'I . . . I don't speak Italian.'

'The literal translation is "noble floor". It's what architects called the first floor of these big townhouses,' he told her, before sipping his tea. 'The basement was the engine room, manned by the poor old servants, the ground floor was for daily life, but this floor was for entertaining the most important guests. It always had the highest ceiling, the biggest windows, and the grandest fittings' – nodding to the imposing marble fireplace.

'How do you know all this?' – trying to keep the disbelief out of her voice.

'Oh, that was my misspent youth in Hong Kong. I was posted there when I was in the forces. It was considered a cushy posting, but you had to have an outside interest or you'd go nuts. So while courting my wife I also studied for a history of art degree at evening classes.'

Blimey O'Reilly, as her father had been fond of saying.

'Army?' she asked, her gaze drawn to the framed photo of Pops on the mantelpiece, off duty and in his gardening gear, a lifetime ago.

Following her gaze, Streaky stood to look more closely at the picture. 'That's an entrenching tool he's got there!' he said, sending her a delighted look. 'Were you an army brat?'

She nodded, amused by his evident delight. 'Six schools in the space of five years before getting sent to boarding school at twelve.'

'Same as me,' he said with a grin.

Worried that he might ask about Pops – too personal – she changed the subject. 'So, we've proved that Ethan lied to us about his whereabouts the day of Bronte's death.'

Streaky nodded. 'Which is a start, but clearly he could've given her the sodding book any time that evening, hours before she died. We need something to put him at the flat later that night. And we still have no clue what he might have fed her to trigger the anaphylaxis.'

'Her mother was all over what she ate, so you'd think she would know if she'd had a reaction before,' said Flyte, frowning.

'Does she strike you as a control freak?' mused Streaky.

'Maybe. Or maybe just overprotective? She had already lost one child remember.' Picturing Poppy, Flyte could absolutely understand how the loss might make her a neurotic mother next time round. *If there was ever to be a next time.* Which, now she was sliding towards forty, looked less likely with every passing year.

She gathered their cups up. 'I like the new suit, by the way,' she said. 'Very smart.'

'If I commented on your appearance HR would have me up on a charge,' he said, pulling what she now recognised as his wind-up grin.

'Hardly,' she said, thinking of the hundreds of sexual assaults by male cops on their female colleagues – and even against victims of crime – that were starting to emerge: crimes that had largely gone unpunished. But debating the patriarchal structures of the Met with Streaky would be a hiding to nothing, as her pops would have said.

'How did you know it was a new suit, anyway?' asked Streaky.

She pointed to his left cuff which bore the remains of the stitch where the label had been attached.

'Busted,' he sighed. 'The wife insisted on a trip to M & S last night' – looking mournful.

'Job interview? Not that it's any of my business.'

He hesitated. 'Strictly *entre nous* and not for the ears of the team, I'm being measured up to head the new Major Crimes team that Borough is putting together.'

Flyte dropped her gaze. She had no wish to revisit her role in the meltdown of the old Major Crimes unit. Despite spending her entire career in the police service – straight out of university – her profound disillusionment with the Met had made her departure inevitable. But she still missed being a detective every day.

The opening bars of 'London Calling' by The Clash sounded on Streaky's phone.

'DI Bacon,' he said into the mic. Then he looked up at her with a smile. 'We're on our way.'

Within ten minutes the two of them, together with DS Craig, were gathered round DC Becca's laptop in the incident room.

'So here it is,' said Becca, frowning intently at the screen.

The clip she played had been captured at night by a CCTV camera positioned above a petrol station forecourt, presumably in a bid to catch drive-offs. She fast-forwarded through a few cars coming and going, their drivers whizzing back and forward to the window to pay. Then she paused it.

'There.' There was no one at the payment window but she was pointing at a guy off to the right who had walked up to what appeared to be a cash machine. He was in half profile but from his gait alone there was no mistaking his identity. *Ethan Fox.*

'It's definitely him, isn't it?' asked Becca, the young female DC.

'It's him all right,' Flyte told her, smiling at her anxious but excited expression. It was a tedious job, tracking down every possible source of CCTV material in the area around Bronte's flat and it had paid off.

'The time stamp reads five past eleven,' said Streaky, squinting at the screen. 'And Bronte's flat is how far from this garage?'

'About ten minutes' walk,' said Becca. 'I timed it.'

'Bang in the right area a couple of hours before Bronte takes a fatal header off her balcony.' Streaky pulled a beatific smile.

'So Ethan not only lied about seeing her that evening,' said Flyte, 'but also about his movements that night.'

'What did his bandmate say again?' Streaky asked Becca.

'That Ethan was at band practice at his gaff in the Holloway Rd that afternoon and slept on the sofa cos it was late when they finished.'

'The last bit made up to protect his chum,' said Streaky. 'In fact, Ethan came back to Camden, and got some cash out a short step from Bronte's.'

'And who uses cash these days? Other than drug dealers,' this from Craig. 'Should I go doorstep Ethan's bandmate, boss?'

Streaky turned to Becca. 'It's your lead, Becca. You should go see the guy, put the fear of God into him for lying. See what else he can tell us about Ethan. You can take Craig here, if you like: it's your shout. Terrific work. Good old-fashioned policing.'

Becca went a fetching shade of pink.

Flyte was pleasantly surprised to see the way Streaky bigged up Becca, but something had been niggling away at her about Ethan as a suspect. She could definitely buy him losing his temper with Bronte and tipping her over the balcony, and of course he could easily have known what it was that she was dangerously allergic to. But was he really capable of the calculation and planning that feeding her an allergen involved? And why risk taking her the gift of a book that might advertise his presence at the flat that night?

'Did you find anything useful in your trawl of Bronte's comms?' she asked Becca.

'Nothing much,' said Becca, pulling up a file. 'But you were right about her planning a Cyprus trip. She had a flight booked to Larnaca and car hire for a week.'

'Just her? When was she supposed to be flying?'

'Ten days after her death.'

Interesting. So much for Chrysanthi's insistence that Bronte had zero interest in the family's home island: maybe she just hadn't liked the idea.

'One other thing,' said Becca. 'Her health problems were ongoing – she had sent an email a few weeks before her death enquiring about an appointment with a gastroenterologist in Harley Street. Using a false name.'

Not that unusual for a celebrity wary that their private info could be leaked.

'Did the consultation happen?' asked Streaky.

'The fee quoted was £350 plus VAT, but she didn't reply.' Becca shrugged. 'And there's no payment going out of her bank account so it looks like she didn't get round to it.'

Streaky returned to his desk and Flyte followed.

'I did some Google research on anaphylactic shock,' she told him. 'Apparently it's pretty rare for the first serious reaction to kill you – there's usually a previous episode. Clearly her murderer knew what she was allergic to. Which suggests they might have been with her when she suffered an earlier reaction?'

'Hmm.' Streaky nodded thoughtfully. 'Bad enough to call 999 you mean.'

'Exactly.'

Chapter Thirty-Five

After what had happened at the club the previous night, Cassie hadn't got much sleep, despite prescribing herself a serious dose of vodka. Every time she closed her eyes, the peeling blue paint of that door filled her vision, she felt the pain in her cheek, heard the relentless *boof-boof-boof* of the music, his voice hissing in her ear, his clammy hands . . .

Stop!

In the early hours she had got up and smoked a spliff in the cockpit, eyeing the darkness of the canal with a new sense of anxiety, twitching at every innocuous sight and sound on the towpath.

As someone who'd had plenty of experience with people facing trauma in the shape of sudden bereavement, she understood in theory that the shock would take some getting over. But the thing Cassie struggled with, the thing that she just couldn't compute, was viewing herself as a victim. She had always seen herself as someone who could take care of herself, who if push came to shove could fight a guy off. But in that endless moment pinned to the door, his hands on her, she had felt completely powerless. The worst thing, the thing she never could have grasped before it happened to her, was the way it had blurred the boundaries of her *selfhood*, leaving her feeling raw and fuzzy at the edges.

A sinuous black shadow jumped silently up onto the boat, only Macavity's golden-green eyes reflecting the light in the night sky. After a moment staring at her, he came over and climbed into her lap, purring. A soft reassuring purr, not the higher pitched 'feed me now' version. 'I'm honoured,' she murmured. As she pulled him into an embrace, she felt a knife-like pain in her wrist – from where SkAR had twisted her arm up behind her back.

The only comfort was picturing how much pain he would be in. Thank God she'd worn the DMs and not some less sturdy footwear: that stomp on his foot had been hard enough to inflict a Jones fracture – a fracture of the fifth metatarsal, the commonest kind. As for his balls . . . well, maybe she had altered the boundaries of his selfhood in return.

Her phone lit up again. Ethan had already texted her half a dozen times asking how it went, was she OK etc., but she couldn't face speaking to him. She had the urge to call Archie, to hear his comforting laid-back tones – but really, what would that achieve? *More confusion*.

Well, she knew now what had happened to Bronte in Berlin, alone with that bastard into the small hours in a soundproof studio. She had pushed back on what they'd been recording, and when she wouldn't budge he'd decided to show her who was in charge. He wasn't just an opportunist who tried his luck – he was a sadistic predator who got off on women's fear. And if Cassie hadn't been able to fight him off, what hope for Bronte? Five foot three and less than eight stone. Easy to rape – and easy to tip over a balcony.

In the morning Cassie forced herself to listen back to the recording on her phone from last night. The phone had been in her pocket so it was muffled and the banging music obscured most of what he'd hissed in her ear. But worse still was the discovery that at no point had she shouted, *No! stop now!!* Why hadn't she? She'd never truly understood how the shock of sudden violence could rob you of the power of movement and speech. It was only seeing Bronte's face that had snapped her out of that, saving her from much worse.

Thank you, she murmured.

Bracing herself, she went online to find out more about SkAR. The bios revealed that his real name was Stefano Makris, born and raised in Enfield, who'd gone to a private boys' school where he was known as Steve. A rare early pic of him showed an overweight adolescent in a blazer, radiating a mixture of neediness and entitlement. After school he'd spent fourteen years working for his father's estate agency business. The whole super-cool SkAR persona, the street veneer, was a total facade.

She decided to think of him as just Steve from Enfield, the uncool pudgy kid turned estate agent. Maybe it would help dispel the feeling of utter powerlessness she'd experienced in his dressing room. One of the bio sites mentioned where in Cyprus his family hailed from – a village called Perdikia – which Google Maps showed as a tiny dot in the foothills of the Troodos Mountains without even a marked road. The accompanying image showed a few dilapidated houses strung along a dirt track, pretty much the 'one-donkey shithole' of the type he had accused Bronte of coming from. Steve from Enfield had only turned his hand to DJ-ing a few years earlier, presumably while on a visit back to Cyprus, where he'd made his name at a club in Ayia Napa – the island's dance music mecca.

What else was it he'd said about Bronte's home village – where presumably Chrysanthi, or George had come from? 'Where they don't marry outside the family'. It sounded like a standard if colourful insult against a remote and backward hamlet.

Closing the laptop, Cassie indulged in a revenge fantasy. Bronte came back from the dead and together they got Steve to a high building where, as he grovelled for mercy, they picked him up by shoulders and ankles like a sack of potatoes and threw him off. The image of his body getting smaller as he fell, his arms windmilling, gave her particular satisfaction.

Had Bronte threatened to expose him as a rapist? Had he killed her to shut her up? Like the film industry before it, the music scene was having its own moment of reckoning with serial abusers. But how would he know what she was allergic to? Maybe there was something in her rider from the record company to say what she could and couldn't eat?

She replayed the vid of Bronte singing the embryonic track 'Skeleton' that Ethan had sent her. The central lyric was about secrets: secrets that she was accusing somebody of keeping, but listening to it a second time Cassie picked up something new. It was the line: 'You feed me, always feed me, but what you feed me is lies.' Something in the way she sung it, staring straight into the lens, made Cassie wonder.

Was Bronte talking to her mother?

Chapter Thirty-Six

Cassie pushed open the heavy oak door of Agios Ioannis, aka St John's Greek Orthodox Church, up on Camden's northernmost fringe. The interior made her gasp. It was a vast space, with upper galleries on either side, but the sombre gloom focused the gaze entirely on the huge image of Christ that covered the entire wall above the altar. Picked out in mosaic his stern face, dark-eyed and bearded, glowered out of a sea of gold, his right palm held aloft in a gesture that could be a blessing – or a terrible warning.

The overriding impression: *Jesus wasn't happy.*

Babcia had called her to say she was on her way to some God-bothering event at Chrysanthi's church. 'Come and meet me there, *tygrysek*,' she had said. 'It's only for an hour and we can have lunch afterwards at that new Polish café.'

Cassie had agreed: she wasn't on call that weekend and she was intrigued to observe Chrysanthi in the place of worship that meant so much to her. A little gaggle of ladies off to one side of the main body of the church caught her eye. From their movements and the chink of china they were clearing up tea things. Recognising Babcia's tiny and shockingly bent figure gave her a jolt – *when did she get so old?*

As she drew near, Chrysanthi emerged through some plush velvet curtains in the rear wall, and leaned down to take a stack of china from her grandmother. She looked taller than Cassie remembered – she must have towered over her daughter. Funny how two tall parents could produce such a tiny child.

Cassie saw a shadow fall across Chrysanthi's face and turning she was met by a startling sight: an elderly priest, tall and stooped, in long black robes, topped with a headdress affair. He had a dirty white beard that reached his sternum and the craggily forbidding features of some Old Testament prophet who'd just spent forty days in the desert. He stared at Cassie's piercings and tattoos, looking aghast.

She stared right back, tempted to say, *What, I look weird?*

It struck Cassie that they must look like a tableau in a medieval illuminated manuscript, titled something like *The Saint is Visited by a She-Devil*. Finally dragging his eyes from her, he turned to Chrysanthi. 'Come into my office, we need to finalise the funeral details,' before sweeping away, his long robe hiding his feet so it looked like he was on castors.

'Nice to meet you too,' Cassie murmured to herself.

In the Polish café, Babcia fixed the young girl who took their order with a beady stare and interrogated her in Polish. The poor girl looked terrified, but whatever she said in return seemed to satisfy Weronika. '*Dobzre*,' she said, handing back the menu.

'What was that about?' asked Cassie.

'I was checking that they use proper dried ceps in the *pierogi* and not some cheap imitation,' said Babcia. 'You can't be too careful, eating out.' Then she took Cassie's hand across the table. 'You have shadows under your eyes. Is something bothering you, *tygrysek*?'

Cassie dropped her gaze. No way was she about to tell Babcia what happened last night. Not only would she be terribly upset – who knew what she might do? She might be old but she was made of tough stuff, forged in Stalinist Poland, might even take the law into her own hands to deal with someone who'd hurt her granddaughter.

'It's Bronte – you know, Sophia. I guess her murder has got under my skin because we were in the same class.' She shrugged. 'I just can't bear the thought of the killer getting away with it.'

Babcia's eyes grew hooded. 'Her mother needs a resolution too.' She stopped to let the waitress lay their cutlery and pour their water from a proper old-fashioned china jug. '*Dziekuje*,' she thanked her, before going on. 'She said a strange thing to me earlier today.'

'What?'

'She said that she had "always been afraid that God would take Sophia".'

'Really? Why?'

'As a punishment for sin.'

'Sophia's sin? What had she done that was so bad?'

Babcia shook her head, her gaze inwards. 'I don't know. The drugs? Sex with bad men? But you should forgive your own flesh anything. *Anything*.'

'Did she say any more?'

'No. I think she regretted saying it. She changed the subject.'

The girl brought their *pierogi*, swimming in melted butter and topped with crispy onion, and they started eating.

'That priest dude gives me the creeps,' said Cassie with a visible shudder.

'Father Michaelides.' Babcia pulled a worldly sigh 'He's very traditional, like most priests of his generation. I heard that he barred a woman in her thirties from taking communion because she had two children, both in their teens, and therefore wasn't in a state of grace to receive holy wafer and wine.'

'Because it meant she must have been using contraception? Jeez.'

Babcia nodded. She impaled a *pierogi* on her fork, but before taking a bite, paused, frowning. 'I'll tell you something strange. Chrysanthi makes *konfesja* every week with the other women, but twice I've been to mass at that church and she didn't go up and take communion either time.'

FLYTE

Monday morning saw Flyte and Streaky driving north to an industrial estate where the ambulance call centre covering Camden was located. Rather than going through the bureaucratic process of emailing a request and waiting for permission, his strategy was simply to turn up in person.

'Nothing concentrates the mind like the flash of a warrant card,' he told her with a wink as he parked in the near-empty car park. He hauled himself out of the pool car and Flyte followed, her nerves still jangling from the ride: Streaky appeared to have picked up his driving technique from one of those old TV cop series.

They made their way into the call centre – housed in a nondescript low-rise red-brick building that could have been a storage facility were it not for the row of ambulances parked outside.

'Why bring me though?' Flyte asked him, after they'd announced themselves at reception. She'd been wondering why he was allowing her to take such a big role in his investigation.

'Oh, it never hurts to have a pretty face along,' he said.

She saw his wind-up grin in time. 'Very funny.' Before going on, 'Just don't go thinking any of this means I'm going to pull my punches when it comes to compiling my report.'

'What, even if I treat you to a pie and mash afterwards?' asked Streaky.

They'd been advised that 8 a.m. would be the optimal time to visit, offering the nearest thing to a lull after a night of mayhem. And as the manager ushered them onto the open-plan call-centre floor, there was a definite 'after the deluge' feel about it, and the smell of sweat and stale coffee in the air. At the first desk they came to a woman in her thirties, wearing a dark-green uniform, stretching and yawning.

'Oh sorry!' she said, seeing her visitors, hastily clearing away a torn-open packet of Doritos into the bin.

'Don't apologise,' said Streaky.

The manager introduced the woman as Holly, the team leader for the emergency medical dispatchers. He left them to it and Streaky explained that they were looking for any call-outs to a 'Sophia Angelopoulos, also known as Bronte'. Adding her date of birth.

Holly's eyes widened at hearing the name, but all she said was, 'And the timeframe?' before starting to tap at her keyboard.

'We don't have one really,' said Flyte apologetically. 'But could we search the last year to start with?'

It was only a moment before Holly shook her head. 'Nothing under either of those names I'm afraid. Do you have an address and postcode?'

Streaky gave her Bronte's last two addresses: her previous place in Gospel Oak – a flat that she and Ethan Fox had shared for several months – and her canal-side apartment.

Holly's hands flew over the keyboard. 'Nothing coming up.' Then she tapped in her latest address.

'Here you go!' she said, beaming and angling the screen towards them. 'Last September the fourteenth, at 1.03 p.m. a 999 call from a woman in distress, breathing difficulties. It was deemed a Category 1 – life threatening.'

The mobile number the call came in from wasn't Bronte's – or Ethan's, but of course he could have changed his phone in the interim.

'When did the ambo get there?' asked Streaky.

Holly peered at the screen. 'Eight minutes. Just outside the seven-minute target.'

'What was her condition?'

Holly pulled an apologetic shrug. 'We can't access the clinical details, they will have been archived along with the 999 call recording. You'll have to apply for those.'

'Did she get taken to hospital?' This from Streaky.

Tapping the keyboard again, she shook her head. 'That ambulance stayed at the address for about an hour before being sent to another location, so no. Unless she was a walk-in to A & E later.'

Streaky and Flyte shared a frustrated look.

Holly's gaze went between the two of them. 'I can tell you the team who attended – they might remember something?' She did some more tapping. 'Here you go . . . Gary Walbrook and Yasmin Chowdhury.'

'How can we get hold of them?'

'You're in luck,' said Holly, checking the clock. 'They were based here last night and their shift ended twenty minutes ago. They'll be in the canteen.'

Chapter Thirty-Seven

Seeing yet another missed call from Ethan, Cassie steeled herself to call him back.

'Oh for fuck's sake, Cassie, it's been three days! I was frantic!' – sounding genuinely worried. 'After sending you to see that SkAR geezer when I knew he might've . . . you know, had a pop at Bronte? Are you OK?'

'Yeah, I'm fine.' Her default method of dealing with trauma: bury it and move on. Always a winning strategy. *Haha*. 'But I think you were right about him, he's a *disgusting predator*.' Unable to disguise the venom in her voice.

'Did he hurt you? Cos I'll—'

'I'm fine,' she broke in. 'But listen, do you know anything about his background? His family comes from the Troodos Mountains, the same bit of Cyprus as Bronte's mum – or dad. He might even come from the same village, a place called Perdikia? Did she never talk about going back there for a visit?

'No . . . But the name does ring a bell. She showed me a pic in a guidebook. Said those mountains were where her family came from. Like she'd only just found out.'

'Chrysanthi's family? Or George's?'

'No idea. But I know her mother would have been dead set against her going there – she hated the place, apparently.'

The conversation left Cassie's brain whirring. Steve from Enfield had told Bronte something about her family history deliberately to hurt her, something that – perhaps even more than a sexual assault – had disturbed her, and made her determined to visit Cyprus, maybe to explore the family history. Was Perdikia where one, or both, of Chrysanthi's parents had been raised, at least until she went into care?

What had Babcia said Chrysanthi told her? That God had taken Bronte as some kind of 'payment for sin'.

Hamartia. Cassie suddenly remembered the grief-stricken Chrysanthi using the word when she first saw her dead daughter. Opening her Greek dictionary app, she looked it up.

Hamartia was ancient Greek for sin – and also for sin offering.

Sacrifice.

Why didn't the devout churchgoer Chrysanthi take communion?

Cassie went online to read up on Orthodox theology, which appeared identical to traditionalist Catholic thinking on this topic. You must not take communion if you were guilty of a mortal sin, unless you had confessed it to your priest and made amends. There was a cheery little injunction she could just imagine that bleak old patriarch Father Michaelides intoning: 'Therefore whosoever shall eat this bread, or drink the chalice of the Lord unworthily, shall be guilty of the body and of the blood of the Lord.'

In other words, you'd be killing Jesus all over again. *Heavy.*

The list of mortal sins was a long one and included masturbation, suicide, abortion, 'invalid marriage', such as remarrying after divorce, rape, and, of course, murder.

Cassie started to pace the cabin. Food was the recurring theme in the relationship between Bronte and her mother: from the specially prepared school lunch boxes that had continued into adulthood in the form of 'food parcels' – home-made dishes delivered to the flat. Then she recalled Althea Knowles, their school nurse, saying Bronte got sick in the afternoons: in other words, *after lunch*.

Were Chrysanthi's attempts to control her daughter's diet designed to avert her lifelong stomach problems? *Or to cause them?*

Then there was Bronte's little brother, the twin who didn't live to see his third birthday. Chrysanthi had always struck her as a disturbed soul, full of hatred for her ex-husband, and obsessed with exerting control over her daughter's life.

What if Chrysanthi had channelled all that hatred against her innocent children?

FLYTE

In the ambulance service's canteen there were half a dozen green-uniformed paramedics sitting around various tables.

They recognised Gary and Yasmin from the employment record images that Holly had shown them: Gary, a bear of a man in his late forties with dark stubble who loomed over the tiny, much younger Yasmin sitting next to him.

After introducing themselves, Streaky showed them an image of Bronte – the one her mother had given police at the start of the investigation. It was a snap of her striking a jokey pose in the market, looking like any other young woman, rather than one of the paparazzi specials.

'Sophia Angelopoulos. Breathing difficulties? It was a Category 1 call to one of the warehouse apartments by the canal in Camden last September?'

Shrugging, Gary shook his head, and after studying the shot so did Yasmin. 'People can look totally different when they're sick.'

He stirred sugar into his tea before adding, 'We get twenty-plus calls a night. We've probably been on a few thousand since then.'

'You might also know her as Bronte?' Flyte prompted, making an effort to suppress the impatience in her voice. 'The dance music celebrity?'

Blank looks from both of them. Gary said, 'Music-wise, I'm more of a Dusty fan.'

'This was an allergic reaction, a serious one,' Flyte tried.

'That's become a pretty common call-out over the last five, ten years,' Yasmin said.

Flyte was losing hope. 'What would the treatment be in a case like that?' Hoping to jog their memories.

'Adrenaline, intra-muscular,' said Gary. 'Works like a charm.'

'But you'd still take them to A & E?' This from Streaky.

'Oh, no question. You can get a biphasic reaction a few hours later. And they need to get referred to the allergy clinic, find out what caused the initial reaction.'

'You didn't take this young woman to A & E, but then I guess not everyone listens to your advice, am I right?' asked Streaky.

'Exactly,' said Gary, nodding sagely. 'It's their funeral.'

Literally, sometimes.

Flyte scrolled through her photos and pulled up the images of Bronte's flat taken after her death. 'Here's her place. Tenth-floor apartment overlooking the canal. Ring any bells?'

Gary's brow furrowed, and he looked over at Yasmin. 'Do you remember that place with the music posters? There was a fantastic one of Nina Simone, proper vintage.'

'That's it! That's the place,' said Flyte.

'I only remember the poster,' said Gary. 'Wasn't that the block where the lift was out of action?' he said to Yasmin. 'And I said I hope to fu—God we don't have to stretcher her down.'

Yasmin peered at the images 'Oh yes! I do remember. We don't see too many places with a piano.'

'Did you ask her what she'd eaten to cause the allergic reaction?' Flyte chipped in.

Yasmin nodded slowly. 'A takeout vegan mezze, which wasn't much help – it would be full of potential allergens – nuts, legumes, soybeans . . . I told her she needed to get tested but she was . . .' she hesitated.

'Dismissive?' said Flyte.

'I was going to say drunk,' said Yasmin with a look. 'And probably stoned.'

Streaky said, 'We think somebody was with her when it happened.' They had to tread carefully – any identification had to come from the witnesses unaided.

Yas nodded. 'Mmm, yes. There was a guy there.'

'Could you describe him?'

'Umm. Tall. Nice-looking,' said Yasmin.

Flyte bit her lip.

'Yaz likes an older guy,' said Gary, sending her a cheeky look.

'Older?' queried Flyte. Yasmin could only be a few years younger than Ethan.

Yasmin blushed. 'Yes, in his fifties, at a guess? He said he was her dad.'

Chapter Thirty-Eight

'I can't talk to you right now,' said Flyte, her voice tense – and raised over the sound of a car being driven fast.

'Listen, Phyllida, you're going to want to hear this,' Cassie told her.

She was at work, the day after the germ of a terrible idea had planted itself in her mind: the idea that Chrysanthi could be seriously – dangerously – unstable. Disturbed enough to have killed her own daughter – and not just Bronte but perhaps her twin brother Alexander too. Was that the dark secret that meant she could never take communion?

Cassie knew that the confidentiality of the confession was sacrosanct. Even if Chrysanthi had confessed to murder, her priest wouldn't report her to the cops, but he would forbid her from receiving communion until she had done appropriate penance – which would mean owning up to her crimes and doing jail time.

A sigh from Flyte, who sounded tense. 'I'll call you back in ten minutes,' she said.

Cassie knew Flyte well enough now to pick up that *something* was going on. Were she and the ginger gorilla still pursuing Ethan? Recalling his flashes of vulnerability stirred protective feelings. Despite his laid-back charm she could tell that Ethan was a bird with a broken wing – a combination she found dangerously appealing.

She went out back to retrieve Bronte from the freezer, where her body had been stored since her forensic post-mortem, to get her ready for collection by the undertakers.

Opening the zip of the body bag, she said, 'Hello there.'

Bronte's face was the colour of a freshwater pearl now, her lips a shade of lavender, her skin the texture of putty or bread dough. *Otherwordly*. Cassie could hardly claim they were friends – she had thrown away that opportunity forever when she was fourteen. But she hoped that Bronte no longer hated her.

'It's your funeral tomorrow,' she said. 'And you'll be at peace.'

Did Bronte's expression have a sardonic edge? As if saying, *At peace? With my murderer still walking around?*

Cassie touched the crucifix locket around Bronte's neck. 'Was your mum there with you the night you died?' she murmured. 'Did she bring you some kind of food, drink, medicine . . .?'

She leaned over her as if trying to inhale her last thoughts, desperate for some clue.

Nada.

Her phone rang: Flyte calling back.

'OK make it fast,' came the clipped tones. 'I'm out on police business.'

Always with the charm.

Cassie took a breath. 'I think you should consider the possibility that Bronte was killed by her mother.' A sound expressing outright disbelief came down the line. 'Listen, hear me out. Have you heard of a mental health disorder called FDIA? – Factitious Disorder Inflicted on Another.'

'Like those nurses who kill the babies they're supposed to be looking after?' Flyte gave an audible shiver.

'Yes. But the most common expression of it is when a mother persistently feeds her own child toxins to make them sick – sometimes even killing them.'

'You're saying she killed Bronte and her son, Alexander?' Flyte sounded incredulous. 'Why on earth would she do such a thing?'

'Who knows why crazy people do crazy things? The theory around FDIA is that the abuser has a desperate need to win attention and sympathy for themselves through the chronic sickness of their child. Chrysanthi was brought up in care, remember. She had no family, she made a disastrous marriage far too young, to a much older guy who turned out to be a serial philanderer. I'm no shrink but it sounds like the perfect profile of an FDIA abuser.'

'But it was Chrysanthi who kicked up the fuss about the police handling of Bronte's death, who complained to the IOPC that it hadn't been properly investigated!' said Flyte.

'Couldn't that be the action of a narcissist? "Poor me, I'm the victim"? Look, we know Bronte's brother Alexander died when he was three. Bronte suffered from stomach problems all her life – and her mother was obsessed with feeding her.' Remembering Bronte's lyric about a skeleton in the cupboard. 'I think she was digging around in her family history, perhaps because she was suspicious about how Alexander died, and suspected her mother. I think she might have been planning a trip to Cyprus to find out more.'

When Flyte fell silent Cassie thought she was taking it seriously, but when she spoke again it was in pure cop-speak – as if Cassie was just another member of the public. 'Thank you for sharing your thoughts. Rest assured that every lead is being considered.'

Engulfed by a wave of anger Cassie hung up.

Going back to Bronte, she eyed her sunken features guiltily.

'I tried,' she murmured. 'I don't know what else I can do.'

Suddenly she was pitched back to the school showers, feeling the hot water raining on her skin, Bronte's piercing scream like a jolt of electricity. A violent shudder went through her.

'I'm just so sorry, Bronte. For everything' – her words coming out in a rush. 'For not being your friend when you needed one. For being a snivelling little fucking coward when I should have been brave. I would do anything now, to change how I behaved. I think . . . I *wish* we could have been friends.'

She remembered what Althea Knowles had said about forgiving herself. But she knew that wasn't her call. That was down to Bronte.

'Can you forgive me?' she asked, holding her breath.

Nada.

Reaching down, she was starting to zip the body bag back up when her hand lost the power of movement. The fluorescent lights flared, forcing her eyes closed, and she was enveloped by that old, familiar sensation. *A feeling of reality slipping . . . A buzzing and tingling in the air . . . the smell of electricity you got before a storm . . .*

Opening her eyes, Cassie stared down at Bronte. Her mauve-coloured lips didn't move but what floated up was a single word, the tone teasing.

'*Friend!*'

FLYTE

At the undertakers, Streaky and Flyte waited in reception; Streaky walking up and down, whistling show tunes, and basically being eighteen-stone of human irritant, while Flyte tried to ignore him. When Streaky had called George to say they had a few questions he said he was here to finalise the funeral arrangements.

It was another twenty minutes before George emerged from the office, followed by his ex-wife. He didn't look especially surprised by their presence, and his wife looked dazed with grief, not quite present.

The undertaker showed them into another office, and Chrysanthi followed them in. DI Bacon told him, 'It was you we wanted to chat to, George.'

But he just waved a hand and said, 'I've got nothing to hide from my wife. I'll do anything I can to help you find my daughter's killer.'

'Something has come up of relevance to the investigation. You told us that you had no prior knowledge of your daughter having had any serious allergic reaction, right?' asked Streaky.

'Yes that's right.' He looked mildly curious but Flyte could detect no signs of anxiety.

'We have evidence that you were present last September when Bronte suffered exactly such an attack.'

Flyte saw him throw a look at his ex-wife, but she couldn't decipher his expression.

'You mean the time she was poorly at her flat and the ambulance came?'

'That's the one,' said Streaky with just a hint of sarcasm.

George looked confused. 'The truth is, she called me, drunk, saying that she'd taken an overdose of something. I drove straight over there and called 999 and made her throw up the pills she'd taken. The paramedics came and gave her some kind of injection.'

'The injection was to counteract anaphylactic shock,' said Flyte. 'An extreme allergic reaction to something.'

'I didn't know that.' George shook his head. 'They treated her in her bedroom and wouldn't tell me anything because of patient confidentiality. All they said was she should go to hospital. I tried to persuade her but she refused point-blank – the press were already on her back by then and she didn't want any more bad publicity.'

'You're saying she had no symptoms of anaphylaxis?' Streaky pressed. 'Shortness of breath, swelling in the mouth and throat?'

George raised his hands. 'I remember her breathing was bad but I'm no doctor. I thought it was the pills that made her ill. She never had any allergies as a child' – turning to Chrysanthi who'd uttered not a word during this exchange – 'did she?'

She shook her head. 'Never,' she said. 'She was a very sick child sometimes, but no, no allergies.'

Flyte silently replayed the paramedics' recollections: believing Bronte to be displaying symptoms of a serious allergic reaction they had administered adrenaline. But they'd also said that they wouldn't have shared the diagnosis with her father without her express permission.

Now Chrysanthi turned to Streaky. 'Why are you wasting your time pursuing my husband?' she asked, quiet fury in her voice. 'I can assure you he had nothing to do with my daughter's death.'

'How can you be sure of that?' asked Flyte.

Chrysanthi bit her bottom lip and shot him a look before dropping her gaze into her lap. 'Because he was with me that night.'

Jumping Jehoshaphat!

Flyte gathered herself. 'The whole night . . .?'

'Yes,' said Chrysanthi, with a trace of irritation. 'Have you never heard of a married couple spending the night together?'

Flyte tried to imagine the devout and dowdy Chrysanthi having a night of passion with serial philanderer George, the husband she didn't live with and appeared to loathe.

'I've been telling you from the start if you would only listen,' Chrysanthi told them, shaking her head pityingly, 'it was that boyfriend of hers.'

'Those two still shagging?' Streaky said, shaking his head. 'I've heard everything now.'

They were on their way back to the nick, Streaky exiting the car park with his usual insouciance.

'Do you think they're telling the truth?' asked Flyte. 'Or could they be in it together?' – her eye fixed on the road ahead and her foot pressed to an invisible brake pedal.

'Why on earth would they kill their daughter?' asked Streaky as he navigated a roundabout one-handed. 'What possible motive could they have?'

Flyte wasn't about to share Cassie's theory, that Chrysanthi killed her children to win sympathy, because she simply didn't buy it: couldn't see her killing her own daughter – *both* her children – in cold blood. 'If it was George – whatever his motive – then why would she give him an alibi? Even if they are having... relations occasionally it's clear she can't stand the guy.'

'You do hear about people having hate sex after a nasty break-up,' said Streaky, with a man of the world nod.

'I suppose she can't sleep with anyone else, because in the eyes of her church she's still married, and will remain so until he dies,' said Flyte. 'Maybe her priest is pressing her to reconcile with him?'

'Maybe.' Streaky shook his head.

Flyte recalled Bronte's planned trip to Cyprus, and Cassie's suggestion that she'd been investigating her family history. *But so what?* It felt more like coincidence than a basis for any plausible motive. How had Cassie come by that information anyway? *It could only have been from Ethan.* The thought prompted a nasty jolt: a feeling that Flyte had to admit bore a strong resemblance to jealousy.

Back at the nick they found Craig and Becca both wearing long faces.

'What's up?' asked Streaky. 'Did somebody's hamster die?'

'Ethan has an alibi for the time Bronte died. A real one this time,' said Craig. 'Tell them, Becca.'

'Ethan's bandmate admitted to lying about Ethan sleeping at his place in Holloway that night.' Becca looked forlorn. 'But he did it because Ethan actually spent the night in Camden with the girlfriend of the band's drummer.'

'And his latest version of events stands up?' asked Streaky.

Becca nodded miserably. 'I spoke to her myself and she confirmed it. She broke down, said she'd have to tell her boyfriend she's been cheating on him.'

Flyte felt a surge of anger at Ethan: not just for spinning them a line to cover his back, but on Cassie's behalf too.

Chapter Thirty-Nine

Cassie had booked the day of Bronte's funeral as holiday so she could watch the coverage from the boat. Naturally, the service at St Ioannas would be a private affair, but the funeral cortege and guests arriving was being live-streamed by a US-based online music and entertainment channel.

She wouldn't be watching alone though – she had an unexpected guest in the form of Ethan, who'd called to ask if he could come over.

'Thanks for this,' he said as he took a seat in the cabin, and she was touched to see that he had shaved and wore a clean shirt, presumably to mark the seriousness of the occasion. 'George would probably have put me on the list for inside but I wasn't about to give social media fresh meat – you know, "evil junkie boyfriend attends funeral of his victim".' Taking the cup of tea she handed him, he added, 'And I didn't want to be on my own.'

As she sat beside him, close enough to feel the warmth of his arm, she realised that her crazy little crush on him had totally evaporated. Ethan had edgy good looks and charisma by the bucketload – but even she could see that he ought to come with a relationship health warning tattooed on his forehead.

What had she been thinking? A lot of it had been their shared connection with Bronte, heightened by Cassie's guilt about the bullying at school. And it wouldn't be the first time that she'd jumped into a new relationship in a bid to paper over her feelings about the previous one. She did still wonder if she'd done the right thing, calling time on her and Archie.

The streamed footage stood in stark contrast with her memories of the Amy Winehouse funeral, back when she'd still been at school. Although she'd been a far bigger star than Bronte, that had been a low-key affair, with only a modest gathering of respectful fans and well-wishers who had kept their distance. This time there was a noisy scrum of spectators and the police had thrown a ring of steel barriers around Agios Ioannis fronted by officers in hi-vis jackets to keep them at bay, and she saw four TV cameras and a bunch of other press in a kind of pen off to one side of the church entrance.

Seeing the funeral cortege arrive, flanked by two motorcycle cops, Cassie lowered the volume so they didn't have to listen to the inane chatter of the presenters. A sea of arms went up from the crowd to capture the moment on their smartphones. 'Look!' she told Ethan, pointing to a neon pink head at the front of the crowd filming herself as Bronte's hearse drew up in the background.

'Oh yeah!' he said. 'That's that Charly girl whose post got me a kicking, right?'

'What happened about that?' asked Cassie.

'She took the posts down.' He shrugged. 'If I could afford a libel lawyer I'd be a few hundred grand richer by now.'

'Do the cops still think you had something to do with it?'

'Nah,' he said. 'I had to give them the name of the girl I was with that night' – he sent her an awkward look. 'She's the girlfriend of our drummer. So as you can imagine I'm persona non grata with the band, but hey, she dumped him and we're legit now.' He sounded more resigned than thrilled by the outcome.

'But you're not watching this with her?' Cassie asked lightly.

'She wouldn't like it.' He gave a half-shake of his head. 'You cared about Bronte. And put yourself in danger to try and find out what happened to her.'

The back of the hearse was so full of flowers you could only catch glimpses of the dark wood coffin within. The report cut to a close-up, filling the screen with the words 'Goodbye Baby Girl' spelled out in red roses on a background of white lilies. The limo directly behind, which presumably carried George and Chrysanthi, had heavily tinted windows protecting the privacy of its occupants.

As the hearse turned into the churchyard entrance a shower of flowers thrown by the crowd fell on and around it, some getting crushed under the wheels.

Once the cortege of cars was inside, a couple of church flunkies came and shut the gates. Cassie threw a look at Ethan and was shocked to see tears spilling from his eyes.

'Oh Ethan,' she said, putting a hand on his arm.

'I'm all right.' Taking a breath, he put up a hand. 'I know I was a totally shit boyfriend but, you know, I really did love her.'

She filled two shot glasses with iced vodka from the freezer.

Raising her glass, she said, 'To Bronte. One of the brave ones.'

'To Bronte,' he echoed, and they both knocked back their drinks.

After Ethan had left Cassie couldn't relax, her mind constantly circling back to her suspicion that Chrysanthi could have been a lifelong abuser, poisoning Bronte since childhood to cause her 'stomach problems'. What if she had contaminated one of the many home-cooked meals she delivered to Bronte after she'd left home? Not with a toxin this time, but with something she had discovered her daughter was seriously allergic to? Even a tiny trace of allergen, hidden in a stew or similar, could have been enough to trigger anaphylaxis.

Then all she had to do was fail to call an ambulance – and suck up the sympathy that would be lavished on a mother who'd lost a second child – the child she was no longer able to control. Bronte heading out to the balcony in a desperate bid to get air wasn't in the script, but the stronger and taller Chrysanthi would have been more than capable of tipping her over, especially with her daughter in the throes of an anaphylactic attack.

Cassie spent the rest of the day down an online rabbit-hole exploring every conceivable known allergen. In addition to the hundreds of foods and flavourings that could cause a serious reaction in the vulnerable, she discovered you could be dangerously allergic to coins, sunlight, textiles, any number of different insect stings – even to your own sweat. Given that anaphylaxis had been incredibly rare until recent years, it was clear that something in the modern lifestyle was scrambling the normal programming of the human immune system.

Cassie wished she'd hung around when Curzon had opened Bronte's stomach in case the contents had held any clue. Then she remembered the crime scene pics that Tina the CSM had printed out for her right at the start. *Where were they . . . ?* Half an hour later she'd unearthed them from the Jenga tower of paperwork stood on her bedroom chest of drawers.

She'd been totally focused on the balcony images before, but now she flicked impatiently past them to find the interiors.

Plucking one out, she murmured, 'Tina, you're a star!' It showed what had clearly been the contents of Bronte's fridge lined up on the kitchen worktop. Flattening the printout on the table she looked for any Tupperware or foil container, the type of thing that might hold the remains of a home-cooked meal. But there was nothing like that – the only containers being jars of mustard and salad dressing, and an ice cream carton. She sighed: remembering Chrysanthi saying that before the police finally called it as a murder she'd been allowed to take 'mementos' like the locket from her daughter's flat, so could easily have removed anything she'd previously missed that might incriminate her.

Cassie wondered whether to call Flyte again, to try to persuade her, but was put off by her outright disbelief from last time. Her anger at Flyte's reaction had subsided. It was totally understandable that someone who had experienced losing a baby would find it near-impossible to comprehend a mother killing her own child.

FLYTE

The day after Bronte's funeral Streaky held a case conference. 'I don't need to tell you that we are drinking in the last-chance saloon here. It's been three weeks since Bronte's murder and there's a limit to how long Borough will fund an incident room when we've delivered jack-shit so far as a meaningful lead is concerned.'

While disapproving of the vulgarity, Flyte couldn't argue with the sentiment. And once the incident room was downsized she'd be back to the IOPC, interviewing intellectually challenged plods all day, a prospect that she realised filled her with gloom.

Streaky summed up where they were. 'So we have a pretty solid picture of the order of events. The night Bronte dies she lets somebody into her flat – somebody we assume she trusts. Someone who knows her well enough to feed her something she is dangerously allergic to with the aim of killing her.' After a pause, he went on, 'Now, we know that her father was with her when she suffered anaphylaxis before but it appears the paramedics gave only Bronte their diagnosis, not him – although of course she could have shared it with George, or anyone else, at any stage afterwards. In any case, his estranged wife has given him an alibi, and it's not easy to see why either of them would murder their only daughter. As you all know, Ethan Fox is out of the frame, this time with a genuine alibi.'

'So what's our new plan of attack, boss?' asked Craig.

'I want you overseeing another shot at door-to-door, see if any possible witness was missed in the last sweep, taking the radius from Bronte's flat out wider.'

'Boss.'

'Becca, you do another trawl of her mobile records and emails, going further back. Any contacts, friends, lovers, we might not know about.'

He stood up and straightened his tie. 'I've got a meeting over at Borough HQ with the brass, so I'll see you all later on.' Flyte caught the ghost of a wink that he sent her and mouthed *Good luck* back at him.

Shortly afterwards, Craig surprised her by sidling over to her desk to consult her on the list of door-to-door targets to revisit. Then Becca called her over to look at something on her computer. Even though Flyte was no longer a ranking officer, in Streaky's absence the team seemed to be treating her as his de facto deputy, as if she were part of the team.

'This is Bronte's email inbox,' Becca said. 'Obviously it's ninety per cent junk, but we check it every day and a new message arrived yesterday that I thought you should see.'

The email came from the Harley Street gastroenterologist to whom Bronte had sent an enquiry about an appointment. Attached was a receipt showing that just three days before her death she had paid his fee in cash – presumably to protect her identity – and two further files: a PDF leaflet titled 'Living with Crohn's Disease' and a document with Sophia's name that was password-protected.

So Bronte had consulted an expert after all – and after tests they had clearly diagnosed her as suffering from Crohn's. Although it was hard to see how it might be relevant to the case, Flyte believed in leaving not even the smallest piece of gravel unturned. She checked her watch. 'Let's get onto the coroner's office and ask them to apply for her records – today if humanly possible.' Coroners had the powers of a judge and could compel healthcare providers to release documentation that could be relevant to an investigation of a suspicious death.

'Yes, boss, sorry, I mean Phyllida.' Becca looked flustered.

Flyte turned to walk away to hide the blush suffusing her cheeks.

Boss. She had to admit she liked the sound of that.

Chapter Forty

'Terrible, just terrible,' Babcia was saying on the phone. Chrysanthi had been to her flat that morning for coffee and told her all about the funeral.

Cassie was on her way into work when her grandmother called, and could tell from her heartfelt tone that she needed to talk.

'It must remind you . . .' Cassie didn't need to finish the sentence. Babcia had had to face the funeral of her own daughter – Cassie's mother – murdered in her twenties, just like Bronte.

'It was the worst day of my life.' She paused. 'But I realise now that I was wrong not to take you to the service. Even though you were so young, it might have been helpful for you to say goodbye to your mama properly.'

'You were just trying to protect me,' said Cassie staunchly. But her grandmother was right. The way her mum and dad had just *disappeared* when she was four had cast a lifelong shadow over her life – might even be the root of her difficulty in maintaining relationships, ones with the living at least.

'Did Chrysanthi say anything more about Bronte's death being a punishment from God?' she asked.

'Hmmm?' Babcia was off in the past, in her own memories.

'She told you that Bronte's death was some kind of payment for sin?' prompted Cassie.

'I don't remember saying anything like that,' she said.

No point contradicting her. 'I assume that spooky old priest did the funeral service?' No doubt his funeral oration would have had plenty to say about sin. 'Not much tea and sympathy from him I'll bet.'

'Oh you non-believers wouldn't understand,' retorted Babcia. 'We don't want tea and sympathy – the comforts of religion are its rules, its constancy. She *relies* on Father Michaelides. When she left here she was going straight to church to see him, to make *konfesja*.'

Half an hour later Cassie was pushing at the massive dark-oak door of St Ioannis, her pulse tapping in her throat. She'd just phoned work and told Doug a rare lie – that she'd had to wait in for a workman.

She had to see Chrysanthi, to try to find out if her terrible intuition about her harming her children might be right – for Bronte's sake. Maybe it was flat-out crazy, but she felt if she could just see Chrysanthi's face again, maybe hint at what she knew, it would reveal the truth.

Inside, the air was hazy, and smelled resinous and faintly acrid – like the aftermath of a forest fire. It must be the spent incense burned at Bronte's funeral: she recognised the piney-earthy smell of myrrh, part of funeral rites that went back thousands of years to ancient Greece.

Constancy. She'd never admit it to her grandmother, but she wasn't immune to its appeal.

Raising her eyes to the huge, glowering face of Jesus in his sea of gold she gave him a nod. He wouldn't object to her mission, would he?

Two oldish ladies were sitting in the front pew praying, but otherwise the church was empty. Looking around for the confession box, her gaze fell on an ornate structure topped by four elaborate pinnacles that stood against the wall of a side aisle. As she got closer a low murmuring from inside and the sight of the old priest's robed legs beneath the curtain on the right-hand side confirmed it.

She took a seat in the empty pew set against the wall beside the box, presumably for those awaiting confession, but despite straining her ears she could hear nothing of the conversation within – couldn't tell if the female-sounding murmur belonged to Chrysanthi. As a child she'd gone to confession now and again at her grandmother's gentle urging, but always on the understanding that once she was a teenager she could choose to stop. *I came to this country because people are free to follow their own beliefs here, not to impose mine on you.* And Babcia had been as good as her word: after the age of thirteen Cassie never went again.

While she was waiting, she got a text from Phyllida Flyte. It said, *It looks like Bronte had Crohn's disease. Connected to anaphylaxis?* Cassie knew next to nothing about Crohn's, except that it was an inflammatory bowel disease, but before she could text back, someone emerged from the confession box.

It wasn't Chrysanthi but an elderly woman. She smiled approvingly at Cassie and tipped her head towards the box, as if to say, *Your turn.*

Ah Jeez, had she missed Chrysanthi?

On impulse she went inside, and pulling the curtain closed behind her, settled on the hard bench within. A rectangle of oak in the partition facing her was pulled back by an invisible hand to reveal the granite-hewn profile of Father Michaelides behind a grille. Even partially obscured as he was, the sight of him made her feel jumpy.

He made the sign of the cross towards her before saying, 'What have you come to tell God before my witness?'

Given how long it had been since she'd been through this malarkey Cassie was surprised to find the words springing easily to her lips. 'Bless me, Father, for I have sinned. It has been ...' she dropped to a mumble '... years since my last confession.'

He raised a bony hand. 'You are Roman Catholic. And it has been *how long*?'

She squirmed: obviously the script was different here. Maybe this wasn't one of her better ideas. 'Yes, umm, fourteen years? I'm here because ... because I'm marrying a boy from a Greek family and I want to convert. I thought this was a good first step.' Feeling a niggle of guilt at fibbing to a priest.

He tugged at his beard. 'Hmm. You would have first to go through many months of catechesis.'

'Of course, Father.' *Sounds like fun.*

When he fell silent, she realised it was her turn. 'I have committed venial sins. Impatience with work colleagues. Sins of lust' – seeing him nod sagely at that one. 'Sometimes I am dishonest but for good reasons ...' It didn't hurt to cover today's transgressions. 'But most of all I'm worried for my soul because I think I know someone, a woman, who has committed a crime.'

'A venial or a mortal sin?'

'Mortal, Father.' Leaving a pause. 'She is a devout believer, and I believe she will have confessed this sin to her priest but ... I'm concerned. I think she is a very troubled woman but she can't receive the treatment she needs because of the seal of the confessional.'

'It is not for you to judge.' He sounded testy. 'It is for the priest and God to rule on such matters.'

'Even if she killed her own child?'

He became utterly still for a moment, before slamming the oak rectangle shut. Then the curtain to her box was whipped aside to reveal the black-robed figure filling the doorway, his face contorted in fury.

Chapter Forty-One

'It's you!' he hissed. 'A godless creature come here to tell lies and make trouble!'

Reaching in, he grabbed her upper arm and yanked at it, his face twisted in fury. 'Out harlot! Out of God's house!'

His bony grip, the shock of her bodily space being invaded, pitched her right back to SkAR's dressing room, the powerlessness she had felt. By instinct, she braced her feet against the doorway, but he just pulled harder.

'Father!' Approaching footsteps and a woman's voice.

The priest tightened his grip, then suddenly released it, which sent her crashing back into the side of the confession box.

Cassie took a moment to try to calm her breathing before coming out. The voice belonged to Chrysanthi, who was clad in her usual dowdy gear – a shapeless beige raincoat and a tweedy skirt that reached just below her knees, the least flattering length.

'Cassandra,' she said flatly. 'What are you doing here?'

'I need to talk to you,' said Cassie.

A look passed between Chrysanthi and the priest and then, turning to Cassie, he raised his long index finger up to her face like he was issuing a curse. 'Those who bear false witness in the sight of God will meet a reckoning.'

Still trembling, Cassie watched him sweep away up the side-aisle. She rubbed her upper arm, which would bear the bruise marks of his bony fingers – *like stigmata*. Recalling that he'd denied a woman communion because he suspected her of using contraception, it struck her that, for all their outward differences, that old bastard and SkAR were fundamentally the same: they both saw woman as objects to be controlled in whatever way men decided.

They took a seat in the pew next to the box and Cassie said, 'To be honest, I was just curious, you know, to see what confessing would feel like after all these years. I didn't mean any disrespect.'

'What is it you want?' Chrysanthi asked, eyeing Cassie through narrowed eyes.

'Look, I met someone who knew Sophia. I think he told her things about Cyprus and something about her family history – that is yours, or George's.' Cassie was watching her face carefully. 'Something that upset her?'

'I have no idea what that could be,' said Chrysanthi, smoothing her skirt over her knees. She would have made a good poker player – but was that a look of alarm that had briefly flared in her eyes?

'Did you know she was thinking of going to Cyprus, to do some family research?' *Pure conjecture, but she wanted to see Chrysanthi's reaction.*

'She never said anything to me about it.' But the way she dropped her gaze told another story.

So Bronte really had planned a trip to investigate her family's history. Had she quizzed her mother about Alexander's death? Cassie remembered the lyric in her song 'Skeleton': 'You feed me, always feed me, but what you feed me is lies'.

'I wondered if it might have had something to do with Alexander?' Cassie went on. 'When did he start having health problems?'

'Why would you ask me that?' Chrysanthi's face twisted in grief, but her eyes remained watchful.

Cassie realised there was something different about her – despite her anxiety over the questioning she was sitting a little taller today. She seemed oddly . . . *at peace* for a woman who had just buried her daughter. Was it simply the comfort that Cassie knew the funeral rites could bring those left behind? Or some twisted sense of liberation in having rid herself of motherhood?

'It was terrible luck having two children with serious health conditions, wasn't it?'

Putting her hands into her coat pockets, Chrysanthi turned her whole body away from Cassie, and started intoning something to herself in Greek. Staring at her back, Cassie picked up the word *hamartia* again. Meaning sin, or sin offering.

Sacrifice.

'When was Alexander diagnosed with beta thalassemia?' Cassie pressed. 'Was that while you were still in Cyprus?'

Chrysanthi had her head down, still murmuring to herself in Greek. Then she appeared to make a sort of tugging movement before half turning back to Cassie, her face pale as death.

Cassie flinched to see Chrysanthi's expression. It reminded her of avenging Furies of Greek myth. *Pitiless. Implacable.*

'It wasn't *bad luck*,' she said. 'It was a punishment for sin.'

Only then did Cassie see that Chrysanthi was holding something. Something metallic that winked as it caught the light.

Oh Christ. She shrank back along the narrow pew, trying to scramble to her feet.

Then the harsh clatter of metal on stone. Looking down, Cassie saw a bright crimson sash unspooling across the flagstones, pooling in the mortar joints. Still her brain struggled to catch up, until she saw the steady trickle of blood falling from the fingertips of Chrysanthi's other hand.

'Sins of the blood can never be washed away,' she said, with a terrible smile, before slipping off the pew in slow motion onto the floor.

Fuck fuck fuck!

Bending over Chrysanthi, Cassie pulled up her sleeve to reveal a long gaping gash from inside her forearm down to her wrist.

No!

Part of her brain went into analytical mode, assessing the damage. It was the worst kind of wrist slash – longitudinal cuts, two of them, each around ten centimetres long. Going by the pulsing flow, Chrysanthi had laid open her radial artery in more than one place.

Cassie used her fingers to apply pressure to quell the bleeding. But the wounds were just too long. As she staunched one leak another would appear, like a grisly version of whack-a-mole. Within seconds her fingers were slippery and useless.

'Father!!' she shouted, her panicked voice echoing in that cavernous space.

The pool of crimson on the flagstones had already grown alarmingly large. *Just like the cartoon speech bubble of Bronte's blood on the towpath.* Hypovolemic shock, followed by cardiac arrest was a matter of minutes away.

Father Michaelides came flapping up the aisle like a giant bat, exclaiming in Greek. Over his robes he now wore a long blue scarf, decorated with gold circles and crosses. Without a word, Cassie yanked it off his neck and in a few swift moves made a tourniquet round Chrysanthi's upper arm and tightened it as much as she could.

The blood flow slowed – *but not enough.*

'Help me!' she shouted at the priest.

Together they hauled on the scarf to tighten the knot.

Chapter Forty-Two

Choosing to have the church janitor drive them to A & E rather than wait who knew how long for an ambo had been the right decision. Chrysanthi desperately needed intravenous fluids, and with the tourniquet slowing the blood loss to a dribble, Cassie gambled on speed over the risk of moving her.

Their entrance to A & E must have looked like a scene from a Tarantino movie: the black-robed priest with the blood-spattered beard and the pierced punky gal, her leather jacket caked in blood, half carrying a white-faced woman between them – her tweed skirt and tights streaked in blood, looking like a sacrificial offering.

Chrysanthi had been whisked straight into resus, leaving Cassie and Father Michaelides sitting side by side on uncomfortable chairs in no less uncomfortable silence. In Cassie's lap lay the box-cutter knife she'd picked up from the church floor, clogged with gore and wrapped in the priest's ruined scarf. It might be needed by the cops – *or the pathologist*.

Chrysanthi might be guilty of murder, but Cassie couldn't face the thought of her dying. There had been too much death already.

Again and again, she pictured the spreading pool of blood, trying to calculate its volume: more than a litre, probably closer to two, getting on for half an adult female's supply, making Chrysanthi's chances of survival fifty-fifty at best. She had seen hundreds of deaths-by-haemorrhage in the mortuary; could hear Prof Arculus saying, *When the heart runs out of blood, it's like a car running out of petrol.*

'I'm sorry about your scarf,' she told the priest, really just to break the awkward silence.

'It's an epitrachelion' – sending her a frosty look.

She narrowed her eyes, dredging up her Greek. 'Oh right *Epi-trachelion*: "upon the neck". Cool.'

Half an hour later, the registrar emerged from backstage.

'You're ... Mrs Angelo-pou-los's niece right?' he asked, referring to her admission notes.

'That's right,' she said.

The priest muttered something in Greek, probably some hellfire curse against lying harlots, but he didn't grass her up.

The news was as good as could be expected: Chrysanthi was still only semi-conscious, but out of immediate danger.

'She's being monitored while we give her blood and IV fluids,' the doc went on, eyeing the pair of them.

'And the arm injury?' Remembering the way the artery had kept springing leaks, she suppressed a shudder: witnessing a dramatic injury in a living person had been a radically different experience to eviscerating a dead body.

'A vascular surgeon will be coming down to assess her. Do you have a contact number for her next of kin?'

Cassie gave it to him. Chrysanthi might not like it but she was still married to George and it felt wrong to keep him in the dark.

With the doctor gone, the old priest unfolded himself from the seat like a waking bat and left. It was a relief to see the bony old back of him, trailing stares and whispers as he trundled out of A & E on his invisible castors.

George wasn't picking up, so after leaving him a message Cassie decided to stay on: knowing Chrysanthi didn't have any other family she could hardly abandon her.

She was on her third battery-acid coffee from the machine, when the automatic doors opened to admit a blonde Valkyrie on a mission: Phyllida Flyte, the big ginger cop trailing in her wake.

Flyte's searchlight stare raked the room, her whole body tense with worry, until she caught sight of Cassie. A look of relief flooded her face and Cassie's heart did the can-can in her chest.

Ohhh, I see.

Flyte came and sat next to her, while the ginger cop stayed standing at a discreet distance.

'The priest called us,' said Flyte, her ice-blue eyes soft.

'He just left.'

'Tell me what happened?'

Cassie told her as best she could, stumbling over her words: her memory of events non-linear and fragmented, like shards of a broken mirror.

'Why would she do such a thing?' Flyte asked gently.

Cassie shook her head slowly. 'Who knows? Grief? She just buried her daughter.'

Frowning, Flyte leaned closer and spoke in a murmur. 'But you told me you thought it was her who murdered Bronte. And her twin brother.'

'I don't know, Phyllida. That was just a wild theory.' In truth, since Chrysanthi's desperate act she no longer had any idea what was going on. 'Could you take this?' – holding up the box cutter wrapped in the bloodstained epitrachelion.

'Sure' – putting out her hand, before pulling it back. 'Actually, DI Bacon will need to take it. Chain of custody.'

Of course, Flyte wasn't a cop anymore.

Just then the unexpected sound of 'London Calling' filled the waiting area and they both turned to see Bacon answering his mobile phone.

The call was brief and after hanging up he met Flyte's eyes and tipped his head towards the door. He looked sombre and his meaning was crystal: *We're out of here.*

Chapter Forty-Three

Just after Flyte and Bacon had left, a different doctor, wearing a more self-important air than the A & E registrar, emerged to take Cassie into a side room.

He introduced himself, his eyes sliding over her piercings. 'Mrs Angelopoulos needs urgent surgery to ligate the radial artery. Put more simply—'

'—you're going to sacrifice her radial artery by tying it off,' said Cassie. 'Will that have any vascular consequences?'

'Are you . . . a medical student?' His look of blank bafflement reminded Cassie of one of her grandmother's favourite Polish phrases: *Like a dog that's been shown a card trick.*

She stared right back. 'Nope, just a lowly mortuary tech. But I've probably seen more complete forearm dissections than you have.'

He gathered himself. 'Right, well, her radial artery is beyond repair and she's very lucky not to have ruptured the ulnar artery. Only time will tell whether there's severe nerve damage, but with luck she'll regain most of the use of her left hand with physio.' He looked at her. 'But only if I can operate soon.'

'She hasn't consented.'

He shook his head.

Oh boy. Since Chrysanthi was a danger to herself the doctors would probably section her to stop her leaving the hospital, but they still couldn't operate on her against her will.

On the ward, Chrysanthi's bed wasn't curtained off and a nurse was hovering. *Suicide watch*.

'I'll leave you two on your own,' she told Cassie with a meaningful look. 'But I'll be just over there' – with a nod towards the nursing station.

Cassie sat in the bedside armchair. Chrysanthi was hooked up to an IV drip and to a monitor displaying her vital signs. In place of Cassie's rudimentary tourniquet was a proper pressurised version and going by the candlewax pallor of Chrysanthi's left hand below the bandages it was pumped so tight as to be seriously uncomfortable – not to mention damaging to her nerves and blood vessels the longer it stayed on.

Cassie smiled at her.

'Listen, Chrysanthi, I know we don't know each other very well. But you really need to give consent for this op – or you could end up losing your arm, or even dying.'

Chrysanthi raised her good hand in a dismissive gesture. Translation: *Like I care*. It was clear that the minute she got the opportunity she'd be finishing the job she started in St Ioannis.

How to argue with someone who had just graphically demonstrated their lack of interest in living? Cassie pictured her wounds – those long cuts right down the mainline had aimed for swift and unstoppable bleed-out. Which is what would've happened if Cassie hadn't been there.

She found herself thinking, *What would Flyte say in this situation?* Visualising those ice-blue laser-like eyes she got her answer: *Put the screws on.*

'Dying by your own hand is against the teaching of your church, isn't it?' she said. 'Which means that if you try again and succeed they won't bury you in their churchyard with Sophia. Do you want to end up in a random plot in Golders Green cemetery, miles away from where your daughter is buried?'

Going by the tremor of regret that crossed Chrysanthi's face, that had hit home.

Cassie pressed her advantage. 'If you choose to live out your natural life you will be laid to rest alongside Sophia one day. Isn't that worth living for?'

'You don't understand!' Chrysanthi burst out. 'It's too late. There has been *too much sin*!' She banged her good arm on the bedspread for emphasis, her dark eyes under those winged brows boring into Cassie, as though willing her to understand.

Cassie got the strangest feeling – that she knew nothing, and the little she did know she'd been viewing as if through a series of blurred and shifting filters. If Chrysanthi hadn't killed her own children then who had, and what was this terrible sin that haunted her?

The nurse came to check Chrysanthi's vitals and her IV line, and Cassie took the opportunity to duck out, miming that she needed to make a call. Outside the doors of the ward, she walked up and down for a couple of minutes before pulling up Flyte's last text, the one saying that Bronte had been diagnosed with Crohn's disease. What Chrysanthi had said after slashing her artery came back to her: *Sins of the blood can never be washed away.*

Then she called Xavier, a mate in the specialist DNA lab which the mortuary sometimes had dealings with, praying that he'd answer.

'Hey, Xav. Can I pick your brains about something?'

Ten minutes later, she was back at Chrysanthi's bedside with a heavy heart – and a powerful conviction about the 'sin' that had led to her desperate act.

'I think I know what happened,' she told her gently, once they were alone again. She was viewing Chrysanthi through new eyes, and with profound compassion. 'And I am so sorry I ever suspected you. You were a loving mother to your two children and you didn't deserve to have them taken from you.' She put a tentative hand on Chrysanthi's uninjured right arm. 'I think you need to share what happened with someone who understands' – her tone and emphasis signalling *not Father Michaelides*. 'Someone who knows what it's like to grow up as an orphan.'

Chrysanthi didn't move her arm from under Cassie's hand. She returned her look, saying, 'Nobody can ever know these . . . things. I will not have my daughter's name besmirched for my sins.'

'You have my absolute promise it will go no further. I swear it, on the soul of my mother.' Cassie crossed herself to demonstrate the unbreakable nature of her vow. In any event, whatever Chrysanthi told her would be inadmissible in any court of law. But if she just took that first step perhaps she might eventually come round to talking to the cops. To ensure that punishment fell on the guilty.

Still Chrysanthi hesitated, and Cassie realised she would have to begin the story for her.

'How old were you when he first came to find you?' No need to utter his name.

George.

'Fifteen,' she said. 'A little girl.'

'So you were still in care.'

A nod. 'In a children's home on the outskirts of Larnaca.'

'But permitted to work in the flower shop, at the weekend?'

'Yes, they approved of us getting "labour market experience" ready for when we left.' She plucked at the bedcover. 'I suppose he told you that was where we met.'

A nod.

'A lie, of course. The first time I ever saw him was in the children's home. I remember him arriving and the female carers all fussing over him, this big handsome man, tanned from years working on the cruise boats. He was a captain by then and charming from dealing with so many foreigners. *Cosmopolitan.*' The way she said the word didn't make it sound like a good thing.

'And what did they tell you?'

Chrysanthi raised her gaze from the bedcover 'That I was one of the lucky ones, because my *daddy* had come to take me home.' Decades of loathing packed into the word.

There it was. The thing that Cassie had taken so stupidly long to work out: George was Chrysanthi's father, their 'marriage' a sham, and their two children the product of incest. When Cassie had picked the brains of Xav, her buddy at the DNA lab, he had confirmed that beta thalassemia, which had killed Bronte's brother, was a rare autosomal recessive disease or ARD.

A child from two unrelated parents who both happened to have the faulty gene that caused it could inherit them in the roulette-wheel spin of genetic blending. But between *first-degree* relatives like father and child the chances of their offspring having an ARD rocketed.

Consanguinity, he had called it. From the Latin for shared blood.

Bronte hadn't inherited an ARD but she had inherited Crohn's – another condition with a strong genetic component, which meant it had a high incidence among cultures where marrying relatives like cousins was still common practice.

The chances of Bronte and Alexander both suffering from different genetically determined diseases was almost unthinkable – *unless their parents were closely related*.

From that realisation, everything else slipped into place: the fact that Chrysanthi and George were both tall while Bronte had been tiny – a common feature of consanguinity ... the wedding photo in which they looked so strikingly alike ... even those winged eyebrows they shared. And of course it explained the vitriolic level of hatred that Chrysanthi directed towards George. It wasn't a result of his philandering but because her 'husband' was also her father and abuser. And both father and grandfather to Bronte and Alexander.

'You don't have to tell me any more, unless you want to,' Cassie told her, seeking those dark eyes – *George's eyes*.

But with a lift of the shoulder Chrysanthi went on, 'My mama was only sixteen when she died of complications after giving birth to me and by the time I was a teenager I'd given up hope of my father ever coming back. To begin with there was the occasional birthday card from some foreign port but that didn't last. But when he finally turned up, I was caught up in the excitement, of course. The other girls were so envious of me. The day

I left they lined up to wave as I got whisked away in a fancy car by this man who looked like a film star. It was like a wedding.'

She fell silent, looking up at the ceiling, remembering.

'He had saved most of his wages all those years away at sea. He took me all over Cyprus, swimming on beautiful beaches, drives into the mountains, always staying at the most luxurious hotels. He bought me silk dresses from expensive shops in Larnaca, and told me I looked just like my mama.' She shook her head, a look of shame on her face. 'And I went along with it.'

'Of course you did!' said Cassie fiercely. 'He was *grooming* you. He was the adult, he had all the power.'

'You don't understand.' She turned to Cassie. 'I fell in love with him. At the start.'

'Listen, Chrysanthi, nowadays people would completely understand. A child without parents, in care all your life. This glamorous man you've never seen before turns up to save you, to lavish you with love and affection – of course you thought you were in love with him!' Remembering George comparing the young Chrysanthi to a flower, she got an image of a beautiful peony, but wilting for lack of water.

There was a long pause before Chrysanthi went on, her voice barely above a whisper, 'We always had separate bedrooms. Then on my sixteenth birthday he booked us into a five-star hotel in Paphos where the rooms had a connecting door. We had champagne at dinner – my first ever alcohol – and it made me tipsy. That night he opened the door.' The hospital bed opposite Chrysanthi's was empty and she stared at it as though replaying what had happened that night in that other bed – her stare fierce, as if she could erase the images. 'I *hated* it. There was so much blood. I knew it was wrong.' She shook her head slowly. 'He told me that he loved me, that we were meant to be together, to be married. After that night there were no more separate bedrooms.'

'Who married you?' Thinking even in rural Cyprus in the nineties they would surely require ID, birth certificates and so on.

'Someone he *told me* was a state official.' She made a scoffing sound. 'Some friend of his in Larnaca he paid to put on a suit and say some fancy words. And I was stupid enough to think it meant something! As if it could ever have been legal in any case.'

'How long was it before you fell pregnant?'

'Four months. And then everything changed.' Her lips curled in a half-smile, for the first time. 'Those children saved me,' she said softly. 'The day I gave birth to the twins, and saw their beautiful innocence, I told him. I said that if he ever laid a finger on me again I would report him.' Sounding matter-of-fact. Then her lips pulled back to show her teeth, an animalistic gesture. 'And if he *ever* laid a finger on my daughter in that way I would kill him.'

Cassie left a pause. 'And you don't think he ever did? Touch Sophia?'

'*Never*. I was always watching him. I would have known.'

'But you do think he . . . killed her.'

'I know he did. I admit, at first I thought it was that boyfriend of hers. Despite what he had done to me I couldn't imagine him killing his own daughter. But then the police said he was with Sophia the first time she had a serious allergic reaction to something. He had never said a word about it to me – and he knew how carefully I watched her diet. The pathologist's report said she had it again the night she died. *Anaphylaxia*.'

She pronounced the word the Greek way, making it sound beautiful. Of course, its roots lay in ancient Greek: translating as something like *extreme guarding*. The armed guards of the body's immune system going rogue, attacking the very thing it ought to be protecting. A bit like George's crime against Chrysanthi – his own daughter.

'It was him who gave Sophia something to make her sick.'

'How do you know?' asked Cassie gently.

'I was there when the police put it to him, and he looked at me.' She widened her eyes for a split second in imitation. 'And in that moment I knew.'

'You could see he felt guilty?'

'Guilty? No!' she scoffed. 'That man didn't know what guilt was. No, he was frightened of being found out.'

'And getting sent to prison?'

The look that Chrysanthi turned on Cassie took her back to that moment in St Ioannis. It was an expression she could imagine on the face of one of the ancient Furies: the female Greek deities who wrought revenge on the wicked, especially on those who murdered their own flesh and blood.

FLYTE

After leaving the hospital Flyte and Streaky had driven east then south through rush-hour traffic. They only had a stick-on blue light that looked like it came out of a Christmas cracker and so Streaky made liberal use of the horn and some rather unprofessional hand gestures to clear the way.

They didn't need the smug female voice on the satnav to tell them they'd arrived at their destination. The cherry-red air ambulance had managed to touch down on an unfeasibly small patch of open ground amid Stratford's high-rises, where it now crouched, blades motionless, looking like a prehistoric insect. It was guarded by a double perimeter of police tape manned by uniformed officers controlling a crowd of rubberneckers who held their arms aloft, phones angled towards a spot some fifty metres beyond. The focus of their attention: a white forensics tent that straddled pavement and road beneath the looming bulk of a skyscraper.

Spotlit in the golden rays of the setting sun, the tent would make a good image on social, Flyte thought grimly.

Streaky flashed his warrant card through the car window and the uniform guarding the access road lifted the tape to let them through. After parking up, they made their way over to the tent.

Opening the flap, Streaky ducked his head inside. Over his shoulder, Flyte could see the outline of a man in a dark suit, face down, who looked as if he were floating on a tide of his own blood – recognisable even in half-profile. The white-suited crime scene manager, whom she recognised as Tina Verity, emerged from the tent carrying an evidence bag.

She handed it to Streaky and Flyte could see it contained a burgundy-coloured EU passport with Greek lettering on the front, opened at the holder's page. 'Georgios Alexander Angelopoulos,' said Tina. 'Place of birth: Perdikia, Republic of Cyprus.'

Aka George, Bronte's father, as Craig had informed them on the phone.

'Good of him to help us out with his ID,' Streaky grunted. 'Any suspicious injuries on the body? Signs of a struggle?'

Tina shook her head. 'Nothing obvious.'

'Pathologist on the way?' asked Streaky.

Tina nodded.

He sent Flyte a meaningful look. 'Belt and braces on this one.'

She nodded: a pathologist wouldn't normally attend the scene of a straightforward suicide, but after the police had so spectacularly dropped the ball after Bronte's death it was a sensible move.

Shading her eyes with a nitrile-gloved hand, Tina looked up to the skyscraper. 'He fell from the garden area, eighteen floors up.'

Following her gaze, Flyte saw that a five-storey-deep slice had been excised from the building around halfway up, leaving the upper floors suspended from a slender cantilever, like a giant Jenga tower on the verge of collapse.

'He left the keys to his Merc on a bench up there – and this.' Digging out her phone, she stripped off a glove and pulled up an image.

His car keys were set on a photograph, which showed Bronte as a child of perhaps nine or ten, on a beach, her little arms and legs stick-thin, her face split in a gap-toothed grin.

'Is the garden accessible to the public?' asked Flyte.

'Just to residents,' said Tina, 'but anyway it was supposed to be closed when he fell, so ... it's not clear how he managed to get out there without triggering the door alarm.'

'Where there's a will.' Streaky shrugged.

As two paramedics ambled over with a stretcher – no reason to hurry – Flyte and Streaky made their way towards the building's foyer and took the lift up to the floor marked 'Residents' Garden'.

'What's your call on this?' asked Streaky, giving his pocket contents a thoughtful jingle.

Flyte narrowed her eyes before ticking off the options on her fingers. 'One, he simply killed himself out of grief at losing his daughter. Two, he killed himself out of guilt because he was involved in Bronte's murder. Three, somebody else killed him because they found out he was involved.'

They found the double doors to the garden area open, noting the security keypad that controlled access, and ducked under the skein of police tape.

Leaning against the wall to pull on plastic overshoes, Streaky nodded. 'My thoughts exactly. If it's one, then not our department. If it's two and he did murder his daughter it would mean Chrysanthi gave him a false alibi for that night. Not to protect him but so she could kill him herself, i.e. number three.'

They walked over to the parapet and Streaky frowned. 'And she has the perfect alibi given she was eight miles away slashing her own wrists at the time. Unless she took out a hit on him.'

'Does she strike you as the type to hang out with hit men?'

'Not really.' Streaky shook his head. 'Anyway, where's the motive? We already considered child abuse – i.e. George abused Bronte, she threatens to dib him in to the cops, tells Chrysanthi . . .'

Flyte made a sceptical face. 'The abuse angle just doesn't add up. Bronte was far closer to him than she was to her mother.'

'My money's on Occam's razor,' mused Streaky. 'Faced with competing theories, always choose the simplest one.'

'Suicide while the balance of his mind was disturbed.'

'Yep.'

Looking at the scene far below them – the sun glinting off the blades of the air ambo, the crowd waiting to catch its take-off – something caught Flyte's eye. At the front of the melee of spectators, with the forensic tent and skyscraper in the background, identifiable by her pink hair, @Charly_Detective was filming her latest unmissable update.

Following her gaze, Streaky made a scoffing sound. 'One person's tragedy is another person's clickbait.'

Chapter Forty-Four

The blood-drenched drama in St Ioannis, followed by Chrysanthi's traumatic revelations in the hospital, had left Cassie feeling drained. After staggering home, she had managed only to feed Macavity before falling fully clothed into bed and a dreamless sleep.

The next morning, she sat on deck in the sunshine with a coffee watching a pair of coots, which she had come to recognise by their black heads and white beaks. At first she thought they were fighting, before realising that she was watching what passed for springtime courtship in the coot world, a male pursuing a female. He chased and chased but she kept evading him at the last minute. Finally, she disappeared, diving right under the water before surfacing a metre behind him, leaving him looking around in comic confusion. *Good for you, girl*, she thought.

She had given Doug a (heavily edited) account of the events that had stopped her from appearing at work the previous day, and he'd insisted she take today off too. She and Chrysanthi had carried on talking until dusk, when Cassie had told one of the nurses that the surgeon could bring the consent forms. Even then, Cassie had held her breath. But Chrysanthi had signed, and the risk of her committing suicide had ebbed – at least for now.

Having kept a lid on the real story of her life and her father's crimes all these years, why had she chosen to share such profoundly private matters with Cassie? Probably as a result of the heightened sense of intimacy that came from Cassie looking after Bronte in the mortuary, while also being a complete stranger.

Cassie could barely control her feelings of rage whenever she thought of George's callous abuse of his own child: a little girl brought up by strangers, who must have thought all her Christmases had come at once when her daddy finally turned up in his fancy fucking car . . .

What a contrast to what had happened when her own father had turned up after a similarly long absence – albeit one that hadn't been his choice. Sure, she and Callum had each struggled to adapt to their roles, but she had known one thing from the start: his every action had been designed to put her welfare, her feelings, her best interests, above his own needs.

Cassie saved a side order of wrath for the role Father Michaelides had played.

As a young mother of twins recently arrived in England, deeply troubled by her sham 'marriage' Chrysanthi had sought out St Ioannis. But she had got cold comfort from her confessor. It was clear that he had denied her absolution for the mortal sins – not of murder, as Cassie had thought – but of incest and 'criminal marriage'. Before receiving forgiveness she'd be required to show a 'firm purpose of amendment' which would have meant reporting her incestuous marriage to the police, and telling Bronte the truth about her parentage – that her mother was also her sister, her father also her grandfather.

Rather than inflict such a terrible revelation upon her daughter, Chrysanthi had silently and bravely borne 'her' sin – 'the sin that could never be washed away' – alone. And as Bronte's star had started to rise, the stakes of keeping the family secret climbed ever higher. It was Chrysanthi and not George who had been punished – without absolution she was denied the comfort of communion, the taking of holy bread and wine with her fellow churchgoers.

Horrible. And Cassie had since discovered that there were other Orthodox churches, with other, more liberal-minded priests who would have taken a very different view of where the sin rightfully belonged.

One thing Cassie wasn't sure about: whether she'd read Chrysanthi right when she'd implied she would be prepared to kill her husband for his murder of their daughter.

She didn't have to wonder about that for very long.

The boat swayed gracefully in the water and she turned to see Flyte climbing on board, her unbending spine marking her out as irredeemable land-folk.

'Come aboard why don't you?' she said with a wry grin. 'But take those heels off before you scratch the varnish.'

Flyte made a face, but obeyed, before inching her way up the catwalk like it was a tightrope.

'George Angelopoulos is dead,' said Flyte, drilling Cassie with her glacier-blue gaze.

'Christ,' said Cassie, her shock genuine. 'How?'

'Threw himself off a high building.' Still staring at her. 'Just like Bronte.'

'Wow.' You had to admire the symmetry. Cassie had no idea how she'd pulled it off but was in no doubt that George's death was Chrysanthi's retribution for her daughter's murder.

'I'm wondering if the two events are in any way related – Chrysanthi's attempt on her own life and George's suicide,' Flyte went on. 'Did she say anything to you before she cut her wrists?'

'Not really,' said Cassie, truthfully.

Flyte swept back her fringe, frustration making her face even more angular, a series of planes, like a Picasso.

Still beautiful though.

'I'm going to talk to her priest, Father Michaelides,' she went on. 'He must surely know something.'

Cassie was reminded of a saying from her grandmother's fund of Polish proverbs: *You'll get no milk from that cow.*

'What's funny?' Those steel ice picks that doubled as eyes didn't miss much.

'Oh nothing,' said Cassie. 'But you do know the sacrament of the confessional is unbreakable?'

Flyte made a face before looking out over the canal. 'It's actually quite . . . peaceful here, isn't it? You could almost be in the countryside.' Her tone wistful, before turning businesslike again. 'Look, we're not ruling out that it was George who killed his daughter.'

'Really?' Cassie sensed that Flyte was simply flying a kite.

'But we can't see any possible motive.'

'Yeah, like why would he?'

Flyte looked at her. 'Is there something you're not telling me?' A plaintive note to her question.

Cassie and Flyte had cooperated in the past, short-term alliances that had helped to solve more than one murder, but this time Cassie wasn't about to help her. *Why?* Because the perpetrator in this Greek tragedy lay dead – and good riddance.

Chrysanthi had been punished enough. Dragging her through court and broadcasting the grisly family history would only throw fresh meat to the social media hyenas. And if Cassie knew anything about Bronte, she knew she wouldn't want that.

Friends.

FLYTE

Cassie had been her usual enraging self, but Flyte had known her long enough now to detect a whiff of duplicity.

She knew something. Was it something that might shed further light on the sequence of events that had seen the entire Angelopoulos family die, or narrowly escape death, within a matter of weeks?

Maybe Streaky was right and George simply couldn't face life without his daughter. She of all people could understand that. For more than a year after Poppy's death the idea of suicide had been constantly at her side – the comforting friend who would whisper in her ear, *I'm here for you if it all gets too much.*

What had stopped her? Poppy herself. Because only by staying alive was Flyte able to honour her brief existence, to ensure she was named, commemorated, her life given meaning. It occurred to her for the first time that Matt, who was still many steps behind her in his journey of denial, rage, grief and acceptance, might be tempted by the dark lure of suicide – an idea that horrified her. She made a resolution to call him.

Before going back to the nick, she had phoned Father Michaelides at St Ioannis. He had pretended he couldn't speak English: they'd clearly get nothing out of him.

Back at her desk, she looked again at the email Bronte had received from the Harley Street clinic that appeared to confirm a diagnosis of her Crohn's. *What had made her seek a diagnosis for her lifelong digestive problems – just days before she was murdered?*

Going out into the corridor, she called the clinic to arrange a call with the doctor Bronte had seen there. She knew she shouldn't be interviewing witnesses without keeping Streaky informed but something told her to fly under the radar until she found out what Cassie Raven was hiding.

Dr Abadi was an urbane character with the trace of a Middle Eastern accent. He had seen the coroner's order requiring release of Bronte's confidential medical information and was keen to help. He told Flyte that Bronte had presented with lifelong and ongoing digestive issues. 'My initial diagnosis was Crohn's and the tests we ran confirmed it.'

'Is there any likely connection to anaphylaxis?' asked Flyte. 'Are Crohn's sufferers more likely to have life-threatening reactions?'

'No,' he said, before adding, 'Anecdotally, they are more likely than most to suffer from allergies but I'm not aware of any proven association with anaphylactic episodes.'

'Did she say why she was consulting you? I mean why now, when she'd suffered these problems all her life?'

He thought for a moment. 'She didn't say. It can take people years before they address the problem.'

Flaming fishcakes, thought Flyte, this was getting her nowhere.

'I remember she did ask about heritability,' he said. 'And it's true that Crohn's has a strong genetic component. So it's probable that one of her parents carried the genes that can cause it, even if neither of them ever had symptoms.'

'OK . . .' Flyte mentally shrugged.

'She also asked whether Crohn's became more likely if the parents were related in some way.'

'Related? Meaning?'

'Cousins having offspring together are at greater risk of passing on diseases caused by faulty genes. It's why marriage between even third-degree relations is forbidden in some countries. It was the focus of my PhD actually.'

Bronte's interest in the heritability of her disorder, days before her death, got Flyte's brain whirring. The more she thought about it, the more an almost-unthinkable scenario kept presenting itself as the key to the bloody trail of murder and suicide in the Angelopolous family.

Chapter Forty-Five

Later that day, Cassie had a second visitor on the boat and this one did ask for permission to board, but then Archie had always had the loveliest manners.

As he climbed into the cockpit she threw her arms round him.

He seemed startled, but after all the shit that had gone down over the last few days, she had a sudden need for the feeling of his lean but solid body against hers, his long arms around her, making her feel safe.

After getting them both cold beers, they went up on deck where she and Flyte had sat earlier. There were two coots near the opposite bank, where part of the canal had been cordoned off for nesting birds. These ones were busy building their nest – a joint endeavour, she was pleased to see – bustling back to and from their new home with strands of marsh grass in their beaks.

She kept sneaking looks at Archie's profile, hearing a treacherous little voice in her ear: *Could they give it another go*? She'd probably have to move into a flat, of course, but hey, life was all about compromise, right?

He told her he was loving the Gloucester placement, before asking, 'How's life at the mortuary? Your guests giving you any trouble?'

Ha! Her guests gave her far less grief than the living.

'You know, same old same old,' she said with a wry grin. The Bronte story was too complicated to get into and no way would she be sharing the SkAR incident with him. She had no doubt that he would believe her, but the dark side of male behaviour was simply beyond Archie's sunny worldview – a view she had no urge to pollute.

'I've missed you,' she told him quietly, frowning into her beer bottle.

'You too,' he said.

But she couldn't decipher his tone.

They watched while one of the coots – presumably the female – climbed onto the new nest, turning one way and then the other, before settling – exactly like a human checking out a new sofa.

'I didn't just come to get my stuff,' admitted Archie. 'There's something I need to tell you' – finally meeting her eye. 'I'm seeing someone.'

Ohhh. The cocoon of comfort his hug had wrapped her in evaporated, leaving a chilly hollow in her gut.

'Congratulations!' Pathetically grateful for the shiny, meaningless word to disguise her shock.

'I know it's . . . really soon after we broke up,' he said, seeking her gaze anxiously. 'But I guess our conversation at the pub made me focus on where I want my life to go. You know, a couple of kids, countryside, fishing, horse riding.' An embarrassed shrug. 'All the Hooray pursuits.'

She had a flash of insight.

'It's Lætitia, isn't it?' Picturing the fawn-faced racehorse blonde who'd come over to chat to 'Arch', her old friend –

and ex-boyfriend – during that ludicrous dinner in deepest Wiltshire.

His look of surprise was followed by a sheepish half-smile. 'You really are a witch. I know it all seems super-fast, and I can't quite believe it myself, but after we . . . ran into each other that night she got in touch.'

I bet she fucking did. Anger elbowed its way into her state of shock. Cassie might have 'feminist' written through her like a stick of rock but she wasn't naïve about the aphrodisiac effect of seeing an old flame with a new squeeze.

'But . . . wasn't she engaged to some other guy?!'

Another grimace 'Yeah, she realised Angus wasn't right for her after all.'

They both watched as on the other side of the canal the male coot paddled towards the nest with a beakful of grass so long and unwieldy that he was struggling to keep it aloft. For some reason the sight made her want to cry.

Recalling her intense, if short-lived, crush on Ethan, Cassie wondered if Archie was repeating her mistake.

'Look, Archie. I wish you tons of luck. You deserve to be happy.' She paused. 'But can I say something as a . . . friend? You do know that emotions can get a bit . . . out of control after a split?'

'You're saying it might be a rebound thing.' He tipped his head, acknowledging the point. 'It did occur to me. But you know, Letty and I do have previous, so . . .'

He looked at her, his eyes serious yet full of warmth. 'You're the best, Cassie. I'll always treasure the memory of our time together.'

Hearing those words, which filed their relationship irretrievably in a box labelled 'the past', Cassie had to bite the inside of her cheek – hard – to quell the tears building behind her eyes. His eyes were still on hers – crinkled with concern. *Seeking absolution.*

'It's all good, Archie. I'll remember it too,' she said, managing a smile. 'Just do me one favour, will you?'

A wary nod. 'Sure.'

'When you move to the sticks, promise me you won't murder any innocent foxes?'

Chapter Forty-Six

It was a fortnight since Chrysanthi had got out of hospital after the operation on her arm.

Cassie had been back to visit her four or five times during her hospital stay. Haunted by the prospect of one day opening a body bag to find that familiar face with its winged eyebrows, she felt driven to stop Chrysanthi giving up on life again. And crazy as it might sound, she had an unspoken deal with Bronte that if she looked after her mother they'd be quits.

Absolution.

So she'd made herself a nuisance with hospital staff, sorting out Chrysanthi's post-release occupational therapy to get her damaged arm working properly, as well as gently encouraging her to think of ways that might give her life meaning again.

Now the two of them sat in Chrysanthi's living room in Hampstead, drinking tea and eating oven-warm *kolaczki* – biscuits made with rich cream cheese pastry and filled with home-made cherry preserve. Babcia had made a batch for Easter, which had fallen the previous weekend, and had given Cassie a tin of them to take to Chrysanthi's.

Cassie sought her eye, pleased to see some colour back in her cheeks at last.

'So have you thought any more about the future, what you might do now?' she asked gently.

Chrysanthi tipped her head. 'I'm going for a visit with my relatives. In Australia' – pronouncing it in the Greek way '*Af*-stralia'.

'Wow! This was the cousin you mentioned?'

'Second cousin – on my mother's side.' They exchanged a look. 'I had never been in contact before but I found her on Facebook and now she sends me pictures and messages every day. Her teenage children call me their *Kamden theitsa* – Camden auntie.'

'How exciting!'

A cautious smile lifted one side of her face, as if smiling was a trick she had yet to master. She still wore the black of mourning but today it was brightened by a coral-coloured scarf round her neck – the first time Cassie had seen her wear any proper colour. It offset her complexion, making her look more her real age – forty-four. *Barely halfway through life*.

'I'd like to ask you a favour,' said Chrysanthi. 'Will you look after my Sophia's grave at St Ioannis while I am away?'

'I'd be honoured.' It struck Cassie that the old patriarch Father Michaelides would be furious at the sight of her on his patch tending Bronte's grave, but that was just an added bonus.

Chrysanthi's eyes scanned Cassie's face. 'I see a lot of her in you, you know. Not in the face but in the spirit. You're both such brave girls.'

Cassie could hardly contradict her, to say that she wished she really had been brave when it mattered, back when they were fourteen: brave enough to befriend her daughter so they could have faced down the bullies together. But time didn't run backwards.

Chrysanthi went on, 'They're not religious, my cousins. But ...' Meeting Cassie's eye, she made a face that married regret and resignation. *That part of her life was over now*. She might find a liberal priest who would absolve her of the 'sin' of her incestuous marriage but now there was the other little matter of a dead husband *and father*.

Thou shalt not kill, was the biggie, after all.

Chrysanthi met her eye. 'I miss the church,' she said simply. 'And most of all I miss the sacrament of confession.'

Picturing Father Michaelides' implacable profile through the grille of the confessional, Cassie failed to see any comfort there. But then religion hadn't been the lifeline it had been to Chrysanthi all these years. 'I can see that it must be cathartic to have someone you can say anything to,' she said.

Catharsis, from the ancient Greek for cleansing or purification.

Seeing Chrysanthi's gaze upon her, an uncertain look in her eyes, Cassie realised something. *She had more to confess.* And by a twist of fate it was Cassie who had become her confessor.

Cassie had never asked, and Chrysanthi had never revealed, how she had exacted revenge on George for their daughter's murder. She clearly couldn't have done the deed herself: at the moment George was falling to his death in Stratford she'd been in St Ioannis with Cassie after all, bent on taking her own life.

Meeting the older woman's eye, Cassie said, 'You know you can tell me anything you want to. In total confidence.'

Chrysanthi started talking, the words spooling out of her gratefully. When it had become clear to her that George had killed their daughter, she said, she'd faced a choice: hope that the police would find enough evidence to ensure he was punished, or take matters into her own hands.

'The police had failed my darling daughter from the very first day,' she said. 'How could I trust them to get justice for her? And I had her memory to think of. I couldn't let the whole world drag her name through the mud, for her parents' sins to be visited on her.'

'Her *father*'s sin,' said Cassie gently. 'You mean that so long as George was alive the whole story of Bronte's parentage might still have come out?'

Chrysanthi nodded. After a lifetime protecting her daughter from the truth about her birth, she was driven to protect her memory in death.

'Once he saw that I had realised his guilt, it would only have been a matter of time before he ran away, disappeared into some hidey-hole overseas. Somewhere that doesn't ask questions of the wealthy.'

'And you feared that once he lost his nerve and ran, the police would be straight on to him, look into the Cyprus angle, and join the dots.'

Chrysanthi nodded, touching a crucifix at her neck. 'There were people in our home village, people who had known my mother, who must have heard things. That after he took me from the care home in Larnaca, I had given birth to twins, and that we were living in England as . . . man and wife' – her voice dropping to a whisper on the last words.

'And in all these years nobody alerted the authorities? To report him as an abuser?' Cassie couldn't keep the outrage out of her voice.

Chrysanthi shook her head slowly. 'Such a shameful thing would only be whispered. They would blame me as much as him. They would say that I should have resisted him.'

Cassie made a sound of angry disbelief.

'When the detectives asked me about his death, I told them that in his grief over losing Sophia he had spoken repeatedly about destroying himself. They believed me.'

Cassie's curiosity got the better of her. 'But how . . .?'

Chrysanthi sighed. 'There's only one person in the world I could ask to deal with something like that. We grew up together in the children's home and he came to London not long after I did. He's like a brother to me. He didn't know the whole story – what George did to me and my daughter. When I told him he just said, "I'll take care of it."'

Wow. Cassie wouldn't mind having a mate like that.

Chrysanthi went to refresh the teapot, giving Cassie time to examine what she felt about her confession.

Vigilantism. A nasty word for a sordid business, and not something she'd ever imagined herself approving of. The pathologist had clearly found no signs of George having fought his attacker. Maybe he'd had a gun to his head. Perhaps had even welcomed his punishment.

Either way, she found she gave zero fucks about George's fate. Sure, he had loved his daughter, but when faced with the risk of exposure, he had put himself first and coldly planned her death. Even at the very last moment when she was clinging on for her life, no doubt begging him to save her, he could have relented and pulled her up.

Picturing her own dad's lopsided smile, she experienced an unexpected rush of love for him so powerful that it snatched the breath from her throat.

That evening Cassie did something she'd been putting off, something that had been weighing on her mind. She was dreading it, but she detested unfinished business.

She walked straight past the queue of youngsters outside the club, their excitement hovering above them like a physical, palpable thing. Looking at the faces, she could see that several of the girls were under eighteen, no doubt using fake ID to get in. Reaching the head of the queue, she looked up at the display that read 'SkAR: New Spring Residency!' before scoping the bouncers for a familiar face. *Nothing.* But just then she saw him emerging from the foyer, the black guy who had checked on her that night. When he saw her he looked alarmed, and then resigned, like he'd been anticipating her return.

Pulling out a pack of cigs, he nodded to the alleyway just beyond the club. After they both lit up, he said, 'I know why you're here.'

FLYTE

A few days after her return to the IOPC offices Streaky called Flyte, offering to buy her lunch at a Greek restaurant off the high street.

As they awaited their meze she raised an eyebrow. 'To what do I owe this honour?'

Grinning at her, he chinked his glass of retsina against hers – mineral water. 'Say hello to the new DCI in charge of Major Crimes for NE London.'

'Congratulations!' And she meant it. He might have some . . . outdated ways of expressing himself, but she had come to realise that he was far from the sexist, racist, cartoon Met Neanderthal that she'd pigeonholed him as when they'd first met.

Prejudice came in all shapes and sizes.

'How's life at the IOPC?' he asked.

'To be honest? It's depressing,' she admitted. 'My current case is some horrible little plod who badgered a sexual assault victim he'd met on the Job for months and then threatened her with a spurious arrest when she said she'd report him.'

'Eurghh.' Streaky made a face. 'Will he get the chop?'

'You would hope so, wouldn't you? But that's not up to us, we can only say there's a "case to answer" and hand it over for the individual force or an independent panel to decide. And they can throw it out, or just give them a verbal warning. So I can't even guarantee I'm taking the bad officers off the street.' She took the slice of lemon from her water and tore the flesh from it with her teeth. 'How's the Bronte case? Still stuck?'

A regretful tip of the head. 'Dead ends at every turn. It's been six weeks since the murder, and I'm down to three people in the incident room. I'm afraid it looks likely that the inquest is going to be concluding "murder by person or persons unknown". The case file will stay open of course but in reality it's game over.'

'And George's death?' Flyte dropped her gaze to pour them both some water: Streaky was a good detective and she didn't want him picking anything up from her expression.

He told her that the last sighting of George alive had been a CCTV image as he left the lift on the eighteenth floor: apparently the camera covering the garden area had gone on the blink. The pathologist had found no injuries beyond those consistent with a fall from height, and there were no lines of enquiry suggesting foul play.

'Straight up and down suicide while the balance of his mind was disturbed by the death of his beloved daughter,' said Streaky.

'Won't there be a backlash over the lack of a result on Bronte?' asked Flyte. 'From all the wannabe sleuths on TikTok and the rest?'

'Haven't you heard?' he asked. 'The jackals are already feasting on a new carcass: some football WAG who drowned in her jacuzzi after a heart attack. And our favourite armchair detective stuck her neck out a bit too far on TikTok this time.'

'What, that silly girl who had it in for Ethan? Charlotte Wiggins?'

'Yep. She quoted a psychic who told her that the woman's husband did it.'

Flyte beamed. 'Ooh. And I'm guessing a footballer has the cash to sue.'

'Indeed.' Streaky grinned back. 'Happy days.'

They fell silent while their first meze arrived: grilled halloumi and lounza, hummus, and deep-fried calamari.

Flyte cut a piece of pitta into neat quarters before spooning some hummus onto her plate: Streaky had 'double dipper' written all over him.

Through his first mouthful he said, 'I could get used to this healthy stuff.'

'You do know that lounza is basically bacon, right?'

He looked sceptical. 'So I assume you'll be publishing your report soon.' He bugged his eyes. 'Should I be putting newspaper down my trousers?'

Flyte shook her head, suppressing a smile. 'The errors were all Sergeant Hickey's. It's not your fault that no detective attended the scene and that proper enquiries weren't conducted straightaway. Never mind the golden hour, they missed five golden days.' She sniffed. 'I don't mind telling you my report will have nothing but praise for the professionalism you've brought to what had been a totally failed investigation.'

Streaky expertly speared three calamari rings in one go. 'Well, that's a relief. Because I'm hoping that this is the beginning of a beautiful friendship.'

She sent him a raised eyebrow.

After dispatching the cephalopod, he wiped his mouth with his napkin. 'I'd like you to join my new team, Phyllida. We'll be dealing with serious crimes, murder, rape, abduction – all the fun of the fair.' Seeing her look of shock, he went on, 'I know you had a grim experience at the old Major Crimes but this will be a brand-new unit. All the old faces are long gone and I want at least fifty per cent girls on the team to keep the boys civilised.'

Flyte was staggered '*Me*? I thought you didn't like me.'

'If I didn't like you, you'd know about it.' He pointed his fork at her and she tried to ignore the hummus on his upper lip. 'You're a good detective. According to Bellwether, one of the best he's ever had.'

'Really?' She felt a deep blush flooding her neck and cheeks.

'His exact words. But before you get too full of yourself, he said there was something I ought to know.'

'Oh?'

'Yeah. He said you had a triple-cooked chip on your shoulder.'

Chapter Forty-Seven

'Permission to board, Cap'n?'

The voice sent Cassie racing up into the cockpit. It was her dad Callum, back from his extended holiday revisiting the Raven clan in Northern Ireland. 'I've missed you,' she murmured, holding his hug longer than usual, which left him blinking with surprised pleasure.

'And who's this?' she asked, wrinkling her brow. Knowing of course that the little girl he'd helped up on board, now standing shyly half behind his legs, was Orla, her five-year-old cousin who he'd brought back for a short stay in London.

'I've got no idea,' said Callum with a shrug and a little wink. 'She followed me here.'

Orla batted him on the leg, protesting, 'Ah, Uncle Callum, you're a *case*' – her accent straight out of the Falls Road. Cassie bent to give her a hug and, looking down on her dark curls, felt a giant hand reach up under her ribs to squeeze her heart.

Orla got over her shyness in a heartbeat and she was soon surveying Cassie's cabin like a miniature estate agent. 'I like the look you've got going on here,' she said judiciously. 'It's cosy but not cluttered. Though these wee curtains could do with refreshing.'

Cassie exchanged a look with Callum, his lips pressed tight, his shoulders doing the silent laughter thing.

Going into Cassie's room, Orla threw herself down on the bed which butted right up to the hull. 'You can hear the *water*!' – her eyes and mouth wide with amazement. 'Oh, Cousin Cassie, can I sleep over? *Pretty please?* I'll be no trouble.'

'No sleepover.' Cassie spoke firmly. 'But you can come over one afternoon and we'll have a picnic up on deck. How does that sound?'

Orla screwed up her face and Cassie was braced for a tantrum or tears, but the next moment her expression cleared and she gave a judicious nod. 'Picnic on deck. It's a deal.'

Then her eyes widened. 'Oooh!' She'd just spotted Macavity entering the cabin. Seeing the creature bearing down on him the cat's eyes flew wide open too. A split second later he was just a tail-tip disappearing through the cat flap.

'When you come for the picnic you can feed him,' Cassie told her. 'Then he'll be your best pal forever.'

Then came the sound of another voice from the towpath: well spoken and sounding borderline irritated. 'Hello? Anyone at home?'

Flyte.

Cassie did the introductions, feeling awkward: she'd never had this many people on the boat at one time and she didn't want to explain who Flyte was – or what she was doing here.

But Callum could be surprisingly sensitive to vibes. 'Come on, missis,' he told Orla. 'You're the one who wanted to go to Camden Market.'

After Flyte's arrival she'd gone all shy again and followed Callum meekly out of the cabin.

But in the cockpit, when Cassie bent down to give her a goodbye kiss, Orla hissed in a penetrating whisper: 'Is that your girlfriend? She's *drop-dead gorgeous*.'

Callum said, 'Hey! Wind your neck in young lady!' – mouthing a *sorry* at Cassie, he lifted Orla down on to the towpath.

But her comment left a wry smile on Cassie's face.

Out of the mouths . . .

Chapter Forty-Eight

She and Flyte sat side by side overlooking the canal, where the sun was starting to sink towards the roofline opposite.

'So, DI Bacon and I interviewed Axel, the doorman from the club yesterday,' Flyte told her.

'And?'

'He's given the police a statement about this SkAR character.'

Cassie repressed a shudder. 'Could we call him by his real name?'

Flyte's eyes softened. 'Of course. Anyway, Axel has detailed all the times he's witnessed young women leaving the club in an upset and dishevelled state, some of whom named Sk—Stefano Makris as their attacker. Axel has two younger sisters and he says he hated what's gone on there. Sounds like it's been more or less common knowledge among the club staff.'

One of Cassie's most vivid memories of that night was the caring expression on Axel's face after she'd escaped Steve. It was something that had been a great comfort to her these past weeks – the concern of a stranger.

'And none of these women pressed charges.'

'No.' Flyte shook her head. 'He even offered to call the cops but the women all said the same thing: they wouldn't be believed, that rapists never get convicted . . . Luckily, Axel had used the club Uber account to get some of them home safely. Which means they can be traced, and the aim is to reassure them that they will be believed.' She looked at Cassie, uncharacteristically hesitant. 'There's a really good female DC on the case, Becca Povey.'

Cassie put her out of her misery. 'Look, I know you need to ask and it was me who kicked this thing off. So sure, I'll give a statement, go to court, etc., etc.' She pulled a wry grin, remembering. 'Although he'll say it was me who assaulted him.'

A dry smile spread across Flyte's face. 'I can believe it.' She went on, 'He might have got away with it indefinitely by relying on women's silence. But maybe the prospect of multiple complainants will give these women confidence.'

It was true, Cassie reflected. Finding out that she wasn't the only one had made her feel less... ashamed. Feeling *any* shame was stupid, of course, but somewhere along the line the idea that women were responsible for their own abuse got baked into the female psyche.

She had no doubt that Steve had assaulted Bronte in Berlin, and that when she resisted, he had turned nasty and thrown the Perdikia village gossip at her – that she was the product of incest.

That had been the catalyst for everything that had followed. Although Bronte wasn't here to see him punished, Cassie was, and would.

But first she had to make a confession to Flyte. Why? Because she felt the need to unburden herself – and to trust her. *If they were to have a future.*

'I need to tell you something,' she said. 'It's about Bronte – and why she was suddenly interested in her family history back in Cyprus. But you must swear to me that it's in total confidence.'

Flyte lifted her hand in agreement – her expression hard to read.

'Chrysanthi was George's daughter, and Bronte was the product of incest,' said Cassie, meeting Flyte's eyes for a long moment before saying, 'You already knew?!'

Flyte nodded. 'After finding out that Crohn's can occur when both parents have the same faulty gene it got me thinking. Bronte's twin brother died from a genetic disease. Then there was the big age gap between George and Chrysanthi, her hatred of him, her rejection of her sexuality – and her extreme protectiveness of her daughter. So I . . . got hold of Bronte's DNA profile.'

Of course. Post-mortem samples from Bronte's body would have automatically been sent to one of the specialist labs where a profile would have been produced. But it wouldn't have been examined or analysed; it would have been held on file solely for exclusion purposes in case someone else's DNA was found in Bronte's flat – which had never happened.

'Her profile was just sitting there, unanalysed. Waiting to one day be deleted,' said Cassie.

Flyte nodded.

'But you're not a cop anymore so how . . .?'

Flyte looked irritated. 'You're not the only one with contacts you know. I was a serving officer for fifteen years. I called in a favour and had it mailed to me. Then it was just a matter of redacting the name and date of birth and getting someone in the know to take a look.'

'What did they say?'

'She was unequivocal – said it was a textbook example of first-degree consanguinity. A highly atypical overlap of the two sets of chromosomes, which proved beyond doubt that the parents were father and daughter.'

Cassie's mind was racing to catch up: if Flyte had worked it out then why hadn't she tipped off DI Bacon, who would have had Bronte's profile officially analysed, and instantly seen the significance?

'Why didn't you share the info?' she asked. 'It gives George a clear motive for murdering Bronte. When she told him she'd booked a flight to Cyprus to explore her roots, he obviously panicked about being exposed.'

Flyte turned to look at her, her eyes hooded. 'Because it would also give Chrysanthi a clear motive for taking out a hit on her husband.'

Their eyes stayed locked for a long moment, a moment of understanding passing between them.

Of course. Having lost her own child Flyte wasn't about to see Chrysanthi pursued and convicted of a crime that she probably viewed as retributive justice.

'Anyway,' said Flyte. 'I wasn't on the Bronte case as a police officer, I'm just a civilian investigating the way it had been conducted.'

Bullshit.

There was a silence while Cassie absorbed it all. She had trusted Flyte to keep a confidence, and Flyte had done her the honour of trusting her in return.

'I think I know what he fed Bronte,' said Cassie.

After her first attack, Bronte must have told him the paramedics' diagnosis of anaphylactic shock, which allowed George to work out what she was allergic to. That offered him the perfect murder weapon: perhaps already thinking ahead to a time he might need it. Something that would silence his daughter forever and in a way that would look like a tragic accident.

Flyte's face was alight with curiosity. 'Go on.'

'Ice cream.'

'Seriously?' Flyte's mouth turned down, sceptical. 'Surely if you're allergic to any of the ingredients in ice cream you'd know about it? Milk, eggs, and so on?'

'Uh-uh.' Cassie shook her head before pulling up one of the crime scene photos on her phone: the one showing the contents of Bronte's fridge lined up on the counter. 'See this? It's a carton for a new vegan ice cream. I recognised the branding' – zooming the image to show the distinctive green diamond pattern. 'When I googled it I found that the dairy protein is replaced by lupin beans.'

'Lupin like the flower?'

'Yep. It's a big new vegan ingredient, but some people are seriously allergic and cos it's only recent they're often not even aware. A kid in Canada had an anaphylactic reaction to lupin flour in a pancake mix – so now any product containing the stuff has to feature a warning.'

Cassie recalled the pic on George's phone of a beaming Bronte outside Marine Ices. *Ice cream was Daddy's treat.* Easy to imagine him turning up with a carton of her favourite flavour that night, encouraging her to try it.

Go on, it's vegan. I got it specially for you.

Flyte's eyes widened, remembering something. 'Could lupin beans feature in a meze? Bronte told paramedics that's what she'd eaten just before her first attack.'

'Absolutely!' said Cassie excitedly. 'You get them in Mediterranean dips and salads.'

Flyte nodded, taking it on board. 'Anyway. It's all somewhat academic now. The guilty have already been punished.'

There was a silence while they watched the female coot on the opposite bank, sitting complacently on the nest in the dying twilight; the male bird nowhere in sight.

Flyte spoke lightly. 'No sign of the boyfriend? Archie.'

Cassie bit the inside of her cheek. 'That went the way of all flesh. Archie is a lovely guy but . . .'

A pause. 'And Ethan?' Flyte was studiously avoiding eye contact.

'Ethan?!' Cassie shook her head with a self-mocking laugh. 'That was messed up. I was on the rebound, I suppose, and then it got all tangled up with me trying to find out who killed Bronte.' Pushing her hair behind her ear, she sought Flyte's gaze. 'You see, Phyllida, I'm a bit of a disaster zone when it comes to relationships.'

Flyte eyes rested on Cassie's, her ice-blue irises taking on a softening hint of jade from the canal. 'Maybe you just haven't met the right person.'

'Maybe you're right,' said Cassie, looking right back at her, suddenly hyper-aware of their hands just centimetres apart on the deck between them.

'I'm eleven years older than you,' said Flyte.

'Age is just a number.'

'And . . . I'm seriously thinking of rejoining the Met.'

Cassie blinked. The idea of dating a cop had always been the insurmountable obstacle to any idea of a romantic relationship between them. Now she realised that, without even noticing it, her thinking had undergone a fundamental shift.

Flyte wasn't like other cops. And yet she *belonged* in the police, as surely as Cassie belonged in the mortuary. She felt a sudden impulse to share her secret – her bond with the dead – before stopping herself: *there would be time for that later*.

Instead, she moved her little finger to touch Flyte's and smiled into her eyes. 'Nobody's perfect,' she said.

Acknowledgements

Once again, my first thanks go to you, the reader. It's a privilege to have my stories published but it wouldn't mean anything without the wonderful, encouraging feedback I get from readers who've enjoyed meeting Cassie and Flyte. I'd love to hear from you via the social media links at the beginning of the book, and if you'd like to receive Cassie Raven series news and be entered into the odd prize draw, you can sign up for my occasional newsletter here: www.anyalipska.com.

You can probably tell that I rely on the input and fact-checking of several 'expert witnesses'. Pathologist Nic Chaston continues to put me right on matters anatomical and medical, and is a rich source of new and intriguing stories from the dissecting bench. (Although mystifyingly, she refuses to perform my PM should I ever need one . . .)

Anatomical Pathology Technologist Barbara Peters ensures I don't drop the ball on mortuary practice, while former murder DI Paula James has once again been a huge help on every aspect of policing. Cheryl Kynaston, former Met Crime Scene Manager is a patient adviser on all things scene-related, while Alison Thompson, former coroner turned North Wales sheep farmer, somehow finds time amid ram-wrestling to advise on coronial matters.

Since EDM and the music biz are a foreign world to me, it was also super-helpful to be able to call on the advice of music maven Mat Smith for *Dead Fall*.

Special thanks go to Tomasz, my ex-husband and still very dear friend (yep, it happens!), who was instrumental in developing an important part of the *Dead Fall* storyline.

I rely heavily on the lovely and supportive community of crime writing chums, including Domenica de Rosa aka Elly Griffiths, William Shaw, Jane Casey, Susi Holliday, Claire McGowan, Angela Clarke, the legend that is Val McDermid, and Isabelle Grey, aka V. B. Grey, who always provides wise counsel.

I am blessed with a smart and hard-working team at David Higham Associates, home to my fantastic agent, Veronique Baxter – the best possible cheerleader a writer could have – and also to talented reader Sara Langham, TV/film wrangler Georgie Smith, and the fabulous foreign rights folk who have helped introduce Cassie to readers in nine different languages.

Finally, huge thanks go to the super-talented Kelly Smith at Zaffre Books who continues to work tirelessly to steer the Cassie Raven series to new heights!

Have you read the first Cassie Raven mystery, BODY LANGUAGE?

When the dead are silent, she will be their voice

Mortuary technician Cassie Raven feels a special bond with the bodies in her care, but when somebody she loved turns up on her autopsy table, her job suddenly gets personal.

Cassie's instincts are screaming foul play, but the police say it was an accident – and uptight detective Phyllida Flyte has no time for a tattooed morgue girl with attitude.

But when Cassie is proved right, she and Flyte must work together to find a murderer – before Cassie ends up on the mortuary slab herself.

Turn the page . . .

AVAILABLE NOW

Chapter One

The zip of the body bag parted to reveal Cassie's first customer of the day. The woman's half-open eyes, a surprisingly vivid blue, gazed up at her, unseeing.

'Hello there, Mrs Connery.' Her voice became gentler than the one she used with the living. 'My name's Cassie Raven and I'll be looking after you while you're with us.' She had no doubt that the dead woman could hear her and hoped she took some comfort from the words.

The previous evening Kate Connery had collapsed while getting ready for bed and died, there on her bathroom floor one week short of her fiftieth birthday. Laughter lines latticed her open, no-nonsense face beneath hair too uniformly brunette to be natural.

Cassie glanced up at the clock and swore. There was a new pathologist coming in to do the day's post-mortem list and with Carl, the junior technician, off sick and three bodies to prep, it was shaping up to be the Monday from hell.

Still, she took her time working Mrs C's nightdress up over her head, registering the faint ammoniac smell of sweat or urine, before carefully folding it away in a plastic bag. The things somebody had been wearing when they died meant a lot to their loved ones, sometimes more than the body itself, which grieving relatives could struggle to relate to. A dead body could feel like an empty suitcase.

'We need to find out what happened to you, Mrs C,' Cassie told her. 'So that we can get Declan and your boys some answers.'

From her first day in the mortuary five years ago it had felt totally natural to talk to the bodies in her care, to treat them as if they were still alive – still people. Occasionally they would even answer.

It wasn't like a live person talking – for a start, their lips didn't move – and the experience was always so fleeting that she might almost have imagined it. *Almost.* Usually they said something like '*Where am I?*' or '*What happened?*' – simple bewilderment at finding themselves in this strange place – but now and again she was convinced that their words contained a clue to how they'd died.

Cassie had never told a living soul about these 'conversations'; people thought she was weird enough already. But they didn't know what she knew deep in her gut: the dead could talk – if only you knew how to listen.

The only outward sign of anything wrong with Mrs Connery was a few red blotches on her cheeks and forehead and a fist-sized bruise on her sternum where either her husband or the paramedics had administered desperate CPR. Cassie looked through the notes. After a night out at the pub watching football, Declan Connery had come home to find his wife unconscious. An ambulance rushed her to the hospital, but she was declared dead on arrival.

Since Kate Connery had died unexpectedly – she'd apparently been in good health and hadn't seen her GP for months – a basic or 'routine' post-mortem to establish the cause of death was an automatic requirement.

Cassie put her hand on Mrs C's fridge-cold forearm and waited for her own warmth to expel the chill. 'Can you tell me what happened?' she murmured.

For a few seconds, nothing. Then she felt the familiar slip-sliding sensation, followed by a distracted dreaminess. At the same time, her senses became hyper-alert – the hum of the body-store fridge growing to a jet-engine roar, the overhead light suddenly achingly bright.

The air above Mrs Connery's body seemed to fizz with the last spark of the electricity that had animated her for five decades. And out of the static Cassie heard a low, hoarse whisper.

'I can't breathe!'

Chapter Two

As always, it was all over in an instant. It reminded Cassie of waking from an intense dream, your mind scrabbling to hold onto the details – only to feel them slipping away, like water through open fingers.

In any case, Mrs Connery's words weren't much help. Cassie could find no history of asthma or emphysema in the notes, and there was a whole bunch of other disorders that could affect breathing. She was still wondering what, if anything, to make of it when she heard the door from the clean area open. It was Doug, the mortuary manager, followed by a younger guy – tall, with a floppy fringe – who he introduced as Dr Archie Cuff, the new pathologist.

Stripping off a nitrile glove, she offered Cuff her hand.

'Cassie Raven is our senior mortuary technician,' beamed Doug. 'She's the one who makes everything run like clockwork round here.'

Although he wore cufflinks (*cufflinks*?!) and a tie, Cuff couldn't be much more than thirty, barely five years older than Cassie. A single glance told her that his navy waxed jacket was a genuine Barbour, not a knock-off – its metal zipper fob embossed with the brand name – and going by his tie, a dark blue silk with a slanting fat white stripe, he'd been schooled at

Harrow. Cassie noticed things like that, had done ever since she could remember.

'Looking forward to working with you, Cathy.' He spoke in the fake, demi-street accent favoured by the younger royals, his smile as glib as a cabinet minister's, but it was clear from the way his glance slid over her that she'd already been filed in a box labelled 'minion'.

Cassie didn't often take an instant dislike to someone, but in the case of Archie Cuff she decided to make an exception.

'Me too,' she said, 'especially if you get my name right.'

A flush rose from Cuff's striped shirt collar all the way to his gingery sideburns, but at least he looked at her properly this time. And from the flicker of distaste that crossed his face, he didn't much like what he saw – although it was hard to tell whether it was her dyed black hair with the shaved undercut, her facial piercings, or simply the way she held his gaze. She had to fight a juvenile impulse to lift the top half of her scrubs and flash her tattoos at him.

Doug's eyes flitted between the two of them like a rookie referee at a cage fight, his smile starting to sag. 'Right then, I'll leave you folks to it.' Cassie knew he would probably remind her later of his golden rule: *'Never forget, the pathologist can make your job a dream – or a nightmare.'*

After Cuff's brief external examination of Mrs Connery, during which they barely spoke beyond the essentials, he left Cassie to do the evisceration.

She placed her blade at the base of Mrs C's throat. This was the moment when she had to stop thinking of Kate Connery as a person and start viewing her as a puzzle to be unlocked, unmapped territory to explore. Without that shift of perspective, what normal person could slice open a fellow human being?

After the initial incision, a decisive sweep down the sternum laid open the tissue as easily as an old silk curtain. Reaching the soft gut area, she didn't pause but let up the pressure to avoid damage to the organs beneath, ending the cut just above the pubic bone.

Within five minutes, the bone shears had cracked open Mrs C's ribcage, exposing her heart and lungs, and Cassie was deftly detaching the organs from their moorings. Once that was done, she used both hands to lift out the entire viscera, from tongue down to urethra, before delivering them gently into the waiting plastic pail. This was a sombre moment, which always made her feel like a midwife of death.

Now for the brain. Going behind Mrs C's head, Cassie repositioned the block beneath her neck. The scalp incision would go from from ear to ear over the top of the head, so that once it was stitched up again the wound would be covered by her hair – especially important since the Connerys were having an open coffin funeral. Combing the front half of Mrs C's thick dark hair forward over her face, Cassie noticed a shiny red patch on the scalp. Eczema? It hadn't been mentioned in the medical notes, but in any case, eczema didn't kill people.

After peeling the bisected scalp forward and back to expose the skull, Cassie reached for the oscillating saw. Moments later she had eased off the skullcap and was coaxing the brain free. Cradling it in both hands for a moment, she imagined Kate Connery as she would have been in life – a down-to-earth matriarch with a ready laugh, surrounded by family and friends in a Camden Town boozer.

When Archie Cuff returned in his scrubs, the atmosphere between them stayed chilly: in the forty minutes it took him to dissect Mrs C's organs, he only spoke to Cassie once, to complain that the blade of his PM40 was blunt. That only confirmed her initial impression of him as the latest in a long line of arrogant posh boys who viewed mortuary technicians as one step up from abattoir workers. A more experienced pathologist would have asked her opinion on the cause of death, and not just to be polite: technicians spent far longer with the bodies and sometimes spotted clues that might otherwise be missed.

As Cuff moved along the dissection bench to rinse his bloodied gloved hands in the sink, Cassie started to collect Mrs C's organs into a plastic bag, ready to be reunited with her body.

'So, what's the verdict?' she asked him.

'There's nothing conclusive to account for her death.' He shrugged. 'We'll have to wait and see whether the lab finds anything useful.' Toxicology would test Mrs C's bodily fluids for drugs, while samples of her organs would undergo histopathology to look for any microscopic signs of disease.

'Did you find any petechiae in her lungs?' asked Cassie, keeping her voice casual.

Cuff turned to look at her. 'Why do you ask?'

So he had.

She lifted one shoulder 'I just thought her face looked quite congested.'

I can't breathe.

Petechiae – tiny burst blood vessels – could signal a lack of oxygen.

Cuff looked flustered. 'She was found face down. It's clear from the latest literature that a prone position post-mortem can cause petechial haemorrhage.' He managed a condescending smile. 'If you were hoping for a juicy murder, I'm afraid you're out of luck: there's absolutely no evidence of strangulation or suffocation.'

Cassie knew as well as Cuff did that asphyxia could just as easily have a medical cause, but she stifled a comeback. Dropping a nugget of kidney into a pot of preservative for the lab, she caught sight of Mrs C's body on the autopsy table – her ribcage butterflied like an open book, a dark void where her organs used to be. Above the ruined body, her shiny brunette hair looked out of place.

The light from the fluorescent tubes overhead flared, forcing Cassie to close her eyes, the ever-present reek of formalin suddenly harsh enough to claw at her throat. Behind her eyelids, images flickered: Mrs C's blotched face, the scaly patch on her scalp. She felt her throat start to close and in an instant, everything clicked into place.

'Just popping to the loo,' she told Cuff, before slipping into the corridor, where she pulled out her phone.

'Mr Connery? It's Cassie Raven from the mortuary.'

Ten minutes later she was back. 'Sorry I took so long,' she told Cuff. 'But I just had an interesting conversation with Mrs Connery's husband.'

'Husband . . . ?' He sounded confused at the idea of a body having a spouse.

'Yes. Before he went out last night, she told him she was going to colour her hair.'

'I don't see what . . .'

'He says that she had suffered allergic reactions to her hair dye twice before. Nothing too serious. But this time, it looks like it triggered a fatal anaphylactic shock.'

Don't miss the next intriguing case for Cassie Raven

LIFE SENTENCE

Families can be murder...

Mortuary technician Cassie Raven was raised as an orphan, which might explain her affinity with the dead. But she's just made a devastating discovery: her father is alive, but served jail time for killing her mother.

He swears he didn't do it – and Cassie wants to believe him. Desperate to find the truth, she seeks help from Phyllida Flyte, the uptight Camden detective who intrigues Cassie as much as she infuriates her.

As the two women close in on the truth they will encounter true evil, and someone prepared to kill again.

AVAILABLE NOW

Look out for the next gripping mystery for Cassie Raven

CASE SENSITIVE

Deadly secrets are rising from the depths

Mortuary technician Cassie Raven has seen thousands of dead bodies in her day job, but when a drowned man knocks against the hull of her narrowboat, it's a bit too close to home.

DS Phyllida Flyte thinks she recognises the John Doe with the golden-green eyes and wants to go the extra mile to give him back his name. Feeling unable to trust her colleagues, a desperate Flyte turns to Cassie for help.

Together, Cassie and Flyte will dredge up deadly secrets – secrets that will draw Flyte down a perilous path. At best she risks career suicide; at worst, she'll end up dead herself.

AVAILABLE NOW